NAFESA'S LOVE SONG

NAFESA'S LOVE SONG

AUSTIN ALSTON

CHAPTER ONE

William stood outside of the Lincoln building and looked straight up. Somewhere up there was his first office, his first secretary, his first new beginning. His stomach was jumping. He wiped the mist of sweat from his forehead and pushed his way through the revolving door. Outside, eighty-nine degrees; inside, a perfect seventy. The building was the newest office building built in downtown Philadelphia. There were fresh cut flowers strategically placed throughout the lobby. The décor was a soft blue azure hardened with Italian marble floors. A large, dark skinned man with ancient frames and a too small navy blue uniform smiled at him. William returned the smile.

"Looking good there my man. Can I help you?"

"Thanks. Today is my first day with Palmer, Hitower, Viscomb and Detmer. I was told to check in on the sixteenth floor."

"I like that gray pin stripe suit. Man, you really hooked it up with that burgundy tie. Hot damn, brotha man got on new shoes too! You musta got that suit at Marcs. I hear you can't get a suit there for less than a thousand dollars. What kinda job you gonna be doing up there for them? You too well dressed to work in the mailroom. What you, a paralegal?"

Before William could respond to the servant, an elderly white woman interrupted them requesting information about the location of a Dr. Benjamin's office. The large, dark skinned servant gave her immediate attention. William accepted the indignation and moved towards the elevators. There were three corridors of elevators. The first set went to the tenth floor, the second set went to the twenty-fifth floor and the last set went to the fiftieth floor. William walked to the middle corridor and positioned himself for the inside elevator. It was a gamble as to which one would open first. The far-left elevator opened. The outer crowd made a surge to get on but, the inner crowd held firm. William watched the subtle maneuvering. The door of his elevator opened. He made a quick move straight to the rear of the elevator. The box filled up and every button on the panel lit up. No one spoke. Everyone stared absently ahead. The elevator spoke to them at each floor. Its computerized voice was calming. William waited for it to announce his floor.

"Sixteenth floor," it informed. William wanted to thank it. He excused his way out. Three other clones existed along with him. As soon as they got off of the elevator, they spoke to each other. William was surprised that these individual who had ignored each other for sixteen floors actually knew one another. He looked around for directions to tell him which way to go. He was looking for suite 1600. The arrow pointed for him to walk to his left. He turned the corner and a large set of glass doors with the firm's name in black italicized lettering was facing him. William quickened his pace. He opened the door and walked through. There was a greeting sign with his name on it.

WELCOME WILLIAM R. JENNINGS, JR.

William was impressed. His light complexioned skin turned bright red. The receptionist saw it on his face and smiled.

"Good morning Mr. Jennings. Have a seat and Ms. Gatlin will be here to get you.

There is coffee and danishes in the dining area if you're interested."

"No thanks. I'll pass on the coffee and danishes. I had a small breakfast before I left home. I'll just have a seat. Thanks anyway." The receptionist continued her smile, but slowly let her eyes move away from him and return to the switchboard. There was a constant soft chime emanating from her switchboard. "Good morning, Palmer, Hitower, Viscomb and Detmer. How make I direct your call?" She took it all in stride, never relinquishing her smile. William watched as a steady flow of bodies entered and disappeared from the lobby. The lobby was dressed in a neutral décor. It appeared that the designer wanted a glass and steel look but settled for glass steel, and a lot of wood. The combination gave it a mixed feel. The longer William sat there; the more he noticed the wood. It began to look more purposeful than haphazard. A well dressed, short, stocky white woman with overly dyed red hair entered the lobby and walked directly towards William. He presumed it was Ms. Gatlin. She extended her hand when she was a couple of feet from him. William rose to meet the greeting.

"Hello Mr. Jennings. I am Margaret Gatlin. You can call me Marge."

"Hello Marge."

"We'll be working together in the Admiralty Division. I'm the typing pool supervisor. Regina Manis will be your secretary. I'll introduce her to you once you get settled in. Follow me and I'll show you to your den."

William twisted and turned through several corridors, walked down a ramp, twisted and turned through several more corridors until he reached an office along a long hall on the fourteenth floor that housed six other offices. Outside of the office was the typing pool. Four young women were sitting at their stations. They all looked up and gave him a polite smile and nod as their finger continued to dance across their keyboards. William returned the greetings. Marge pointed to an empty office to his left.

"This is it. This is your new home away from home. I'll give you a little time to get settled and then Regina and I'll pop in and get you up and running. If you need anything in the mean time just push the first intercom button on the phone. Do you have any questions?"

"No. Not at this time. I just want to jump in and get my feet wet."

"Mr. Jennings, when you jump in around here, you get more than your feet wet." Marge smiled at William and walked back to her station. William stood outside of his office savoring the newness. There was a name plaque on the wall outside his door.

William R. Jennings, Jr.
1404

William stepped into his new abode. Everything felt new; no, it felt fresh. He walked over to his mahogany desk and placed his brief case on top of it. The brief case was a gift from his mother. William was not sure how he was going to decorate his office but, he was certain that Marla would take care of that task for him. He walked around and stood behind the burgundy leather chair; no, he stood behind his burgundy leather chair. William smiled to himself. He paced off his office. It was twelve by twelve. Three of his walls were painted off white. His fourth wall was a solid pane of tinted glass. It gave him a full view of the southern end of Philadelphia and the Walt Whitman Bridge. Sitting on the fourteenth floor of the Lincoln building gave him a sense power. He felt as though he was as new as the furniture in his office. He had arrived. But this was all expected of him. His father was Judge Jennings, President Judge of the Court of Common Pleas in Philadelphia County. His uncle, Robert Jennings was the first black District Attorney in the history of the city of Philadelphia. All four of his cousins were prominent doctors. William knew that he had to make it, failure was unacceptable for a Jennings. His life had been scripted for him from the time he was born. He had attended West Chestnut Academy, Pemrose Academy, Harvard undergrad and Yale Law School.

He looked out of his wall-sized window to take in the beauty of the view. It was a clear day, he could see for miles. The Walt Whitman Bridge was teaming with rush hour traffic coming into the city from New Jersey. The streets looked like ant trails. The city was alive and he was a part of it. He looked at his watch; it was 10:10 a.m. The buzz from the intercom on his phone startled him, causing him to jump. He bumped his head against the spotless windowpane. The receptionist's voice rolled through. She had interrupted his solitude. He had become so absorbed in his own little world that he had forgotten he was a part of a firm that had two hundred and twenty-three employees, of which, he was the latest addition. Palmer, Hitower, Viscomb and Detmer was the second largest law firm in the city. They had satellite offices around the world. Their Philadelphia office only accepted two new associates a year. William was the third minority to ever get an offer from the firm. He was the first minority to accept their offer.

"Mr. Jennings, a Ms. Bertrem is here to see you. Are you available?"
"Yes. She's my fiancée. I'll come up to get her."

"Regina will escort her down to your office. Now that I know Ms. Bertrem is your fiancée, I'll always try to get her through to you with as much ease as possible."

"I would appreciate that," thanked William. William could not wait for Marla to walk into his office. He knew she would be impressed. Not overly impressed, but impressed. Marla had been surrounded by affluence virtually all of her life. She came from old money. Her early ancestor, Prince Richards was the richest black man in the city of Philadelphia in the eighteen hundreds. He amassed a fortune in the ship building business, employing whites, blacks, freemen and slaves. His heirs maintained their stature, status and light complexion throughout the years. Her father was the Mayor of the city and her aunt was the Lieutenant Governor of the state. But all in all, William was certain she would be impressed with his office. Not overly impressed but impressed. Marla had been surrounded by affluence virtually all of her life. She came from old money. William watched as she strolled through the door. Marla's runway walk was perfect. She was beautiful and, as always, meticulously dressed. She was wearing a light green Versace dress with a double-breasted mellow green jacket to match. She smiled more with her eyes than she did with her mouth. Her legs were long and slender. She was slender and long. She surveyed the office with the excitement of a child on Christmas morning. Marla walked around giving the office a professional going over.

"Your secretary, Regina is a cute dark skin girl. I'm surprised they let her wear her hair in braids. I had to walk through four or five corridors and I must have passed fifty offices to get to yours. This is a very large firm. Oh honey, I'm so proud of you. Your office is spectacular. I can't wait to decorate it for you. You know I did daddy's office and he loves it. Mrs. Williamson hired me to do her home. I'm so glad I took those courses in interior design. They're really starting to pay off for me."

William stood back watching and listening. "You like it? All it needs is your touch and it'll be the best looking office in the firm, bar-none. Even the partners will be jealous," boasted William with a slight smile on his off white face. He moved from behind his mahogany desk and held out his arms inviting her to walk into them. She complied. She was a perfect fit. There was no doubt in William's mind that Marla was the prettiest woman in the world. Her legs were long and slender and she was slender and long. She stood five feet, eight inches tall bare foot. Her skin was as light as could be without being white. In fact, she was often mistaken for being white. You had to stare to tell that she was black. Starring made her mad. Once, while waiting in line to purchase tickets to the play "The Nutcracker", an elderly black woman starred so hard that Marla felt compelled to tell the woman that she was indeed black. The woman was so embarrassed that she exited the line and walked away. Marla wore her hair long and dirty blonde. People often became so enamored with her beauty that they overlooked her intelligence. Marla scored fourteen twenty on the SAT's and, graduated Magnum Cum Laude in three years from Princeton. She was a trophy par excellence. William leaned over to kiss her. She pushed herself out of his arms.

"Now William, you know I can't have you smearing my lip stick all over my face, so be nice. Besides, you're not supposed to use your office as a bedroom," scolded Marla as she refused his kiss.

"All I want is to taste the sweetness of those ruby red lips of yours. How can you fault any man for wanting that?" begged William. Marla ignored his plea. "The next time I come, I'll bring some color patterns along. You need some bright colors in here to offset this masculine flavor. The full window gives me a lot to work with. I'm already starting to get some excellent ideas. You definitely need some plants in here. Well William, I have to go now. I just stopped by to congratulate you on your first day of work. I'm quite sure this firm is not paying you eighty-five thousand dollars a year to play around. I just hope you have time for me when they let you out of this place at night. Or, should I say midnight?"

"OK baby. I'll call you tonight when I get out of here. It may be a little late. Some of the senior associates are taking the newer associates out for a little get together. I think we're going to a jazz club over on Broad Street. I hear it's called the OFFBEAT. I'll call you when I get home. Tell your family I said hello. By the way, are we still having dinner with your family on Sunday?"

"That's a definite. Daddy is really looking forward to talking to you about your future in politics. He said if you play your cards right you could become Mayor someday. So think about it. I'll wait for your call. Try not to make it too late. See you later honey."

"Bye baby. I'll call you as soon as I get home." William watched the sway of her walk as she left his office. He smiled. There was no doubt in his mind that she was the prettiest woman in the world.

William returned to his window and restarted his outward gaze. He was certain that this period of solitude was just the quiet before the storm. He was told that he was expected to do eighty billable hours a week. He had heard about the billable hours nightmare in law school, but he was yet to experience it. There was a soft rap at his door.

"Come in he invited." Frederick Detmer stepped into his office and announced himself with an outstretched hand.

"Hello William. We've never met. I'm Fred Detmer." Frederick Detmer was an average height, thin, no; skinny man with manicured nails and slicked back blonde hair. At thirty-four years old, he was the youngest partner in the firm. He was always meticulously dressed. He looked as though he had just stepped off a Parisian runway. Even when he was casually dressed his outfit was perfectly coordinated. It was rumored that he had his own personal fashion consultant. He was GQ. His three button charcoal blue suit was hand tailored to a tee. The cuffs on his pants stopped a quarter of an inch above his heels. His jacket sleeves stopped at the crest of his palms. His white shirt sported a blue trim on the collar that match the blue trim around the cuffs on his sleeves. There were no initials on the shirt, he knew who he was. His cuff links were oval shaped three carat diamonds set in a rather non-descript setting. The tie brought the whole outfit together with a perfect balance. His tan was deep. The story was he literally bought himself a partnership. His father, Richard Detmer was an A- type personality. At the age of sixteen he was a worker on the docks. At the age of twenty-two he was a ship boss. At the age of thirty-one he was part owner of a ship. At the age of forty-two he was majority owner of a shipping company. And, at the age of fifty he owned the largest shipping company of the eastern seaboard. His motto was "always know a little more than the person ahead of you". Unlike his father, Frederick Detmer was far from a go-getter. His motto was, "Why sweat life when your dad is a multi-millionaire?". Fred had been spoiled all of his life and, had come to like it. He rarely ever came to the office. He spent most of his time jet-setting in highbrow places where the weather was warm. He loathed the cold weather. To keep him somewhat respectable, his father made a deal with the firm. The deal was, the firm would bring Fred in as a full partner and in return, the firm would get to handle thirty-three percent of Detmer's Shipping, Incorporated's legal business. Thirty three percent represented over ten million dollars. And so, Frederick Detmer arrived on his first day at the office to find his name being added to the firm's letterhead as a full-fledged partner. The strange thing about the situation was, Fred Detmer was not the least bit bashful about the manner of his elevation to partnership. His motto was "Why sweat life when your dad is a multi- millionaire?".

"I hope you don't mind me barging in on you like this, but I'm leaving for Australia in a few hours. The WORLD POLO Championship is being held in Sydney. Although, I don't play, I love to watch the sport. I wanted to formally meet you and welcome you to the firm. I was told you will be part of my team in the Admiralty Division. I need sharp people to help me keep the ship afloat," he quipped.

"Thank you for the welcome Mr. Detmer. You can rest assured that this mate will tow his line," joked William, following the theme.

"You and I will get along a little bit better if you call me Fred. My father is Mr. Detmer. I dread the thought of being of the age when I'm thought of as a mister," laughed Fred.

"No problemo."

"Well, I've got a plane to catch. Check with Heleen, my secretary to see what my schedule is like for the rest of the month. Richard Basil, my team leader will sit down with you and show you which projects I need you to start on. In the mean time, take this last opportunity to relax and again, welcome aboard."

"Thanks again. I'll check with Heleen. Have a safe trip," obliged William. *"Gosh, he was a pretty cool guy. I hope he sets the tone for the rest of his team. If he does, it should be pretty relaxed working in his division."*

William began to unpack the few belongings he brought along in his brief case. The brief case was a gift from his mother. They were mostly pictures he wanted to set up in his office. The most prize worthy of which was a picture of him and President Bush on a quail hunting trip in West Virginia. He interned at the White House during the summer following his second year of law school. His contracts professor at Yale, Professor Bultman served as a fighter pilot in WWII with George Bush, Sr. The two had become very close friends over the years. Professor Bultman adopted William during his law school years. So, when it came time for applications to be submitted for the internship at the White House, William's application was hand delivered to President George Bush, Jr. However, William would go to his grave believing that his application would have been selected without the aide of Professor Bultman. William carried a three-point-four G.P.A. throughout law school. William's father joked that his law school G.P.A. was higher than William's. William reminded his father that there was a big difference between Howard's law school and Yale's law school. William searched around for the best spot to place the picture. It had to be displayed. He remembered how he and the President went shot for shot for the first seven birds. When the day ended, the President had out shot him by nine birds. The memories of that day brought a smile to his face.

Lunchtime had come and gone and William had not met anyone except Marge and Fred. He was still waiting to meet Regina. He had gone out to a small sandwich shop and had a Philly cheese steak, a bag of chips, a sprite and a cup of coffee. He loved cheese steaks. Every time he returned home from college or law school, the first thing he had to have was a cheese steak. The thinly sliced steak with sautéed onions, melted cheese on an Italian roll filled with mustard and ketchup was a gastronomical delight. After lunch, William walked around Center City. The streets were full of hurrying people. He did not want to stay away from the office too long. He walked a couple of blocks down to the Love Park. There were tourists taking pictures standing beside the "Love Sculpture". Other people were mingling around the fountain. Some kids were playing in the fountain. The heat and humidity were stifling. William turned around and headed back to the Lincoln building. The servant was manning his position.

"Yo, homeboy. What's your name?"

"William Jennings. What's yours?"

"Levi. Levi Jones."

"Nice to meet you Levi. By the way I was hired as an attorney, not as a paralegal"

"No shit? You must be the only brother lawyer they got up there. I know they got a couple of young boys working in the mailroom and a lot of sisters working as secretaries. That's all right! Homeboy, I'm proud of you. Can I ask you a question?"

"Sure."

"If my landlord try to say I ain't pay my rent but, I had to get the plumbing fixed out my pocket, do I have to pay him?"

"I just took the bar exam and haven't gotten my results back yet. So, I can't advise you as a lawyer. Besides, I don't specialize in landlord and tenant law. You should check with the People's Law Center. They specialize in that type of law."

"Oh. OK. Thanks. You take care Mistah Jennings."

William nodded himself away from Levi trying to figure what just happened there. Did Levi think that William had blown him off? William tried to erase the whole conversation from his mind. He walked to the middle corridor and caught the middle elevator to the fourteenth floor. He circumvented the maze back to his office. He was certain that someone would greet him and get him up and running. But, there was no one waiting for him when he got back. He checked with Marge. She looked up at him with a "no smile". William returned a smile. He walked into his office and sat down. He was looking at his watch when his door flew open.

"Mr. Jennings, are you, or, are you not a part of Mr. Detmer's Admiralty Division? Because, if you are, then I would think that you would be seeking out your assignments. It is almost two o'clock and no one has heard from you. This is a very busy office and no one can take the time to slow down for you. At the salary we start our new associates, we expect them to hit the ground running. So, I would suggest that you grab a pen and pad and let's get started. That is, if you are a part of this team."

"I'm sorry, sir. I was expecting someone to come around and bring me into the fold. Mr. Detmer told me that a Richard Basil would stop by to get me acclimated," apologized William, feeling as though he had cheated the company out of a full day of work.

"I am Richard Basil and I am here to help you get acclimated. However Mr. Jennings, I am not here to hold your hand. So get with the program. Now that we have introduced ourselves, let's get started. There is a freightliner off the coast of Charleston, South Carolina that has a small oil slick trailing it. When I say small, I mean minute small. But, the damn EPA with all of its regulations has frozen the freighter. The problem is, we have a client in New York who has to have the two million dollars worth of garments that are loaded on that freighter. If he doesn't get those garments in the next two weeks, he'll be out of business. Hell, just the analysis of the oil slick alone is going to take them more than a week. So what we need for you to do is find a way around those stupid regulations and get that ship unfrozen. Remember, there is always a way to get around a government regulation. That should keep you busy for the rest of the day. Make sure you keep a track of the hours you spend on this assignment. One more thing, never, ever call me Dick! My name is Richard." Richard stormed out of the office in the same manner that he entered it.

"What a dick! If opposites attract, then Fred and Richard must truly be lovers." William scrambled for a pen and pad. Richard was the exact opposite of Fred. For every dollar Fred spent adorning himself, Richard must have stashed away under his mattress. Richard was the proto-typical geek. He had the personality of a photocopier. In fact, the copier had more color than Richard. He was a little guy who could run a tight ship. And with Fred gone, Richard was all supreme and he let everyone know it. He created tension and thrived on its thickness. Needless to say, there were daggers everywhere waiting to strike the target on his back. *"What a dick!"*

William asked Marge for directions to the library. He meandered his way back up to the sixteenth floor. The firm's library was impressive. It consumed one third of the sixteenth floor. There were two full time Librarians. They had Westlaw and Lexis with a dozen terminals. And, it was heavily used. Young faces were scurrying everywhere, moving from shelf to shelf, workstation to workstation. The workstations were piled high with books. It looked sci-fi; programmed robots in dark blue suits. Even the females were clad in the same uniform. The library lacked personality. Fred Detmer had personality, the library did not. *"Well I guess I better get a couple of blue suits."* William found an empty workstation and dug in. First he looked at the federal regulations that the EPA used to freeze the freighter. Then, he looked up the South Carolina statutes that applied to the situation. Next, William pulled all of the cases he could find on the subject. He had three piles of books, stacked six books deep. William looked at his watch, it was three-ten. After reading seventeen pages of regulations and countless pages of case law, William decided to close his eyes for a minute to give them a rest. He pushed the books off to the side, folded his arms and rested his head.

William felt something tapping him on the shoulder. He jumped up and realized that he must have dozed off. He looked at the clock on the wall. It was six-forty. He turned around to see who had awakened him.

"Hey William, my name is Phillip Wyse, but just call me Phil. I'm part of the welcoming committee. We're supposed to hang out tonight. I stopped by your office earlier. Your secretary told me that you were pounding the books. I see you didn't find the regs to be interesting reading. Dude, what a drag, huh?" laughed Phil.

"Gosh, I guess I must have dozed off for a second, or two, or three, or four. Right, we're supposed to go to a jazz club on Broad Street. Phew, I just need a few seconds to get myself together. Boy, I can't believe that I fell asleep. I'm really sorry," apologized William. Phil knew how he felt. "Hey dude, we've all been there before. It happens to the best of us. Don't sweat it. Besides, if you hadn't fallen asleep, we would have probably labeled you a Richard Basil disciple and shunned you. So get yourself together and we'll meet you down stairs in the lobby. Say in fifteen minutes?" Phil patted William on the back and disappeared.

William stood up from the workstation and gave a heavy stretch. He grabbed his jacket and headed down to the fourteenth floor. He had to use the bathroom and remembered that there was a bathroom around the corner from his office. There were still scores of people running around the office. He used the bathroom and freshened up. When he returned to his office, there were six messages on his desk. His mother, both sisters, and three cousins had called him. William smiled, turned off the lights and headed for the elevator. When he entered the lobby area there were fifteen people waiting for him. The other really new person was a woman named Leslie Conway. She was recruited out of Stanford. The East Coast was a totally new environment to her. Phil approached him.

"I would take the time to introduce everyone, but you won't remember their names anyway. Besides, you'll get to meet everyone throughout the course of the night. So troops, let's move out."

William and Leslie clung to Phil. The rest of the pack seemed to break up into familiar groups. Based on the conversations, it appeared there was very little communicating across divisional lines. The talk was definitely shoptalk. Phil did everything he could to stay away from shoptalk. He wanted to make the new kids feel welcomed. Both William and Leslie appreciated his effort. Leslie was assigned to the Commercial Real Estate division. She had a nonchalant attitude about the position. William felt that she was playing it safe. Say the wrong thing to the right person and you could be out the front door.

They stepped out of their climate controlled building, into a lingering August heat. A full moon hung slightly above William Penn's hat. The sky was relatively clear. A few clouds lay dormant off to the north of the city. The area was in desperate need of rain. It had sprinkled on Saturday, just enough to coat the pavement, but it was still five inches below normal. A drought alert had been put in place. The cities fountains were given an exception to the drought alert. A police van sirened pass them. Philly was a big, small town. It still believed in neighborhoods. The downtown was expanding. Although the skyline was no match for New York's, it was still impressive and, it had a lot of room for growth. The city was fairly clean and seemingly safe. You could feel the police presence. The walk to the club was only three blocks. A blind man with a cigar box, singing gospel songs stood against a wall of an office building at 15th and Market Streets. Leslie walked over and placed a ten-dollar bill in the cigar box. William gave her a puzzled look.

"But for the grace of God, there goes I," she answered.

William smiled in agreement. When they reached Broad and Sansom Streets, a soft neon light flashed "THE OFFBEAT". There was a small line outside the club. The marquis featured a local talent with a picture of a chocolate brown woman with a pearl-like smile. The name "Nafesa" was beneath it. The girl was beautiful. *"Probably just good camera work."*

"Hey William, by the way, do you go by William, Bill or Will?"

"I go by William. My mother never liked nick names for her children."

"Well William, wait until you see this gal who sings. Dude, she is one nice little number. You're going to fall in love with her. And, she can sing," quipped Phil.

"No, I don't think so. She's very attractive though. But, she's not my type. Besides, my parents would have a heart attack if I brought her home. And, I'm engaged."

"Why would your parents have a heart attack if you brought her home?" asked Leslie.

"First of all, she's a night club singer. Secondly, she's too dark. My parents would kick me out of the house if I brought home a dark skin nightclub singer. It would upset them even if I weren't serious about her. Just knowing that I was dating her would drive them crazy."

"Dude, you have got to be kidding me. Hell, you're all black. You mean to tell me that just because your skin is almost as light as mine and your hair is straighter than mine you can't date a person darker than you?" I never knew black people discriminated amongst themselves. That is some whack stuff Dude."

"It's not discrimination, its preference."

"Wait a minute William, you're practically a lawyer. You know the difference between preference and discrimination. Preference is innocent, discrimination is purposeful. It sounds as though your refusal to date a dark skin person is more purposeful than innocent. The majority of black people I know are darker than you. You look more like an Italian than a black person. If you can't date a person darker than yourself, your selection of friends is very limited," piped in Leslie.

"Hey! I don't want to get into a pissing match about the type of women I choose to date. If I don't want to date a Nafesa, for any reason, I don't have to date a Nafesa. And, if either of you want to date a Nafesa, then you can feel free to do so. OK?"

Phil sensed the tension mounting beyond necessity. "Yo Dude, whatever you say. But, if I thought I had a chance to date Nafesa, I'd date her in a heart beat."

They walked up a small flight of stairs that ended at two large smoke colored glass doors with stainless steel handles. Outside, noise. Inside, sounds. A tall slender brown skin woman dressed in solid black greeted them. Her eyes twinkled. At first, William thought it was the way the light bounced off her face. But, the more he studied her face he realized that it wasn't the light. Her eyes twinkled.

"Hey guys, welcome to the OFFBEAT. How many people are in your party?" Phil stepped up and engaged the maitre de. He had called ahead and made reservations. They exchanged unheard words and visible smiles. Twinkles let out a hardy laugh in response to something cleverly said by Phil. She motioned for them to follow her. She led them to a set of four tables situated up front, off stage right. There were small "RESERVED" placards on the tables. She removed them and wished everyone a good time. The group played musical chairs until everyone was seated. An average height, average looking red-head came over to their section and introduced herself.

"Hello. My name is Mia and I'm your server tonight. Can I get you guys anything from the bar?" She systematically took their orders and promised a speedy return. She kept her promise.

The club was much larger than it appeared from the outside. The atmosphere was upscale buppie-yuppie more so than juke joint. Everyone seemed to have been let out of the same office building at the same time. It was recess time. Smoking was not cool, but it appeared to be necessary. Communal packs of Marlboros, Newports, and Camels lay everywhere. The smoke filled William's nostrils with every breath. Ten of the fifteen people in his group were smokers. He couldn't complain. It was part of the vibe. Besides, he was the new guy and didn't want to make a fuss over a non-work related issue. Hell, they were all out to meet, greet and have a good time. Leslie abstained from any alcoholic drinks. She attributed her abstinence to personal reasons. Randy, the supervising attorney in the Real Estate division was a heavy drinker. He belted down shots of Southern Comfort like glasses of water. They were taking their toll. With every shot he got louder and louder. Phil pulled him to the side and warned him to cool out. The drink of choice for the majority of the group was beer. Pitchers of beer came and went. William played it safe and stayed with beer. It was the first time he had gone out to have a good time since his last day of law school. Right after graduation, he had to begin studying for the bar exam. Right after the bar exam, he had to report for work. He needed the relaxation; it felt good.

Activity started to happen on the stage. Stagehands tested and retested the equipment. Various members of the band began to take the stage and test their instruments individually then in syncopation. A microphone, a piano, guitars, horns, and drums. The colored stage lights flickered on and off. When everything seemed to be in perfect order, a short, stocky, dark skin guy with long braids and a beautifully tailored tan suit took the stage. He softly tested the mic. It worked.

"Good evening." He paused to allow the crowd to absorb the deep, full, rich tone of his voice. He was a professional. It was similar to the workings of a bat that sent out sonar to get a feed back as to what was out there. He was waiting for his feedback. The singular voice of the crowd began to subside. Soon it trickled down to a few isolated voices hurrying to finish their thoughts. Then, there was silence. His feedback was complete. "My name is Brother Haki and I am your host tonight. I want you to all sit back and continue to enjoy yourselves. You all seem to be having a good time. I know that I am. Now, the OFFBEAT is both pleased and proud to bring to you one of Philadelphia's very own up and coming stars. This young lady and her band have backed up some of the greatest singers in the business. Aretha Franklin, Natalie Cole, Nancy Wilson, and Luther Vandross to name a few. And, with any luck, because they have the talent, pretty soon they'll be in a recording studio producing their own sound. So, sit back, drink and eat up, and, enjoy one of the jazziest voices in the business today. Ladies and gentlemen, please give a warm and hardy hand for Nafesa!"

The crowd obliged him. The lights dimmed throughout the club and floated to the center of the stage. The band began. William recognized the tune. It was *"MY FAVORITE THINGS"*. Within seconds the entire club was enveloped by the smoothest voice William had ever heard. Bodies began to bounce and heads began to bob. There was a musical sway of the crowd. The voice seemed to be coming from everywhere. It had forced him to close his eyes and try to feel it. It permeated him. He opened his eyes to meet the person who was emanating out such a melodic manifestation. It was her. The beautiful chocolate brown girl on the marquis. The dark brown girl that his years of being a Jennings had forbidden him to date. Her beauty was juxtaposed to everything that he had been taught about beauty. She was elegant. A liquid elegance that seemed to flow from her. If he touched her, the elegance would saturate his hands, his mind, and his heart. Her beauty was not the work of a cameraman, it was real. In fact, the picture did her no justice. She appeared to be about five-feet, six inches with her heels on. She wore her hair in small twisted braids. Her teeth glistened. Her smooth dark skin captured the light, and gave it brightness. She was majestic. She mesmerized him. *"Maybe it's the beer."* But, the more she sang, the more he stared. The more he stared, the lovelier she became. It frightened him. She frightened him. He had never thought of a dark skin woman being more beautiful than Marla. Dark skin women were exotic, not utterly beautiful. Maybe it was his conscience getting back at him for his conversation with Phil and Leslie. Whatever it was, she was the focus of it all. And, she was consuming him. He broke his eyes away from her, but her voice forced him to respect the enchantment of her prowess. His head was spinning. The beer he reasoned. His heart was pounding. He left that unreasoned. She seemed to be starring at him; giving him all of her attention. He had to leave; this was all too unnatural. He abruptly stood up and headed for the door. It frightened him. She frightened him. The dark brown skin girl that his years of being a Jennings had forbidden him to date. Her beauty was juxtaposed to everything that he had been taught about beauty.

CHAPTER TWO

Nafesa could not go back to sleep. She had tossed and turned through out the night. She watched as the sun slipped into the bedroom erasing the pervading darkness that haunts the night. A single sea gull gawked as a harbinger of the arrival of the new day. *"A new day is the holiest concept known to man. Only Allah could have conceived of such an idea."* The new day always brought to man the possibility of a fresh start. Yesterday was gone and its mistakes forgiven by the newness of the same old sun. All praise be to Allah. She was in need of Allah's blessing. She needed newness. She needed a fresh day to rid of her of yesterday's staleness. She turned over and looked at the person who lay next to her in bed. *"How had she allowed this to last so long*?" They had met at the cemetery four years ago. She had gone there to place some flowers on her mother's grave. She felt tired and alone. It was always an emotional ordeal for her to visit her mother's grave site. Normally, the tears would start as soon as she rolled past the wrought iron gates that shielded the cemetery. And, the tears wouldn't stop until she was back in her apartment, stretched out across her bed. On this particular day, even the sky was crying. She placed some blue gladiolas, her mother's favorite flower on the grave site, said a quick prayer and headed back to her car. When she tried to start it up, the car wouldn't kick over. She tried and tried until the battery completely died out. The tears stormed. She sat there not knowing what to do. A cream colored Jaguar pulled up next to her with a tooting horn. She rolled down her window and looked into a sympathetic face that housed a set of confident eyes. They were life rafts in her sea of loneliness. The driver offered her a ride to a service station. She was too embarrassed to tell him that she didn't have enough money to get the car repaired. She asked him to take her home, and she would have a family member pick up the car the next day. He obliged her. He offered to take her out to dinner. She accepted. He was kind, considerate, and confident. He told her how his parents were buried out at the cemetery and how he made it a point to visit them on their birthdays. Today was his father's birthday. After diner, he took her home. They exchanged phone numbers and said good night. She could not stop thinking about him. She waited for two days for him to call her. Her phone never rang. On the third day, she decided to call him. He sounded extremely pleased to hear from her. He told her that he had been out of town for the past couple of days and that he had every intention of calling her once he got back into town. She was happy that he was interested in her. They arranged a date for dinner and dancing for the following Friday. The date went well. He was fun and full of life. The dating continued. The more she saw of him, the more she wanted him. Sex was a minor issue. That's not to say that it wasn't good, but it was secondary to his most appealing quality. It was his strength that she longed for. He possessed the only thing that she ever needed in a man, strength. There was no weakness to him, mentally or physically. But, there was a certain air to him that made her internal danger sensors tingle. He reeked of drug dealing. His money, his style, his attitude all said drug dealer. She asked. He denied. He told her how he had come into the money as a result of a wrongful death settlement. He told her how his parents had been killed by city officials when he was only six. She believed what she wanted to believe. They continued to date. Her suspicions became evident as time went on. How he had initially gotten his money was one story, how he maintained his money was a completely different story. But, he was new and the life was exciting. She decided that she would hang for a couple of months. What she thought would only amount to a quick fling, had lasted for four years. Her womanhood had evolved so much over the past four years. The nineteen year old Nafesa was far different from the twenty-three year old Nafesa. Nineteen year old Nafesa needed shelter from the hardness of an imposing world. Twenty-three year old Nafesa needed warmth from the coldness of life without love. She was young and wanted to be young and in love. As a little girl, her mother had fantasized with her about the beauty of love. She wanted her fantasy. If her mother were still alive, she would not feel so alone. True,

Shamsadeen was always there for her. However, she needed someone to be there with her mentally, physically, and spiritually. Shamsadeen satiated her material nature, but starved her inner essence. It was time to move on. It was over between her and Shamsadeen. But, Shamsadeen was overly compelling. His body alone was enough to make her want to stay with him. He was six-feet, two inches and weighed one hundred and ninety-eight pounds. He carried less than seven-percent body fat. Shamsadeen loved his body and was fastidious as to what went into it. He never smoked, drank or did drugs. In fact, he never understood why anyone would put such harmful chemicals into their bodies. His workout was ritualistic and strenuous. It lasted a solid two hours. His vitamin counter looked like a mini drug store. And, for what it was worth, he was good to her. They stayed in a two thousand dollars a month apartment that overlooked the Delaware River. The apartment was decorated with first edition paintings by artist from all over the world. He drove a V12 Mercedes and she drove a convertible 325i. He was twenty-seven and had never worked a day in his life, that is an honest day of work. Shamsadeen Baku had an organization that was well known and well feared. Nafesa knew that for as much as he tried to shelter her from the perils of his profession, she would someday, some way get caught up in it. There were signs that things were starting to unravel. She wanted out.

Shamsadeen rolled over and reached for her. She removed his hand from her breast and got out of bed. Shamsadeen sat up and marveled at a small ray of light that braved through the separation of the curtains, landed on the small of her back and danced across her African evening skin.

"Baby, could you get me a glass of V8? I wanna put something in my system before I start my workout."

Nafesa walked over to the junk chair in the corner of the bedroom and searched for her fusia satin robe. Then, she walked over to the picture of her mother that sat on the red oak dresser that her grand father had made by hand. She smiled at the picture and blew a kiss to her mother. She needed to get away. She had to come up with a believable reason to get away for a few days. The problem was, Shamsadeen was not the type of man who you could tell you needed to get away from. You could never tell Shamsadeen that you needed to clear your head of him. In fact, Nafesa could never tell Shamsadeen anything. She had to ask him for everything. He had taught her this lesson a couple of years ago when she told him that she was going to the islands for a week to get her head together. Shamsadeen told her that since she had not asked him if she could go, if she went, she went at her own peril. She went anyway. When she returned, he met her at the airport with a big smile on his face and showered her with words of missing her. When they pulled into the parking lot of their apartment building, her Mercedes C230 was smoldering. "That was just a warning. What I giveth, I can also taketh" he told her.

She shuffled into the kitchen and poured him a glass of V8 juice and walked back to the bedroom. He was sitting beside the bed doing isometric exercises and watching the two-inch thick, flat screen, plasma TV that hung on the wall. He was watching CNN Business. He needed to know how the stock market was doing. His partner, Lil' Larry had taught him well. His body rippled with muscles as he stretched. *"He is so beautiful."*

"Hey Boo, I was thinking about going up to New York for a week or two. I was talking to my brother, Rasheed and he said it would be cool for me to stay with him for a minute. It'll give me a chance to see what's happening in the Big Apple. Maybe I could take in some clubs and get to meet some people in the business. You know, help get my music career moving a little faster. Philly can be slow. It's all right being the big fish in a little pond, but sometimes to learn you have to be a little fish in a big pond. Rasheed said he ran into a couple of guys who are looking for a jazz singer with a different sound. So what do you think?" She was lying, but hoped that he couldn't tell that she was lying.

"Fesa, why you always trying to get out of Philly? I mean, don't I always try to make it more than comfortable for you? If you leave, who's gonna take care of me? I know you don't want me running back to Lorraine."

"You fucking bastard!" Nafesa hurled the glass of V8 at him. He ducked and began to laugh. The glass bounced off the wall and landed on the bed. Juice was everywhere.

"Girl you crazy as shit. Now suppose you had hit me with that glass? I'd have to call the cops on your ass and you'd have a case. Yes sir your Honor, the defendant did strike me with a large glass thereby causing serious injuries to which I have yet to recover from. No sir, I don't think five years is too much," he joked.

"Then at least I'd have time to myself. I wouldn't have to ask your ass for permission to leave. And you could spend all the time you wanted with that stink ass Lorraine."

"Look Fe, I'm trying to keep everything together here. Shit is starting to get a little crazy. Mutha fuckas been trying me lately. I got to put an end to some of this shit before I won't be able to walk down the street. I got a whole lot of people depending on me here. If I slip, I could get a lot of people killed, including myself."

"But, what does all that have to do with me going to New York for a week or two?"

"It's just that if you're up in New York, then I'm gonna have to worry about you while you're up there. And, if I have to worry about you while you're up there, I can't give my full attention to my business down here. And, if I can't give my full attention to things down here, then like I said, a lot of people could get hurt." His voice was becoming more authoritative.

Nafesa was determined not to back down. "You know that shit doesn't make any sense at all. Besides, I'll call you every day. And, it's more dangerous for me down here than it is for me up in New York. Nobody up there knows that I'm Shamsadeen's woman. Down here I could get kidnapped or some shit by some young thugs trying to come up." She waited for his response, but none came. She knew it was time to move in for the kill. She walked over to the bed and stood between his legs. She opened her robe and forced his head between her breast. He pulled her down to her knees. She stared him in the eyes then slowly moved into him with warm lingering kisses against his neck. Then, she slid down and began to place soft, small pecks on his inner thighs.

"Please, baby please? I'll make it up to you before I go and when I come back," she cooed.

"Stop that shit Fe. You better make it up to me before you go, when you get back and, right now." He lifted her up and placed her on the bed. They exchanged wild random kisses.

"Take off your robe," he commanded.

"You take it off," she countered.

He felt his body temperature rise as he unrobed her. Her breasts were round and ripe. Gravity had not yet begun its downward pull of them. Her body was hairless. She was a walking wonder of loveliness. Her curvatures were subtle, not pronounced. Her skin gleamed like melting chocolate from summer's heat. His lips began to search her. He found her spot and lingered there. She buckled. She let her fingers play through his hair. She was dissolving. The more she moaned, the more he pursued. She grabbed him by the shoulders and beckoned him to enter her. She quivered as he complied. His body danced with each thrust of himself into her.

"Oh Allah," she screamed, "forgive me, please forgive me?" A solitary tear raced down her face.

Nafesa was just getting out of the shower when the phone rang. It was Flavor, her keyboard player and manager.

"What's up Flavor?"

Flavor's voice was slow and deliberate. What's up Fe? You know that piece that me and Mel been working on? Well, we finally got it finished. Wait until you hear it. The piece is made for you. So do me a favor and come to practice a little earlier so we can give it a try. It ain't hard or nothing. It's real smooth. I'm telling you, this song is the piece that could get us a record deal."

"You know me Flav, I'm always down for a new piece of music. I mean especially something brand new. Now don't have me out there singing no jingle bell shit. You know what I mean?" she joked.

"Fe, they'll be singing Jingle Bells for the next thousand years. I wish I had wrote that piece. I'd be rich. I'll see you at rehearsal at two-thirty. Peace out my Nubian sista."

"Cool. I'll see you at rehearsal." Nafesa loved Flavius Johnson. He was her brother, her father, and her friend. His shoulders were never too weak or too small for her to rely on. When he was six, he starting playing the piano with so much style and energy, that his uncle nicknamed him Flavor. By the time he was twelve, he was playing keyboards for his school's jazz band. When he was seventeen, he was playing for a local jazz band. By the time he was twenty, he was touring with some of the biggest names in the business. He spent a year touring with Miles. But, the fast life caught up with him and slowed him down. At the age of twenty-four, he had spiraled out of control. Flavor spent the next four years eating what he could, sleeping where he could and bathing when he could. He sold everything he had to support his three hundred-dollar a day heroin addiction. Then one day while he was inside of a pawnshop trying to pawn his grandfather's watch, he heard Stevie Wonder's "Jesus Children" playing on one of the radios inside the shop. The song grabbed him and would not let him go. He ran out of the shop, sat against the wall and began to cry. He got up and walked to Jefferson Hospital and checked into the drug and alcohol clinic. That was nine years ago. Now, Flavor was too cool to be cool. He was the most talented one in the group. Every sound was music to him. He would analyze the ring of a door bell in notes and tones. Voices sang to him. He could even hear music in the backfire of a car. Being on the streets for all of those years had taught him to listen to the sounds of life. Flavor was too deep to be deep. Nafesa knew that if he said he had written a song for her it would be tight. She became excited thinking about it. "*Allah is good*," she smiled.

Nafesa was standing at the doorway of the apartment building when Shamsadeen roared into the driveway in his silver V12. His blue tinted windows were up, but the Eclipse sound system was pounding beyond its borders. Shamsadeen was an air conditioner person. He loved to keep his car cold. "*Here we go with that rap shit.*"

"Baby, how can you be with me, a jazz singer for all these years and still listen to this rap junk? This stuff is noise. I mean, haven't I taught you anything about music? Haven't you learned anything from me?"

"Look Fe, don't start that shit today. I'm not in the mood for all that stuff. I got too much on my plate to listen to you bitch about my music. And how you gonna say that Tu Pac ain't music? That's bullshit. Fe, listen to this shit. You know PeeWee right?"

The look on Nafesa's face said no.

"PeeWee, the little hustler from West Philly who's always in jail. He came around that day with that hand held DVD player. Remember? Anyway, he came to me last week and asked me to front him for some Colombian guy. I was hesitant at first, but he promised me that he was on the up and up. So I fronted him on a piece of weight. Then the little faggot called me up and told me that the Colombian had set him up and robbed him. I put out my feelers and found out that he owed the mob some serious money from some bets he made. The word is he paid his debt and paid some dudes to make it look like he got beat-up. How do you think he got the money to pay them back?"

Nafesa really didn't want to be a part of this conversation. She wanted to be free from this whole mess. Shamsadeen was giving her more information than she needed to know. He had never done this in the past. Something was wrong. And, this was just another sign that he didn't really love her. If he did, he would insulate her from his ugly world. She wanted to be in love with someone who truly loved her. Loved her for her voice, loved her for her smile, and loved her for the way she made love. She was tired of being a trophy. To Shamsadeen, she was just a prized possession. She knew she meant little more to him than his prized art collection. She was certain that she meant less to him than his beloved V12. Shamsadeen bought love, he never brought love. She wanted love in its simplest form. Nafesa figured she would play along with the conversation in a dumb way. "I don't know where he got the money from baby. Where do you think he got the money from?"

"Damn Fesa, ain't nobody that damn stupid. That negro sold my weight and moved the money over to the mob. So what he was saying is he's was more afraid of the mob than he is of me. I can't have that little mutha fucka fuck me like that. If that shit hits the street and I didn't do anything about it, my whole shit would start to fall a part. Everybody would think that they could burn me and get away with it. I'd be out of business. I wouldn't be able to get my new V12. You should see the new one. The dude at the dealership said he was going to call me as soon as he gets the info for ordering the new one. How about you? The dude said it was about time to trade in your beemer. Maybe this Saturday I'll take you down to the dealer and let you pick out something new. What do you think about that?"

Nafesa knew that this was coming. Every time he thought she was trying to get away from him, he would offer her an extravagant gift. But what the hell, it was always hard to turn them down; especially, a brand new BMW. In fact, she had been looking at the new convertible 325i. However, she also knew that if she accepted the car, she would only be prolonging her agony. She also knew that if she refused the gift, he would think that she was up to something. And, only Allah knew what he would send her through. She was damned if she did and damned if she didn't. "Well, I guess it's better to be damned with a 325i convertible then to be damned without one," she reasoned to herself. Nafesa knew that it was pleasing time.

"Oh baby, you're so good to me."

Shamsadeen pulled up to the intersection of 10th and Locust Streets and dropped her off in front of the recording studio. He sat there waiting for her to give him a kiss. She didn't.

"Baby I can't wait until Saturday," she said as she shut the door. He looked at Nafesa trying to figure out if her failure to kiss him was deliberate or accidental. He accepted it as being accidental. His ego would not let him think otherwise. Nafesa watched him speed off, running a red light. She shook her head in disgust.

The band was rehearsing when Nafesa walked through the door. They held their rehearsals in a small garage that Flavor had purchase at a foreclosure sale. He gutted they building and rebuilt it to his musical needs. It was small, but comfortable. Flavor noticed that Nafesa wasn't bouncing when she walked through the door. He recognized the sour look on her face.

"What's wrong baby? Come on over here and talk to Uncle Flav. You know you can talk to Uncle Flavor."

"I'm alright Flav. I just gotta clear my head of the trivial stuff."

"Fe, how many times do I have to tell you that the shit you going through, or, should I say sending yourself through, ain't trivial? When you gonna wise up and step from Shamsadeen? You and I both know that he is going to cause you a life time of grief if you don't drop him. You just let me know when you're ready to walk away from him, 'cause you know I ain't scared of him. I'll step to his ass in a second. See, the problem is, he thinks that you're out here all alone with no back-up. But, you know I got your back!"

Nafesa knew that if Flavor stepped to Shamsadeen, Shamsadeen would break every bone in each of Flavor's fingers to teach him a lesson.

"It ain't about fear Flav. I just gotta get my ducks all lined up before I step off. It took me a while to get in this mess and it's gonna take my some time to get out of this mess. I'll be all right. It's just a head thing. Hey, let me hear the song y'all wrote for me."

"I'm telling you Fe, you don't have the time you think you have to deal with the situation. Shamsadeen is a nightmare waiting to turn into your ugly reality. Wise up baby. But, enough of the negative talk. Check out this song. I want you to close your eyes and listen. You gotta feel this song before you sing it." Flavor walked over to his piano and began to play a slow, mellow sound. Nafesa closed her eyes and let the song marinate into her soul. She felt it. It was an old feeling longing for newness. It was her. It was in her heart. It was in her mind. It was in her tears. She began to hum the hook. Flavor watched her become one with the song. He knew she liked it. She kept her eyes closed well after the song was over. Flavor knew not to disturb her. She opened her eyes with a smile on her face.

"Flav, that song is live. It's perfect. I love it."

"Me and Mel knew you'd fall in love with it. Mel can't wait for you to sing it. Ain't that right Mel?"

"Damn straight. Soon as we were done, all we did was talk about how you were gonna give it life," answered Mel.

"I would like to put it into the second set. Do you think we'll have it down by tonight?" she asked.

"Ain't nothing to it but to do it?"

Nafesa knew she would have the song mastered before they hit the stage tonight. *"See, Allah always provides light in the midst of darkness,"* she prayed to herself.

Nafesa took a cab home. She seldom took her car out of the garage. She had three hours to get herself together before she had to be at the OFFBEAT. She needed a little rest. She was tired from not getting enough sleep. She laid across the bed and turned on the TV. Oprah was interviewing Halle Berry about Halle's new movie. Before she knew it, she was sliding down a wall with Shamsadeen and the police chasing her. Her mother was screaming for her to get up and run. She couldn't right herself. The ground was getting closer and closer. She was about to crash into it when she jumped up. Nafesa opened her panic stricken eyes. She was back in the comfort of her bedroom. She took a deep breath and looked around for the picture of her mother. Her mother was still sitting on the dresser that her grandfather had made, looking over her. It was six- forty; she had to get ready to go.

Nafesa loved the aroma of the jazz club. Each club had its own scent and its own feel. She had performed in some of the sleaziest clubs in the city. But, even in the sleazy clubs, once the music started playing, everything always seemed to flow. The OFFBEAT was the best jazz club in town. As far as the Philly scene was concerned, she had made it. She was at the top of the heap. This was where people were discovered. You never knew who would be sitting in the club on any given night. So, each night you had to come prepared to make it big. You had to bring a bucket of verve. When the lights went out, you had to light the club up. If you didn't, the club could be brutal. The crowd would drown you out with personal conversations. And, because of the club's reputation for bringing in good talent, you wouldn't get invited back the next night if you bombed. Nafesa had been there for two consecutive weeks. Each night she had brought the house down. She loved it. And, she showed the audience that she appreciated their love.

The host, Brother Haki was on the stage pumping up the crowd. His introduction alone was enough to make a talent scout take notice. However, Nafesa knew it took more than a good introduction to get a record deal. The band began to play their opening number, "MY FAVORITE THINGS". She was on! Nafesa grooved onto the stage and surveyed the crowd. They were feeling her and the band. She felt a good night coming. Mel, the bass player jumped into a solo. The amplified bass banged through the sound system and reverberated through the souls of the crowd. They gave him a strong applause. Mel stepped back and surrendered the stage to Nafesa. She increased her volume. There was a lawyerly looking group off to her right. They were in her groove. She moved closer to them. After a few songs into the second set, she noticed a guy staring at her. His eyes were piercing her. It was a mysterious stare. She puzzled him. She was an answer to a question that was buried somewhere deep within him. He wanted to learn her. He wanted her. His stare was mesmerizing. She forced her eyes to focus on him through the dimness. She was having a hard time telling if he was black or white. He had white features, but there was something about him that looked black. He had that in between complexion. He could not take his eyes off of her. And now, she could not take her eyes off of him. It had become personal. She felt herself singing to him. He got up from the table and moved towards the exit door. She could not let him leave. She had to stop him. She refused to let him get away.

"This next song is a new song. I want to dedicate it to anyone out there who is searching for newness; to anyone who is searching for new love." He stopped in his tracks, turned around and walked back to his table. Did she have him? Or, did he have her? Who had whom? It was all too unnatural.

CHAPTER THREE

It was Saturday night and PeeWee was out for a good time. He had a few bucks in his pocket and the mob off of his back. *"That was too close for comfort, "*he told himself. He had needed money badly, but he had burned too many bridges to get a loan on the street. PeeWee was a hustler extraordinaire. He stole and sold what ever he could get his hands on. He lived his life trying to stay one step ahead of the cops and two steps ahead of all the people he owed money. He was home only eight months from sitting on a three year hit. He was getting too old to be doing prison bits. The young boys in prison were changing the way you did your time. They were too violent. Everything resulted in fights and stabbings. It wasn't like in the old days when most fights occurred over faggots and cigarettes. Now, too long of a stare could get you killed. He was glad to be home. But he was broke. Money was more plentiful, but it was harder to get. You had to move drugs to get any real money. The credit card schemes were getting too risky. The Feds took over the prosecution of those cases. And the Feds gave out time like you had two lives; they used up the first one. For the most part, the State still handled most of the drug prosecutions. You had to be a part of a major organization or, a kingpin before the Feds moved on you. So, as long as you stayed within the limits, you were OK. But, PeeWee had graduated to the career felon level. The next time he was caught spitting on the sidewalk he was looking at twenty-five years. He had to be overly careful. He decided to place a big bet on the Sixers game to get some up front money. Tony Dimaia agreed to front his bet.

Those stinking ass 76ers. He laid down twenty-five hundred dollars at three to one on the Sixers with the points against Houston. All they had to do was win by six points and he would be sitting pretty.

The paper had them favored by ten points going into the game. The Sixers were up by five with six seconds to go. The Sixers' guard, Mike Bradley stole the ball and made a long outlet pass to their strong forward David Anderson. Anderson made a strong move to the hoop, but was fouled hard by Houston's center, Jake the Fake. Bobby Walker, the Sixers' coach wanted an intentional foul call. The ref wouldn't give it to him. David Anderson was an eighty-nine percent free throw shooter. He was perfect from the line all night. This was a sure thing. No fucking way he could or, would miss two free throws. This was money in the bank. PeeWee was on his feet. The crowd's roar had subsided to a tensed silence. PeeWee had the seventy-five hundred dollars spent in his mind. The first thing he was going to buy was a new set of rims for his car. He would break his mom off a nickel. He would party for a week straight. And, he would pick up some weight to get himself started. PeeWee squeezed the program in his hand as he watched Anderson walk up to the foul line. The giant TV screen showed the sweat pouring down Anderson's face. The referee tossed him the ball. He stepped up to the line, studied the basket, and gave the ball a hard twirl. Mike Bradley came over and gave him a soft pat on the butt. Anderson bent his knees and raised his shooting arm with the ball poised perfectly on his right palm. Then, there was the release. PeeWee watched as the ball seemed to move in slow motion. It hit the inside of the rear of the rim and ricocheted out. The crowd let out a long, slow "awe". The muscles in PeeWee's stomach tightened. "That's OK baby. You just gotta make the next one and we'll still be fine," he shouted. Anderson stepped away from the line cupped his hands and blew into them. Then, he re-approached the line and restarted his free throw ritual. Mike walked over to him and gave him a little harder of a pat; a slight slap. Anderson smiled, assumed his position with the ball in his shooting hand and made his release. Again, the ball seemed to travel in slow motion. PeeWee's eyes followed and counted each rotation of the ball before it entered the rim. Seven turns. It hit the inside of the rim, spun three times around the inside and edged its way off to right before it spun out of the rim. Jake the Fake swooshed it out of the air, and with two seconds left tossed the ball towards his basket at the opposite end at the court. He missed by five feet and the buzzer sounded. The game was over. PeeWee stood there in amazement. He had just witnessed Dave

Anderson miss two free throws with six seconds left on the clock. What were the fucking odds of that happening? He felt like the biggest loser on the planet. His bank had just been robbed of seventy-five hundred bucks. And, what was even worst, he was now twenty-five hundred dollars in the hole with the mob; twenty-five hundred dollars that he didn't have.

Tony DiMaia gave him three days to come up with the money. PeeWee was certain that if he didn't pay, he would be in a wheel chair for life. His debt wasn't large enough to get him killed, but it was big enough to get him permanently maimed. He thought about leaving town, but realized that he had lived in Philly all of his life and didn't have any other place to go. Nor, did he have any contacts that would help him get away. More importantly, he would have to leave his family at the mercy of the mob. And, if there was one thing PeeWee was sure of, the mob did not know of Mother Mercy. The only person who he felt comfortable with was Shamsadeen Baku, the biggest black player in Philly. PeeWee knew he could approach Shamsadeen and, Shamsadeen could make things happen at the drop of a dime. He and Shamsadeen went back over fifteen years. They had grown up together in West Philly. Shamsadeen always respected PeeWee as a hustler and, PeeWee was always square with him. PeeWee called Shamsadeen and asked to meet him. Shamsadeen told PeeWee to meet him the next day at noon, in Love Park by the water fountain. PeeWee got there fifteen minutes early. Shamsadeen arrived twenty minutes late. PeeWee told Shamsadeen that he had met a Colombian who was new in town needed to make a strong purchase real fast. The money was already in place. PeeWee played the high-low game. He asked Shamsadeen for two kilos hoping to get one. Although Shamsadeen was doubtful with two kilos and reluctant with one, he fronted PeeWee a kilo of powder without too much of a fuss. PeeWee had always returned good in the past. However, Shamsadeen had never fronted PeeWee that much powder before. The last thing Shamsadeen wanted was to lose a friend over drugs or money. But, business was business and PeeWee understood that from the door.

Tony DiMaia gladly accepted the kilo in lieu of cash. In fact, he kicked a little bit of change back to PeeWee. To add a taste of realism to the lie, PeeWee paid some young boys fifty dollars to work him over a little. Not too much, just enough to make it look convincing; and, definitely no serious damage to the face. Then, he called Shamsadeen and told him that the Colombian had set him up and robbed him of the kilo. He promised Shamsadeen he would square up with him in a week. Shamsadeen gave him exactly one week. Anything was possible in a week. Besides, he'd rather have Shamsadeen on his ass than the fucking mob. Tonight, it was time to have a good time. He still had five days to come up with a scheme. He figured he would stop in Gretta's Sweet Spot. There was always something happening in there. And, there were always young girls looking for oldness. *"Yeah, this is the spot tonight."*

He parked his gold colored 1998 Acura Coupe a few feet from the front of the club. The corner was alive. Young boys were trying to hustle the girls and women going into the club. The flashing neon light that hung atop the entrance gave the corner a surreal look. The black asphalt on the street glistened from the rain that had fallen earlier. He could hear the music and the crowd as he got out of his car. He smiled in anticipation of a good night. A fire engine red Hyundai Elantra Coupe with a spoiler pulled up behind his car. PeeWee stared at the Hyundai to make sure that it didn't get too close to his bumper. The last thing he wanted was to have to bang his way out of the parking spot. He watched as the driver backed the car away from his and shut the car down. The driver's door opened. PeeWee watched as a long set of legs emerged from the car. They were thick, smooth, bare, and well shoed. *"Damn, I hope the rest of her is as bad as those legs."* She only got better. She was an Amazon. She stood almost six feet with her fuck-me-pumps on. Her hot red dress covered just enough to keep her legal. Her platinum blonde wig was perfect. She was perfect. PeeWee was only five feet, six inches tall, but he loved big women. She could put him in paradise.

"S'cuse me. You probably hear this all day long, but I have to tell you that you are fine!" complimented PeeWee.

"Believe it or not, you are the first brother to tell me that in a long time. I needed to hear that. I just want to have a good time tonight. It's been a long time since I've been out and I just want to enjoy myself. My girl friend told me this place is always jumping, so I came down here to let my hair down."

"Well, that's why I'm here. I just wanna have a good time too. I been in some shit and I just wanna free up from all that tonight. Maybe we can have a good time together?"

"Why not?" she answered. The two of them walked into the club together. PeeWee stepped to the side and opened the door for her. He watched as her body made deliberate movements as it passed him. Her movement was smooth. He wondered if she knew he was studying her. The club was loud and getting louder. The smoke surrounded them as they waded through the crowd. The bar was standing room only. There were a couple of empty booths off to the side in the rear. PeeWee preferred to sit closer to the front of the club, but there weren't any seats up front. He ushered his Amazon to one of the booths in the rear. She held his hand as they walked towards the booth. He felt a slight erection at the touch of her hand. He watched as heads turned. He was walking on clouds. PeeWee pointed to a small semi circular booth and stepped to the side to allow her to slide in. Then, he slid in next to her trying not to crowd her too much. The last thing he wanted was to frighten her. But, by the same token, he wanted everyone to know that she was with him. He searched around until his eyes found a waitress. He nodded at her and she gave him a nodding reply.

"What's your name?" he asked his Amazon.

"LaShonda," she answered. "What's yours?"

"PeeWee. And it ain't why you think either."

"Now PeeWee, how do you know what I was thinking? I was always told that big things come in PeeWee packages."

PeeWee grinned. "Yeah, you right, big things do come in PeeWee's package." The waitress walked up to their table. She eyed LaShonda with a "don't I know you?" look. "Where I know you from? You look like someone I went to high school with. Did you go to North Philly High?"

"No, I don't think so. I went to school in Wilmington. I just moved to Philly six months ago. Everybody is always telling me I look like someone they know. I must have a real common type of face," replied LaShonda.

"Ain't nothing common about your pretty face," complimented PeeWee

"I'm sorry, but you remind me of somebody I know. What can I get y'all to drink?"

"Yeah, I'll have a Bombay Sapphire and Tonic with a twist of lime and she'll have . . . ."

"I'll have a Cosmopolitan."

"We also have a dinner menu if y'all interested."

"I'll pass on the menu, but if she wants something that'll be fine."

"No, I ate before I left the house. The Cosmopolitan will be fine for now."

The waitress disappeared into the mass of folks that were swelling into the club. Pee Wee looked over at LaShonda and smiled. Her skin was a soft light brown, the color of coffee with the perfect amount of cream in it. Although he was never good at guessing a woman's age, he figured her to be about twenty-sevenish. Her hands were heavy, but well manicured. The red nail polish was three shades softer than her dress and five shades softer than her car. She appeared to be a woman who took very good care of herself. PeeWee guessed she worked in an office building. She looked too well kept to do any real hard work. She wore a little too much makeup for PeeWee, but hell, nobody's perfect. The tennis bracelet she wore looked like it cost her every bit of five thousand dollars. The stones were big without being gaudy. *"Yeah, I could roll with her for a minute."*

PeeWee and LaShonda played casually with words trying to hit on the right conversation that would take them through the night. They talked about each other in the typical manner in which people speak of each other when they first meet. The waitress returned with their drinks. She looked at LaShonda trying to remember where she knew her from. She was certain she knew her. LaShonda picked up her glass and held it out for a toast. PeeWee lifted his glass and bumped it against hers.

"To having a good time," he toasted.

"To having a good time," she rejoined. LaShonda let her eyes drift over PeeWee for a moment. He was short with little hands. Some of the littlest hands she ever saw on a man. He looked a little worn in the face. She figured him to be about thirty to thirty-four years old. He looked older. His brown skin lacked enthusiasm. It reminded her of her Uncle Sam's skin. Her uncle had spent most of his life working the docks on the waterfront. His skin had leathered before its time. PeeWee's skin was leathering. It wasn't a bad thing, just a thing. But, his hands were little. The littlest hands she had ever seen on a man.

His clothes were caught between hip hop and a suave look; like he couldn't make up his mind so he wore some of each. But, he did have pretty teeth. They were full and bright and white; like he just had them polished. He had the prettiest teeth she ever saw in a man's mouth. He looked at her and gave her a silent smile. *"Yeah, he's got pretty teeth."*

There was a tiny dance floor off to the side. Couples made their way on to the floor for a song or two. LaShonda declined PeeWee's requests to dance. He didn't persist. The waitress kept the drinks flowing. After three Cosmos LaShonda refused her next drink.

"Don't want to get caught driving drunk".

"Fuck that. I'm out to have a good time tonight. I don't care nothing bout driving drunk. Shit, I done made it home plenty of times drunk as a skunk. Besides, I'm quite sure you'll make sure I get to bed alright."

"Now PeeWee, don't you start nothing," retorted LaShonda.

"Don't worry baby, I never start nothing that I can't finish."

"Well, I'm sure you ain't all talk and no action, PeeWee."

PeeWee and LaShonda began to toy with each other throughout the rest of the night. He rubbed her legs. She was more than receptive. She placed her hand on his private and began to massage it. PeeWee almost choked on his drink.

"Look, I don't know about you, but I would like to get out of here and go some place where the two of us can be together," suggested PeeWee.

"What's wrong with the way we're together right now? I'm enjoying myself."

"Don't get me wrong, I'm digging this too. But, I would like to be alone with you."

"PeeWee, I definitely want to get together with you, but I'm nervous about going to a secluded place with someone I barely know. Maybe I've seen too many TV shows. I don't want to be a plot for a Lifetime movie."

"Then how about if we go back to your place?" countered PeeWee.

"Hell, that's even worst. If you are some kind of a crazy, then you'll know where I live. The last thing I want is to have a stalker running up in my spot."

"Then let's go to a hotel?"

"PeeWee, I ain't going nowhere with you until I get to know you better. I want to do something with you, but I have to be careful. Shit is too crazy out here right now. You be reading about shit like this all the time. Some unknown woman's body found in the woods. Or, some guy she meets in a bar rapes her. I can't afford to take that chance. I'm out here all by myself. But I swear I wanna give you some. I ain't had none in a long time. My shit is soaking wet. Hold on for a second, I'm feeling a little daring tonight. Let me check something out and maybe we can both be happy." LaShonda got up from the booth, grabbed her Louie Vuitton saddle bag and walked towards the bathroom in the far rear of the club. PeeWee watched her ass jiggle as she walked away from him. He was exploding with anticipation. When she returned, she motioned with her forefinger for him to follow her. PeeWee almost tripped as he hurried from behind the booth. His drink tumbled to the floor. He looked around to see if anyone noticed his clumsiness. The rest of the crowd was too absorbed in their private worlds to notice. He followed her to the back of the club. She stopped at the door of the men's room. She looked around to make sure they wouldn't be seen. The rest of the crowd was too absorbed in their private worlds to notice.

"The men's room is empty. No one is looking, let's go," she ordered. PeeWee looked at her with amazement. He had fucked in a lot of places, but never in stall of a men's room. *Fuck it, I'm down.*" As soon as they were both in the stall, they moved in for the kill. There was no time for foreplay.

"Pull down your pants," she whispered in his ear.

"I'm trying Baby, but there ain't that much room in this mother fucka." PeeWee managed to pull his pants and underwear down to his knees. LaShonda pulled her dress up and her panties down. She had her rear facing him.

"Bend down a little so I can get it in. You too tall with those heels on unless, you want me to bust that ass for you. In fact, turn around I think I can get it in better from the front."

"I'll turn around for you mother fucka," said LaShonda in a voice that was at least three octaves deeper.

PeeWee looked startled. "Hey man, I ain't no fucking faggot. I don't play that shit. I ain't fucking no man. I never fucked a faggot in all the bits I did." He was trying to pull his underwear and pants up, but couldn't get his underwear to cooperate.

"I ain't here to be fucked, at least not by you. Somebody else might take care of this ass tonight, but I'm here to take care of your little ass," retorted LaShonda. PeeWee looked down and saw that LaShonda was holding a large carving knife in her left hand.

"What you gonna do with that? Man, what's this shit all about? I don't know you. What you some kind of crazy killer or some shit?" asked PeeWee in a panic stricken voice. PeeWee tried to swing at LaShonda. She grabbed his fist and twisted him to the floor. Then, she plunged the knife straight into his heart. His head fell back and his eyes began to roll up into his head. She saw the look of "why" on his face.

"Shamsadeen told me tell you that nobody fucks him. How you gonna try and get over on him to pay some white mother fuckas?" LaShonda watched as the blood slowly oozed out of PeeWee's body. She lifted him up so that his blood drained into the toilet. Then, she reached down, grabbed his dick, sliced it off and stuck it in his mouth.

"Now go fuck yourself. I guess little things do cum in PeeWee's package," she quipped. LaShonda reached into her purse and pulled out a large trash bag. *"I'm so glad you a little mother fucka."* She said to herself as she stuffed him into the bag, tied the bag and left it in the stall. Then, she walked over to the mirror and fixed herself up. A guy stumbled into the bathroom, saw her in the mirror and continued to stagger towards the urinal. She washed her hands and sprayed herself with a quick dash of Marc Jacobs. She left the bathroom and headed straight for the door. The waitress rushed over to her.

"Hey, you or your friend owe me thirty-three dollar and twenty-seven cents on your tab."

"Oh, I'm sorry. That cheap bastard told me he had taken care of the tab," apologized LaShonda, as she searched in her bag looking for her wallet. "Here is forty, keep the change."

"Thanks. Before the night's over, I'm gonna remember where I know you from."

LaShonda gave her a polite nod and left the club. She sat in her car. A fire engine red Mustang 5.0 pulled up beside the Hyundai. A boyish face white boy was driving. He looked over at LaShonda and smiled. She returned the smile, opened her door and got into his car.

"How'd it go?" he asked.

"Almost perfect. The fucking waitress recognized me. I went to high school with the bitch. I gotta do her. Let's just wait here until closing. What time is it?"

"Twenty till two."

"Cool. She should be getting out pretty soon. We'll follow her and when the time is right I'll drop her." The two of them sat in the Mustang smoking a blunt and listening to Madonna's new CD. At 2:00 the club started to empty out. At 2:20 the staff began to filter out.

"There she is, the bitch in the K Mart outfit." They watched as the waitress parted from the crowd and walked down Sixth Street towards South Street. The Mustang slowly rode up beside her. LaShonda took off her wig and pushed the button to let the window slide down.

"Hey Verna. That's your name right? Class of 93? The waitress looked over to the side and recognized LaShonda's face but not the voice. The voice was deeper, at least three octaves.

"Yeah. I knew I knew you. You got a twin sister. In fact, you're a . . ." she caught herself.

"A fag?"

"I didn't mean it that way."

"It don't matter." LaShonda exposed a small thirty-eight and pointed it at the waitress. The waitress froze, fright filled her face. Three bangs filled the air. Three holes filled her face. She dropped to the ground. The Mustang's window glided back up. The car slowly pulled off.

"Don't forget, we have to go back and get my car."

"Girl, you need to get some descent rims for that thing."

CHAPTER FOUR

William drove up to the entrance of the Bertrem's estate and entered his code into the security box. The gate parted and allowed him entrance. The house was a spectacular Contemporary that sat fifty yards off of the main road and was inhibited by a twelve foot wrought iron gate. It sat on a one acre, heavily wooded lot that gave it a secluded appearance. It had a twenty-five by fifty foot pool with a pool house and a separate carriage house. That was the outside. Once the door opened, the opulence continued. It housed its own spa for six and sauna for eight. There were six bedrooms, a billiard room, an entertainment room, a great room, a formal dining room, a state of the art kitchen with a separate breakfast nook, and four full baths. It was a spectacular Contemporary that sat fifty feet off of the main road and was inhibited by a twelve foot wrought iron gate. Thaddeus Jackson, Mayor Bertrem's personal body guard was stationed out side of the entrance of the home. Jackson was big. Real big. He stood six- feet, eight inches tall and weighed at least three hundred pounds. Jackson was caught in a time warp. He still wore safari suits from the seventies and kept an immaculate gerry- curl. But, behind the physical awesomeness was a warm hearted, practical joker. He loved to laugh and loved to make other people laugh. The Mayor selected him because of his easy going manner.

"Hey Jackson, how are things going?"

"Boy, if I had your hand, I'd be in the islands sipping gin and tonic." That was Jackson's standard line.

"Jackson, all you have to do is start spending some of the money you have saved. The Mayor tells me that you're a stock market guru. You can't take it with you. All you're going to do is leave it behind for someone else to enjoy. Now, if you like, I can draw up some papers that will give me full and complete control over your assets."

Jackson let out a big man's laugh. His laugh was toothy and contrasted with his weathered black skin. "I got too many ex-wives that done beat you to that Mr. Jennings," said Jackson, as he pulled out a handkerchief and wiped the concoction of gerry-curl oil and sweat from his forehead.

William walked up to the front door with a big grin on his face. He rang the door bell and listened as the chime bounced from note to note. Donna answered the door.

"Good afternoon, Mr. Jennings." She refused to call him William. During his adolescent years she had referred to him as Master Jennings. "Everyone is in the great room. Did you go to church today? You know, if you want the Lord's blessings, you gotta let him see your face on Sunday morning."

"Well Donna, I'll have you know that I did go to church today. So God did see my face. And, seeing your lovely face is a sure sign that he is granting me my blessings."

"Now Mr. Jennings, you know better then to be flirting and using the name of God," scolded Donna.

William let it go. Donna looked like an elderly, black, Christian grandmother. She even wore her hair in a small perfectly shaped bun, held tightly with a starched white lace bun cover. She had been with the Bertrems for over thirty years. She was family. And, she wielded more control over the children than did either of the parents.

The three story atrium defined the grandeur of the home. William stepped into the foyer. The sunlight sprinkled through the glass and filled the foyer with artificial diagonal forms that seemed to play amongst themselves on the backdrop of the wall. William interrupted their playing area and so, they used him as a backdrop until he eventually left the area. Donna escorted him to the great room. Her formality forbade her to leave a guest unattended prior to them being announced.

"Mr. Bertrem, Mr. Jennings has arrived."

William was certain that Donna had her PhD in Butlerology. It was a familiar scene, the men in the great room and the women in the living room. The usual cast of characters had assembled for another meaningless pow-wow of political gibberish, but, William knew that his attendance was mandatory. His career was tightly interwoven with the power structure that sat in the great room. Mr. Earl Bertrem, the mayor; Mr. James Bertrem, better known as Uncle Jimmy the director of the Philadelphia chapter of the N.A.A.C.P., Mr. Francis Holstein, brother-in-law to the mayor and chairman of the Philadelphia Democratic Party. The only two faces that were not a part of the norm were J.R. and Lance, Marla's younger brothers. They were usually too busy running the streets to attend these power sessions. They both were impersonating thug rappers. They had the look and lingo down, but neither of them had any real street experience. They learned their thuggery from BET and MTV. They had both attended exclusive private schools and both were now attending Princeton. To keep their maternal grandfather happy, they had taken classes in Judaism. The Mayor did not disagree with this, he also felt that it was important that they maintain an identity with both of their cultures.

Mr. Bertrem welcomed William into the room. "Hey William, it's good to see you. Marla told me that she stopped in your office the other day. She said it was very impressive. I guess you're going to let her decorate it for you?"

"As if I have a choice in the matter," joked William.

"Yeah, I know what you mean. But, she did do one hell a job with my office. I still get lots of compliments about it. Have you met all of the partners yet?"

"No sir, I haven't. In fact, I've only met Palmer and Detmer. I met Palmer at my initial interview and Detmer stopped into my office to welcome me aboard. I'm supposed to meet the rest of the partners on Tuesday. Their having the annual office meeting and everyone is supposed to be there."

Marla's uncle, Francis Holstein joined in the conversation. "I hear Hitower is a real go-getter. From what I'm told, he's the back bone of the firm. I played golf with him once. I kicked his butt. The entire time we played, he was milking me for information about my health clinics. How many did I have? How often did I use a lawyer? How many employees did I have? Who was my real estate broker? I finally had to tell him that I was quite satisfied with my attorney. He still gave me a card and a brochure on his firm and asked me to call him if I ever became dissatisfied with my current attorney. You all know that I would never take my business away from the family.

"Well, I haven't been there long enough to know who is who. I'm still trying to figure out where I stand. Boy am I hungry," lied William, trying to change the conversation. There was a chorus of "me too's" from the rest of the men in the room. Once, William attempted to break the gender barrier by going into the family room and sitting with Marla and the rest of the women. The room became pin drop quiet. Mrs. Bertrem reminded William that there are some conversations that were not intended for his ears. William, feeling the imposed uncomfortabilty, stood up and immediately left the room. He never again tried to link the gender separation.

Donna came into the room and announced that dinner was ready.

"Word," shouted Lance.

"Tru-dat," added J.R. The rest of the group all turned and stared at William, hoping that he could interpret what was just said.

"I think they're ready to eat," interpreted William. The rest of the group laughed and shook their heads in amazement. They all meandered into the formal dining room. The women were already seated. An empty chair separated them. The men filed into their respective seating spots. Lance sat between Marla and Mrs. Bertrem. J.R. sat between Mr. Bertrem and his aunt, Lillian Holstein. William was happy to see Marla. He had not spent any time with her during the past week. He was too tired. Over the past week he hadn't left the office before eleven o'clock. By the time he got home; he just wanted to hit the sack. Mental work was more draining than physical work. Physical work hurt, mental work emptied you. He had called Marla every day, but he had not seen her. Yesterday, she went on a shopping expedition with his sisters. Today was the first time in a week that he had an opportunity to be with her. He really missed her. *"Besides, maybe she'll help get Nafesa out of my head."* He could not shake Nafesa. She lingered within him. He could hear her sassy voice singing to him. He could see her gleaming smile that lit up the room. But, he could not figure out why she was haunting him. She was a dark skin girl who was juxtaposed to everything he had been taught about beauty.

"William! Honey, daddy is asking you a question."

William's mind was adrift.

"William would you like to bless the table?" asked the Mayor.

"Sure, Mr. Bertrem." They all bowed their heads and joined hands as William thanked the Lord for the food that they were about to partake. As soon as William completed his amen, Marla began her mothering of him.

"William, are you O.K.? I swear you don't look well. Your sisters said that all you do is work and sleep. Your mother said that she never gets to see you anymore. And I haven't seen you since I stopped in your office last Monday. William, I hope this is not a trend."

Mrs. Bertrem came to William's rescue. "Marla, please! Leave William alone. He has to get adjusted to his new schedule. When your father first started practicing law I never got to see him. And, it was a miracle that he was able to get up in the morning. He was working eighteen hours a day. Once he became use to his schedule, there was no problem at all. So you see, William just has to get use to his schedule."

"That's right," added the Mayor. "And the proof is you and your two brothers."

Mrs. Bertrem blushed while the rest of the table laughed.

"So William, how long do you think you're going to travel the corporate route before you throw your hat into the political arena?"

"Right now Mr. Holstein, all that I want to do is make some money and start to pay off my student loans. And don't forget, Marla and I are only ten months from the big day."

"I understand, but keep the thought in the back of your mind. The city is wide open for a young aggressive guy like yourself. You're bright, you have the right family background and, you have the right look. Whites won't fear you and blacks will look up to you. Look at the Mayor."

The Mayor was chewing and nodding in agreement. As soon as he swallowed, he joined in. "That's right William. You could stroll into politics. Not only is the city wide open for you, but so is the whole state. Hell, who ever thought that Gladys would become the first black and female Lieutenant Governor. She was at the right place at the right time with the right package. And that's what you have William, the right package. Francis is absolutely right about the right look. I don't care what they say, having a light complexion helps a whole lot in politics. My great, great, great, great grandfather understood the importance of skin color. He was the product of a inter racial relationship. His mother was raped by her slave master.

He never felt ashamed of that fact. He looked at it as a blessing. He wrote in his dairy how beneficial it was for him to be a mulatto. He attributed half of his success to his skin color. And, he always stressed that fact to all nine of his children. None of them dared marry a person darker than themselves. You know, I don't think there has been a dark skin person in my family since his mother. Now, we all know that there isn't a bit of difference between us, but, it's the perception that counts."

William felt not only compelled to say something, he also felt compelled to say the right thing. "I agree with you sir. The dark skin blacks that I met in school weren't quite as accepted by the whites as were the light skin blacks. It's funny, now that I think about it, they all liked me. Maybe it was because my upbringing was very similar to the whites students. I don't know. Most of the black students were there because of affirmative action. Not all of them, but I would say most of them."

"You know, I'm in agreement with Clarence Thomas on the affirmative action issue," said Mr. Holstein. "I don't think it does a thing for black people if the standards are lowered to allow them to get into college. I know that if my grades were not acceptable, I would not want anyone to lower the standards to let me in. I would be too ashamed to accept the offering."

"S'cuse me! I believe the name of the game is to get in regardless of how you get in. Ain't nobody was crying when they were raising the standards to keep us out," countered J.R. The entire table stopped eating and stared at him.

"Boy, what do you know about being under-privileged? And listen to the way you're speaking. Too much TV. I'm spending thirty thousand dollars a year on you. I do not want to hear you saying s'cuse me. How do you think anyone is going to respect your opinion if you use Ebonics?" attacked Mr. Bertrem, in a tone of voice that signaled it was time to end this conversation.

Mrs. Bertrem, the perfect hostess moved in on queue. "So Marla, how are the wedding plans going?

"I was going to ask the same question," bolstered Uncle Jimmy.

"Oh mother, I don't think I'll ever have everything together. And with William working all day, I'm left to do it all by myself. Thank God for his sister, Vanessa. She's been a blessing."

"I've learned the less I do or say, the better off I am and the happier she is. Every time I give her my take on something, I'm wrong! So now, I just nod my head in agreement with whatever she says or wants," said William.

"You're learning," laughed Uncle Jimmy.

William was not feeling the atmosphere at the table. It was too staid. He wanted out. He wanted to be alone with Marla. He feigned fullness. "I think my eyes were bigger than my stomach. I can't eat another bite. Besides, Marla and I are supposed to go apartment shopping. We just want to see what's out there and the cost of a nice apartment in the Center City area. We may even look in the art museum area. Although, I'm a little hesitant about the art museum area. Some of the people at the firm live around there and they're always telling stories of having their cars broken into for the change on their center consoles. I don't feel like being bothered with that kind of nonsense."

"Well, you know how I feel about it, if I can't live in Chestnut Hill, then the only place that I'll live is in Center City," piped in Marla.

"I think the best area is the Society Hill section. It's downtown and well protected," added Mr. Holstein.

"Like I said, we're just looking around right now. We still have ten months."

Both William and Marla excused themselves from the dinner table. William could not wait to put his arms around Marla. He held her hand and walked into the living room.

"I can't believe that it's been almost a week since I last held you. It feels like a year," he whispered in her ear. He loved the way she smelled, it was of human freshness. She was beautiful, but he could no longer say that she was the prettiest woman in the world. She was wearing a soft, off-white cotton dress that accented her high-lights. Her long, dirty blonde hair crescendo just below her left shoulder. Her long slender legs were bare and shoed in Diane Jones. Her legs were long and slender and she was slender and long. He pulled her into him so that he could feel her. She felt safe, a maternal safe; secure. He pulled her into him so that he could taste her. He kissed her on the nape of her neck. She tasted of his favorite piece of candy in first grade; the piece he savored, but could never fully consume because Mrs. Bradley always made him spit it out. He wanted consummation. Marla resisted him.

"Now William, we're in my parents' home. That's why it's so important that we find an apartment. So let's hurry up and go to Center City and look at some apartments. And if you're nice now, I'll be naughty later. Deal?"

"Why can't you be naughty now and I'll be nice later?"

"Business before pleasure," she chastised.

"I bet Nafesa would not reject her man." "Come on, let's get started," he snarled.

"Oh William, don't be upset with me. We'll have plenty of time for the other stuff once we're married. It's just that it's real important that we take care of business right now. You're going to be surprised at how fast our wedding day is going to get here. I just want to make sure that everything is perfect on that day. You understand, don't you?" Her voice flat-lined. He knew it was her way of being final.

"I understand and, I'm not mad," he lied.

They drove around Center City checking out ads of apartments for rent. There were a thousand of them. William's intention was to see no more than five of them. Marla wanted to see them all. She was in her glory. He was in despair. After the eighth one, he knew he had to put an end to his torment.

"Baby, I think that we've seen enough apartments for one day. We have ten months before we're going to need one. They're all starting to look alike. I can't take it anymore. Let's get back to the pool house. I've been nice, now it's time for you to be naughty."

"O.K. I guess we can come back next Sunday and look at the rest of them. I'm getting a little tired also. But, I don't feel like going home just yet. I hear there's a nice club a couple of blocks down from here. Let's stop and have a quick drink. Then, I'll take you home and be naughty."

William knew that as always, she was stalling. There would be something else before they would actually make it back to the pool house. But, she was in charge so he had to oblige her or she would send him home totally empty.

"Sure. It's called the OFFBEAT. That's the club I went to the other night when the guys took Leslie and me out. It's a real nice spot. They have a wonderful jazz singer. I don't think she comes on until eight o'clock."

"I'm not interested in listening to any jazz. I just want to have a quick drink."

William decided that they should leave the car in the garage and walk the few blocks to the club. He found himself hurrying to get there. The weather had cooled off over the past few days. The temperature remained high, but the humidity had fallen considerably. Center City was active. It was far from the old Center City that William remembered. The restaurants were packed, the boutiques were busy and people filled the sidewalks. The old Center City was a ghost town. The new Center City was a bustling, modern metropolis.

"I'm really surprised at the amount of activity downtown," admired William.

"Daddy has really done a lot to get Philadelphia up and running again. Mayor Finkleman spent most of his focus on getting corporations into the city. He totally neglected downtown. Daddy's strategy was to bring life to downtown and the rest will follow. Well, the rest are following. It's going to be hard to beat Daddy if he runs again."

"Yeah, you're probably right."

When they arrived at the club there was an elderly church going group working their way up the stairs. William stopped at the marquis and looked at the picture of Nafesa.

"That's the jazz singer. She's really good. Her voice is strong and soothing. I think she writes her own music."

"Well, well aren't we the jazz aficionado. She looks ghetto to me. What is it with these people wearing their hair in plats? They look like pic-a-ninnies. A woman should take care of her hair."

"I think her hair fits her style. It's kind of an artsy look. In fact, the picture does her no justice," replied William in a unawaring tone.

"Well, maybe your little pic-a-ninny will take you home and get naughty with you," scoffed Marla.

William saw that Marla was getting upset with him. "Oh, come on now. Why are you acting like that? You know I'm all yours so stop acting like a spoiled child."

"I'm sorry," she apologized.

The club seemed completely different from last week. It was subdued; polite. There was no verve. There was no Nafesa. The elderly looking church going group who had worked their way up the stairs, felt right at home. William searched the club hoping to see Nafesa. He tried to keep his search for her discreet. He could not find her. The server came to take their order.

"Welcome to the OFFBEAT. Have you been here before?"

"I have," answered William.

"Good. Welcome back and greetings to the lady. Are you having drinks, or would you like a dinner menu?" she asked.

"No, we'll just have drinks. What will you have Marla?"

"I'll have an apple margarita with sugar."

"That's one of my favorites. And what will the gentleman be having?"

"Let me have a Jack Daniels with a glass of ginger ale on the side."

"Thank you. I'll be right back with your drinks."

"Excuse me. What time does the band start on Sundays?" inquired William.

"The band starts at eight every night."

William felt Marla staring at him. He knew he had to clean this up. "Good, we'll be out of here before the place starts to fill up. I'm not in the mood to deal with a crowd." He hoped that it worked. Now, it was time for small talk. "Marla do you ever think that you could seriously date a dark skin person?"

"You mean like a Nafesa? I doubt it. That's not to say that there are not some great looking dark skin men out there. Like every woman wants to date Tyson, the model, but he is the exception. I could never imagine a dark skin person holding me. I'm not saying that there's something wrong with dark men, they're just not my preference. The truth of the matter is I'm proud to look like I do. I don't delude myself into thinking that I'm not black. I know who and what I am. I want my children to look like me. You heard my father, my family has been very careful about that kind of stuff. And so has yours. Your parents would be highly upset with you if you brought a Nafesa home. Are we going somewhere with this conversation?"

"No. Just an idle question. You're probably right, my parents would be upset with me if I brought a Nafesa home," sighed William. The waiter returned with their drinks. Marla was overly pleased with the blending of her drink. The two of them sat there with little to say to each other. They both had other matters on their minds. After the second round, William could see the drinks taking hold of Marla. She flitted her eyes when she drank. Her eyes were flitting. He hoped that it would last until they got back to the pool house.

They finished their drinks and prepared to leave the club. Just as William had predicted, Marla wanted to make another stop. This time she wanted to stop at the Four Seasons Hotel where the wedding reception was going to be held. It was an unnecessary stop, but he obliged her. William was beginning to believe this was her idea of foreplay. They could never have spontaneous sex. Marla always made sure he hurtled a million obstacles before they made love. After walking around the hotel for a half an hour, she finally agreed to go to the pool house. William tried to use the car ride home as an opportunity to get Marla in the mood. He ran his hand up and down her thigh. Then, he tried to maneuver his hand beneath her panties. She stopped him.

"William, wait until we get to the pool house. It's un-lady like to do that kind of stuff in the car in broad daylight."

The pool house was really an apartment. It had all the luxuries of a one bedroom apartment. William was surprised that the Bertrem's did not use it. He and Marla had made it their secret little place to go. However, William was quite certain that their actions weren't that much of a secret. Jackson and Donna both know what was going on. Marla disappeared into the bedroom. William flopped on the couch and turned on the TV. He heard her call him. William walked into the bedroom and saw her lying nude under a sheet. She patted the bed, gesturing for him to get in. He took off his clothes and submerged under the sheets. He worked his way up her legs with his tongue.

"Lick me baby, lick me," she moaned. He began to lick her. His head bobbed up and down as his tongue lashed against her wet vagina.

"That's right. Oh, William you know how to make love to me." He moved up the rest of her body, kissing her as he moved up. When they were face to face, he tried to kiss her. She turned her head; she did not want to taste herself.

"Put it in William. Hurry up, I want to arrive." He placed himself inside her. She began to buck. He pumped up and down until he could feel the begging of his eruption.

"Here I come! Here I come!" he groaned.

"Me too," she shouted. They laid there for a minute or two before she excused herself. She had to make a couple of phone calls.

CHAPTER FIVE

It was a beautiful Sunday morning and Nafesa was feeling new. She was cruising with her top down and spirits up. Germantown Avenue was slow and congested. She wanted open space. She made a right hand turn onto a narrow street of neatly kept row homes. Flowers and plants adorned most of the enclosed porch fronts. A green and white city issued signed welcomed her to the block and proclaimed it a "CLEAN BLOCK". Nafesa pulled up to the curb of a light green front that was decorated with orange Mums and a smiling ceramic frog that held a sign that read "3927 Powell Street". Jasmin was sitting on the porch waiting for her. Jasmin Scott was Nafesa's best friend. As soon as she saw Nafesa, she sprang to her feet.

"Oh my Lord, Fesa, that car is the shit. It's beautiful. What you call that color?"

"Girl, it's called plum."

"Fesa, that car is beautiful. Check you out with the top down and shit. Girl, you betta be careful around here with your top down. One of these fools around here will snatch your little ass out that car and keep getting up."

"And Shamsadeen would make sure that it would be the last car he ever jacked."

"Oh yeah, I forgot about Shamsadeen."

Eighteen months ago Jasmin weighed two hundred and four pounds. On this beautiful Sunday morning, she weighed a hundred and thirty-one pounds. She had carried excessive weight all of her life. She was the fat girl with the pretty face. Now, she was in love with her body and she enjoyed letting everyone know it. Everything she wore was revealing. Jasmin was a head turner. Men lusted after her. She knew how to work her new look. Take her to a bar and she would have drinks pouring into her. Once, a homeless man wanted to spent all of his begging money on her in a bar. She let him. There were a couple of guys who she swung with, but for right now, she was too busy enjoying herself to be serious with anyone. Tyrone Gibson was the man closest to her, but even he had a long way to go before he could honestly say she was his. She hated Shamsadeen and he hated her. They tolerated each other for Nafesa's sake. Jasmin knew that he was not right for Nafesa. She could see that Nafesa was not the same happy person she knew before Nafesa met Shamsadeen. Nafesa was her best friend. They had met in their freshman year of high school. They shared four out of their six classes, but never spoke to each other. Jasmin had a serious crush of Louis Matthews. Louis was Nafesa's brother's best friend. Louis was always in Nafesa's house. Nafesa thought Louis was the biggest jerk in the world. One day during lunch period, Nafesa was having lunch with Brittany when Jasmin ran and slammed her books down on the lunchroom table. Nafesa looked startled. Jasmin began a tirade of threats. She threatened to kick Nafesa's ass if Nafesa didn't stop messing with Louis. Nafesa and Brittany looked at each and laughed and laughed and laughed. When they stopped laughing, Jasmin started to cry and cry and cry. Then, Nafesa started to cry. She walked over and placed her arms around Jasmin. They cried and cried and cried together. They've been best friends ever since.

The two of them had planned to shoot over to Atlantic City and hang out in the casinos for a few hours. Nafesa and the band never rehearsed on Sundays. Shamsadeen had given her five hundred dollars to play the slot machines and ordered her not to give that "use-to-be-fat-ass Jasmin one penny". As soon as Jasmin got into the car Nafesa gave her two hundred dollars. Jasmin was her best friend.

"Here girl, this is for you to play with."

"Now, that's what I'm talking about." Jasmin had on a two piece sun-kissed bikini and a wrap around orange skirt. She wanted to go back into the house and change into something that would match the color of the car. Nafesa had beat her to it. Everything Nafesa had on matched the color of the car. She was plummed down. When they stopped at an intersection for a red light, they turned heads. A couple of brothers in a black Mercedes E320 pulled up next to them.

The passenger let his window down and tried to talk to Nafesa. She gave him a polite smile and pulled off. It was their day and they were not having any outside interruptions. Jasmin searched through her Kenneth Cole bag an pulled out a JayZ CD.

"Damn Fe, we gotta drop the right sounds in. Turn that corny oldie shit off. I brought my JayZ CD. It's live!"

"Jasmin, you just like Shamsadeen. All y'all listen to is that rap shit. Check it out, I'm wearing plum Armani sunglasses, a two piece plum DKNY linen suit and sporting a plum 325i BMW. I'll be damned if I'm going to have some rap shit screaming in my car. I need some Nina Simone."

"See Fe, you wrong. Everything about us is shouting and you trying to keep us quiet. Those brothers that pulled up on us wasn't sweating us because look like Nina. They were sweating us 'cause we look like JayZ. Fe, we in a JayZ world. Now drop it in and pump that shit up. I should have brought me one of those Dorothy Dandridge scarves to wear. Shit we look good!"

Nafesa could not argue with Jasmin. She was right. They would JayZ down to A.C. and Nina Simone back home.

"You're right girl, drop it in and pump it up." The party started. Their heads were bobbing and their bodies were swaying. It felt good. The sign said they were forty miles from Atlantic City. Nafesa turned down the music, it was time to talk.

"Jasmin, have you ever had someone stare at you so hard that it made you sweat? I don't mean that the person stared at you in a bad or nasty way, but rather, in a longing way. Like you were watching a person fall in love with you right before your eyes. And, they gave off a force so great that you felt yourself being drawn into that person. You know what I mean?"

"Girl, I know what you mean. When I was in the fourth grade there was this little boy named Ronald Wallace and he used to look at me like I was a big fat taffy. And, he wanted to lick every inch of me. RONALD WALLACE, HERE I AM. COME LICK ME. I'M ALL YOURS!" she screamed at the top of her lungs.

Nafesa laughed. "Stop playing Jasmin, I'm for real. Last week in the club, there was this guy who looked at me in a way that no man has ever looked at me before. He wanted me. I mean, he really wanted me. And I found myself wanting him. Now, I can't get him out of my mind. The funny thing is, he isn't even my type. I mean he was all light and shit. He damned near look like a white man. He had that in between complexion. I ain't never liked no red or light bright man before. Give me my brown or black brother any day. But, I'm telling you, there was something very special about him. I miss him and I don't even know him."

"Oh shit! Girl, your ass just got this car, so don't start no shit. Shamsadeen will kill his white ass and beat the shit out of your's. Hell, that crazy negro might beat my ass just because you told me about it. Besides Fe, how you gonna miss somebody you don't even know? I can't get with that. Fe, you're tripping. You know I can't stand Shamsadeen, but look before you leap."

"Yeah, you're probably right. I'm tripping. Like I said, I ain't never liked no light skin man. They be all stuck up and shit. They want you to kiss their ass all the time. I don't have time for that."

"Well first of all, I don't give a damn about a brother's complexion. He could be a fucking rainbow, as long as he's a brother. And, if he says that we're rolling and he's mine and I'm his, then it's him and me against the world. What difference what color the ass is, if you're gonna kiss ass? Get me drift? Nafesa heard Jasmin loud and clear.

"You know what's funny about you Fe?"

"Jas, ain't nothing funny about me."

"No, I'm being serious. You know what I mean. The real funny."

"I know what you're saying."

"Look Fe, you've always had your choice of men. Men have always been knocking at your door. But, for as much as that should be a blessing, for you it's a curse. 'Cause you always choose the wrong man. Remember when Kelvin Stoops wanted to date you and you turned him down for Florida Boy. I mean you chose country ass Florida Boy. Fe, he had a gold tooth in the front of his mouth. But, he had money and a car. Whereas Kelvin was just a young boy trying to get an education. Florida Boy never set foot inside of a school building. He was too busy hustling. Now where are they? Kelvin is a big time banker and Florida Boy is doing seven to fifteen. By the way, what was Florida Boy's real name?"

"Mason Hutch."

"Damn. I see why he went by Florida Boy. Then there's Shamsadeen. What in the fuck were you thinking? I know your mother had just passed and you and your father were both tripping and shit, but Shamsadeen was whack from day one. You have to stop jumping in heart first. You gotta sit back and check things out for a minute. For as much as I can't stand Shamsadeen, like I said, look before you leap."

Nafesa remained silent. She had to respect what Jasmin had just told her. Jasmin was her best friend.

The closer they got to A.C. the heavier the salt air became. They exited the Atlantic City expressway and took King Boulevard into the city. Each casino had its own appeal. Nafesa and Jasmin chose the Resorts because Jasmin had won two-hundred and seventeen dollars on the slot machine the last time they were there. They pulled into the valet parking area. A pimpled face, white boy ran over to the car and opened the door for Jasmin. Nafesa searched through her bag and found the valet key for the car. The boy ran around to her side of the car and opened the door for her. She stepped out of the car and gave him the key and a twenty dollar bill.

"My old man told me that I better bring this car back looking just like it was when I left the house, or he is going to kick my ass. Now, here is a twenty, please, please, please do not let anything happen to this car!" warned Nafesa.

CHAPTER SIX

I t was Tuesday, the day of the State of the Firm address. A week of work had passed and William was beginning to question what he had gotten himself into. He had spent the entire week, close to eighty hours in the library. He bounced from one legal issue to another. The only time he ever saw the inside of his office was when he first arrived in the morning and when he left at night. The time in between was spent on the sixteenth floor. Trish and Jackie, the librarians were becoming two of his best friends. His enthusiasm was waning fast. He could not believe that he had gone through twenty-two years of schooling to sit in a library all day looking up case after case. He had specifically asked Palmer during the interview if he would be a part of a litigation team. He had voiced his desire to be a trial attorney. Palmer assured him that he would be part of an active litigation team. The last thing he ever expected was to become a research specialist. Some of the drones that worked the library believed they were the backbones of the litigation teams. "Without us, there would be no litigation team. Most cases are won in the trenches." William saw it differently, grunts worked in the trenches and Generals worked in war rooms. William wanted to be a General. He knew that he had to apprentice as an officer, but he did not want go out as a grunt. Let the grunts prepare, he wanted to be in the war. He pushed his books to the side. *"Enough is enough!"* William decided to go to Richard and ask to be transferred to a litigation division.

Richard's office was on the fifteenth floor. From the look of the floor, it was the home of the big shots. It was well dressed. The offices were spacious and the atmosphere was extremely quiet. The secretaries were better looking and better dressed. The art that hung on the walls appeared to be originals; not the re-prints that hung on the fourteenth floor. Richard was standing beside a busty blonde who was working and nodding at the same time. From the expression on her face, it was obvious that she wanted Richard to drop dead or, at least go away. His mouth was moving a mile a minute. He appeared to be wearing the same suit he had on a week ago when he barged into William's office. He looked up and saw William approaching him. His face said it all, *"How dare this grunt break rank and approach a General without permission?"*. William steadied his course and walked directly up to Richard.

"Excuse me Mr. Basil, can I have a word with you?"

"It depends on what it is that you want to talk about."

"Well, I know that I've only been here a week, but I would like to know how do I go about getting transferred to one of the litigation divisions?" I think I'm better suited for the courtroom than I am for the library. That's all I've done for the past week."

Richard looked at William as if he was from Mars. Then he gave William a big smile. "Well Mr. Jennings, aren't we Mr. Eager Beaver. So you want to move to a litigation division? When the firm is ready for you to move from the library to the courtroom, they'll let me know. Then Mr. Jennings, I'll let you know. You have only been here for a week and you want to be trying cases. Don't you think you should wait for the bar exam results before you start to whine? There are attorneys who have been with the firm for five years and have never set foot in the courtroom. Maybe you don't understand how money is made in this business. Let me assure you of one thing Mr. Jennings, more money is made outside of the courtroom than inside of the courtroom. If we're in court, we've already lost. Do you get my drift?"

"Yeah, I get your drift. But I felt compelled to ask."

"Well, Mr. Jennings, I felt compelled to answer. Now, if you don't mind, I have work to do. And, I'm quite sure that you also have work to do. So let me go back to my office and I assume you will be returning to the library."

William put his tale between his legs and limped away. There was no doubt in his mind that Richard was indeed a Dick! William had been there for a week and already he had a serious dislike for Richard. He knew that a showdown was forth coming. He made his way back to the library. His workstation was just as he had left it, piled high with books. Trish came over and tapped him on the shoulder and informed him that a Lexis terminal had opened up. William thanked her and made his way over to it. He was starting to believe that he had made a serious mistake by not going to the District Attorney's office with his uncle. He had been advised that the corporate ladder would be far more beneficial for him. He was warned that prosecutors, like defense attorneys were a roguish lot who usually burned out at an early age with only poor health, no money, and a broken family to show for themselves. Had he started with his uncle as a prosecutor, he would be developing his own case load. And once he passed the bar, he would immediately be in the courtroom trying cases. Cases that matter. Cases that decided whether a man lost his freedom or, his right to live. Not cases about whether or not a supplier was going to get his garments on time. But, here he sat, researching cases for another project.

At four o'clock, all of the drones stopped what they were doing and made a procession to the other end of the sixteenth floor. It was time for the State of the Firm address. The address was held in the partners area. The area surpassed the General's quarters. It was meticulously dressed. But it was too packed with employees to be enjoyed. William saw Phil standing off to the side. He wormed his way through the crowd and stood beside Phil. Phil gave him a short smile greeting. William returned the greeting. He looked for Leslie, but could not find her in the crowd.

"Now you're about to see why the big boys get paid the big bucks. Once you learn how do what it is they do, you'll be on your way to the big time. Me? I'm still a big-shot in the making. But, one day I'll get there. One day."

Phil was correct. The partners had perfected the art of form over substance. They each took a turn describing the vitality of the firm without going into details. Everyone was expected to dig a little deeper in their effort to help make the firm the biggest and the best in the city. A better sense of teamwork was needed. It was a locker room pep rally. Richard Basil, the consummate cheerleader gave a rousing applause at the completion of each of the partner's pep talk. His boss, Fred Detmer had his message read to the team via Heleen, his secretary. Richard was like the extra point kicker on a football team, no one respected him, but the team couldn't win without him. After the rally, the workers were directed to return to their stations and keep the ship afloat. William needed change. The monotony of his life was redirecting his personal journey. It was robbing him of his hopes, his ambitions, his youth. This was not the answer. He had been lied to. Climbing the corporate ladder required the sacrificing of something he could not sacrifice, his soul. He needed to get away to be refreshed, rejuvenated, revitalized. William looked at his watch, it was seven-fifteen. He unfastened his cell phone from his belt and dialed for Marla. Her voice box answered. He had not heard from her all day. He had heard from Nafesa. She was constantly calling him; in his mind. *"That's it, I'll go out to the club tonight. I need the relaxation. I'll go by myself and have a good time. I don't need a crowd. I'll just sit back and enjoy myself."* William closed all of the opened books in front of him and headed for his office. Once there, he grabbed his jacket, turned off his lights and headed for the elevators. He could feel the heads turn as he walked towards the elevators. It was seven-thirty and he was leaving early.

The evening air was warm and breezy. *"Yeah, this is a good thing,"* he told himself. The walk to the club seemed long. Maybe it was because he took in more of the surroundings as he strolled along. The streets were full of people who had places to go, but were taking their time getting there. William joined their pace. He had some place to go, but he was not in a rush to get there. The night city was completely different from the day city. The day city was hostile, relentless, without mercy. It looked for victims and devoured them. The night city was casual and soft, it took the time to smell the urban aroma that only a city can give off. The day city was a race. The night city was a stroll. William continued his stroll to the OFFBEAT.

The line outside the OFFBEAT was a little longer than last week's. He waited. William looked at the picture of Nafesa and smiled. He noticed the writing across the bottom of the marquis, "FINAL WEEK". His heart raced. A heavy set woman in a pink dress that was three sizes too small for her, tried to start a conversation with him. He was not having it. He was here to see someone and did not want anyone to think he was alone. He stepped into the club. It was alive. Couples seemed to be everywhere. He saw the table he and Marla had sat at on Sunday. It was taken by a couple who could not stop smiling at each other. *"Why hadn't the table captivated him and Marla like that?"*

he silently questioned. He wiggled his way through the masses and found an empty seat up front and off to the side. *"This is the perfect spot to test her powers. If there is a mystical connection between him and Nafesa, he would surely find out tonight."* There was a couple sitting next to him. They eyed each other. William gave the brother the obligatory nod. The brother returned the nod. William looked at his watch, it was seven-forty-eight. He smiled to himself. *"Perfect timing."* A young waitress came over and introduced herself as Charmaine. William ordered a Becks in a bottle. She left and promptly returned with his bottle of Becks.

"That'll be four-fifty. Or, would you like to run a tab?"

"Yeah, you can run a tab." The band members fumbled on to the stage to test their instruments. The stage hands fumbled around, testing the sound system and the lights. All was in order. The host made his way on to the stage. It was he same person from last week. This time, his suit was not as perfectly tailored. He tapped into the mic. A ping echoed through the sound system. The crowd hushed.

"Good evening."

The crowd responded with a shared "good evening".

"Alright! Hey, you guys sure look good out there. My name is brother Haki and I am your host tonight. Boy, oh boy, can you believe that our performers have been here for three weeks already?"

"They can stay for another three weeks," someone shouted from the crowd.

"OK now, don't try to do my job. I need my job. I have five children and two ex-wives. So, you know I need my job!"

The crowd laughed.

"As I was saying, it's hard to believe that three weeks have gone by already. I guess it's true what they say about time flying by when you're having fun, because I've had a ball with this group. They're the baddest group in Philly. Word is, they're moving up to the Big Apple. Let's just hope that they won't forget where they came from. With all of that being said, please give a warm . . . to hell with warm, let's give a hot welcome to Nafesa!"

The crowd bought it. They were cheering, applauding and whistling. William was levitating on the excitement. The music began. It was a different opening number. He recognized the tune. It was Stevie Wonder's "Jesus Children. Then, he heard her voice. She bopped on to the stage. She was wearing a silk powder blue blouse with only the last four buttons fastened and a pair of dark linen pants. Her sandals exposed her toes. She had on baby blue toe nail polish. William searched her hands to see what type of jewelry she wore. More specifically, he searched to see if she was wearing a wedding band. She had on a African cowry shell bracelet on her right wrist and a diamond tennis bracelet of her left wrist. She wore a total of six rings, but none of them adorned the second finger of her left hand. Then, his mind raced to Marla. She was wearing his three-carat diamond engagement ring. He had sworn himself to her by way of a marriage proposal. Now, here he sat, in a nightclub admiring, no falling for a dark skin jazz singer. His world was spinning. He closed his eyes and erased the scenario from his mind. He opened his eyes and returned to Nafesa. He watched her feel the crowd. She was searching for something. No, she was searching for someone. No, she was searching for him. He felt it. He knew it. He waved his head back and forth with the music. He was dying for her to see him. He knew it was just a matter of time before their eyes met. It seemed like an eternity. At last, her eyes found his. With their eyes they met and embraced. It was there. He was hers and he knew she wanted him to be hers. She descended the stage and worked her way over to him. They smiled at each other as if they were old friends. They were. They were primal lovers. They were soul mates. She edged her way closer and closer to him. It was personal. He held out his hand for her to touch him. She stuck out her hand just enough to let their fingers brush. *"She was real. It was real,"* he told himself. For the rest of the night, she gave her voice to the crowd, but she gave her soul to him. The night was long. Some people left, but he stayed put. He had to talk with her and feel the warmth of her voice. He had to let her know every thought he had of her. He had to hold her and feel himself melt into her. Nafesa announced the last song.

"You know, every now and then, I like to bring someone up on stage and give them a special performance."

"Take me baby," someone shouted from the audience. Nafesa smiled. Everyone in the club knew who that special person was. She offered out her hand to William. "Would you like to come up on stage with me for a private performance?"

"What man could or would refuse?" answered William. The

crowd fed into it with a cool applause. Nafesa held out her hand as an invite. William accepted the invite and moved on to the stage. Flavor was trying to figure out what in the hell was going on. The band was trying to figure the queue to bring it all together. This was something totally new, but it was working. The crowd was feeling it. William was totally oblivious to everything and everyone except Nafesa, the dark skin girl who was juxtaposed to everything he had been taught about beauty. Nafesa turned to the band and gave them a quick nod; the instruments rained in. She smiled, nodded her head and returned to William. It was Jon Lucien's "What is Love?". If Jon Lucien didn't know what love was, William was certain that he did and she was standing right before him. He lowered his head and tried to join in on the flow. He wanted to shake in utter disbelief that he was on stage, in a jazz club, being serenaded by a woman whom he had only seen twice in his life and, he was falling in love with. But, it was a wonderful disbelief; a new and wonderful disbelief. Nothing like this had ever happened to him before. But it was happening to him and he didn't want it to stop happening to him.

Nafesa had all but given up on ever seeing the in-between complexioned face that housed the eyes that had stolen her heart a week ago. Was it all real? Or, she was just tripping as Jasmin had said. Maybe he was a talent scout or someone who worked in the music industry. Maybe he was just a jazz fan. But deep within her heart she knew what she was feeling was real. And, she knew the feeling was too strong for him not to reciprocate. For the past week, every night when she took the stage she searched for him, hoping she would feel his presence sitting some where out there in the audience. It had not happened. But tonight, she was clicking. The band had a real funky rehearsal, Shamsadeen was in Atlanta taking care of business, and her father had called her just to say hello. That was rare. The posi-vibes were definitely flowing. Flavor had decided to change the opening set. He chose Stevie Wonder's, "Jesus Children" as the opening number. He loved that song. It had picked him up when he was down. When the band started to play, she closed her eyes and moved into the song. The atmosphere was a sweet groove. She was half way into the song when she felt him. He was out there. No crowd had ever put out that much love. She tried to remember where he had sat the last time he was here. She looked over to her right but he wasn't there. She looked for his starring eyes. The feeling was pulling her to the left. She turned to the left, squinted her eyes and saw him sitting two rows from the front. *"Oh Allah, it's him."* Now, she was singing on pure instinct because her mind was on him. He was calling her. No, he was beckoning her. He held out his hand but, she was too afraid to give him hers. She had to touch him. She extended her hand just enough for their fingers to brush. She had to figure out a way to be with him. She wanted to touch him, hold him and let him know that she knew. She decided that she would bring him up on the stage as part of the act. It was working. The crowd was feeling the vibes that she and her mystery man were emitting. *"Oh Allah, thank you, thank you,"* she prayed within her heart.

After the show was over, William remained in his seat hoping she would come out and spend time with him. The couple at the table next to him smiled at him.

"Man your old lady sure can flow," complimented the brother. William accepted the compliment. "Thanks." Charmaine came over to him.

"Why didn't you tell me that you were Nafesa's guest? If you her people then I would have let you drink for free."

"That's OK. I'll settle up with you."

"Naw, it's not like that. I'll have my manager sign off on the bill for you. Give me a second and I'll be right back." Charmaine ran off with the bill before he could explain that he was not Nafesa's guest; well at least not her formal guest. Charmaine returned with a disappointing look on her face.

"I'm sorry but my manager said that Nafesa has a person by the name of Shamsadeen down as her nightly guest. And he said that he knows Shamsadeen. I'm sorry, I tried. That'll be thirteen seventy-five."

"No problem. I appreciate your effort. Here is a twenty, keep the change." William was crushed, devastated. He had imagined that she was free to be his. She wasn't. She belonged to a Sham-Sardine. He was confused. *"What was up with all of that feeling she had just put out?"* He was certain that is what not just a stage act. It was too real to be fake. Then he thought about Marla and himself. *What was the difference between his relationship with Marla and Nafesa's relationship with Sham-Sardine? Hell, he was engaged to Marla.* He would ask Nafesa for an answer to the puzzle. She would have to tell him that what they were feeling was not real. He had to hear it from her before he surrendered. He got up from the table and moved over to the bar.

The band was congratulating each other back stage. It was a hell of a show and they all knew it.

"Man, that shit was too live," bragged Mel.

"Dig it! We tore it up out there," boasted Greg, the drummer.

"Fe, what in the hell was going on out there with you and that light boy? I mean the crowd took it all in, but it seemed too real for me. You know that dude or what?" asked Flavor.

Nafesa knew that she could not tell them about the situation. Not just yet. Really, she didn't know what to tell them or, how to tell them.

"No. It was just something that I thought the act needed. It was spontaneous," she sort of lied.

"Check it out, there is this little honey who was sitting in the back by herself. Me and her were making eye contact all night long. I think I'm going to introduce myself. I'll see y'all around, but hopefully not for long. If we miss each other, tomorrow at one o'clock for rehearsal," reminded Flavor.

Nafesa could not wait to go out into the club area. She knew that her mystery man would be out there waiting for her. She checked herself out in the mirror. She looked OK. Her outfit was still somewhat fresh. Well, maybe not that fresh. She had sweated pretty heavily throughout the show. He would have to take her as she came. *"It's now or never,"* she told herself.

William watched as Nafesa emerged from the rear of he club. Her eyes fanned the club. She was searching for him. People were coming up to her complimenting her on her performance. She gave them a polite smile and continued her search. He decided that he would meet her half way. Then, he decided that he would watch her move towards him. It was as though she was a panther out on a hunt. Each step was deliberate and graceful. She was tight. He stood erect as she walked towards him. When they were within a few feet of each other, he held out his hand to formally meet her. She shoved his hand away.

"I thought we were past that," she said with her arms outstretched.

"We are," he answered as he moved into her arms. Nafesa tightened her arms around him and let go of every ounce of emotion she had damned inside of her. It poured; it flooded. She wanted to inundate him with it. She took in a deep breath of him. She was beginning to feel as though she knew everything about him. Yet, she didn't even know his name. *"Who needs a name when you have love?"* she convinced herself.

William felt himself weaken as she held him in her arms. He had always held Marla, she had never held him. He wanted to kiss her on her neck, but restrained himself from doing so. He wanted passion, but she deserved respect. She smelled of a foreign exotic fragrance. He felt himself rising. He moved from within her. She was far removed from Marla. There were no similarities. She was night city and Marla was day city. He was tired of daylight. All of his life he was told to fear the night now, he wanted it. He wanted to roam in the mystery of darkness. The daylight was safe, he could see what was coming. He wanted the night with all of its happenstance. William introduced himself.

"Hello Nafesa, my name is William."

"Funny, you don't look like a William. I would have guessed you to be a Shawn or Troy, or some name like that; a pretty boy's name."

"A pretty boy's name? Why, do you think I'm pretty?

"You're very handsome but . . ."

"Hey, I'm not here to talk about me. I want to talk about you. I want find out just who you are. If you have time, I'd like to buy you a drink and find out who is this woman who has so much mystical power over me."

Nafesa felt somewhat relieved that he wasn't some pretty boy who got off talking about himself. He wanted to know about her; he wanted to know of her.

"Come and follow the Voodoo Queen," she joked in a poor Caribbean accent. Nafesa took William by the hand and led him to a table in the rear of the club. She was flattered by his offer to seat her first. They both sat and stared at each other for a while. They were not probing for physical attractions, they were beyond that. They both liked what they saw. They were searching for answers to their cerebral and ethereal attractions. William placed his hands in a folded school boy manner on the table slightly into her space. He hoped that before the night was over she would touch them. Nafesa recognized the move. Before the night was over, she would oblige him. Arthur Prysock was serenading in the background. He filled them with conversation. They listened as he told them what they both wanted to hear. They listened to words of beauty, happiness, warmth, and love. The waitress came over and broke up their melodic conversation. Their minds joined, *"how dare she?"*.

"Nafesa, do you want your usual?"

"Yeah Charmaine, that'll be good," sighed Nafesa.

"How bout you sir, you want another Becks?"

"No. I'll have a coke with a twist of lime and no ice."

"Cool, I'll be right back," smiled Charmaine.

"So Nafesa, how long have you been singing?"

"William, talk to me, please don't interview me. I think you have a lot of other things that you want to talk to me about. You can interview me the next time we meet. But to answer your question, I've been singing since I was five. My grandmother use to tell the story that when I was five, she took me to church one Sunday and when the choir started to sing, I ran out of the pew and joined the choir. And I've been singing ever since."

Nafesa was right, he really didn't want to know how long she had been singing. It was a safe question to start with. But, he was tired of safe and she was the type of woman who would not accept safe. He moved away from the security of safe and plunged into the unknown. She was overly receptive and refused to let him return to his world of safe. In between glasses of coke and bottles of Perrier, they spoke of their whens, their wheres, and their whys. She told him of her dreams and fantasies. William smiled, wishing they were his.

Charmaine walked over and reminded them that the club was going to close in ten minutes. They had not realized that they had sat for almost two hours talking to each other. Nafesa reached across the table and placed her hands on top of his.

"William, this may sound corny, but this is one of the best nights of my life."

William raised up his glass in a toasting motion and whispered, "here's to many more of the best nights of your life."

Nafesa returned the toast, "and may they be toasted with you." They both stood up from the table. William allowed her to walk out first. He followed her. She was just as beautiful from the back.

"Where did you park?" she asked.

"A few blocks from here. The night air will do me good."

"And some young thug will do you bad. I'm parked in the lot next to the club. I'll give you a ride to your car."

"Thanks. I appreciate that."

Gee, the club manager was standing at the door thanking everyone for coming and inviting them back.

"See you tomorrow Gee," parted Nafesa.

"See you tomorrow Nafesa. You really kicked it tonight. By the way, tell Shamsadeen I need to see him about some business matters." Nafesa knew that Gee did not need to see Shamsadeen. She had known Gee for four years and he had never used her as a messenger before. No one ever used her as a messenger for Shamsadeen. Shamsadeen would not have it. She would not have it. That was Shamsadeen's world and she tried to stay as far away from it as possible. This was Gee's way of warning her about what she was getting herself into. Suddenly, she could hear Jasmin's voice in the back of her head, "look before you leap."

"I'll do that when I see him Gee. Good night." Although William did not know the extent of her relationship with this Sham-Sardine, he could feel the chilling effect of Gee's comment.

"Is everything OK?' he asked.

"Sure, everything is fine," she lied. Nafesa reached into her pocket-book and pulled out her keys. She pushed a little black button and the car chirped.

"Nice car," he complimented. "It still has that new car smell. How long have you had it?"

"Thanks. I just picked it up on Saturday. So what does that make it, three days? Now, where are we going?"

"19th and Market. I'm in the Heritage lot. You have to go in off of Market Street. Nafesa did not want small talk. She wanted mood. She flipped through her cd case and pulled out the Best of Aretha Franklin and slid it into the cd player. She turned up the volume to signal a request for silence. She wanted to feel his presence rather than hear him. William caught the vibe. She let her hand relax on the gear shifter. He eased his hand close enough to hers so that they might accidentally touch in a turn. Nafesa saw the parking lot's big neon sign and pulled up beside it.

"Thanks for everything," he said, not knowing what else to say.

"No, thank you," she said, knowing exactly what to say.

"How do we stay in touch?" he asked.

"With feelings," she smiled.

"Well, here's my card with my office number. I'll write my home and cell numbers on the back of it. You can feel me anytime you want."

"I'll give you my cell number, but I must tell you that I always seem to leave it in the house or forget to turn it on. I never really wanted one, but necessity dictates."

"I've had my cell for the past three years. I can't live without it."

"Come here William," she ordered. He surrendered and leaned into her. She ran her hands across his face. She closed her eyes and pulled his face towards hers. She wanted to give him a long passionate kiss, but settled for a cordial kiss on the side of his cheek. Jasmin's voice re-entered her head, "look before you leap". William was set a blazed with the kiss. It was more than he had expected.

When William got home, he took off his clothes and laid across his bed. His head was still swimming. He ached for her.

Nafesa walked through her front door expecting a barrage of questions from Shamsadeen. Then, she remembered that he was in Atlanta. She took off her clothes and washed what little make-up she wore from her face. She dried her face and stared into the mirror that hung over the face bowl. William's scent was still fresh in her senses. *"Oh Allah, guide me and protect me,"* she prayed.

CHAPTER SEVEN

William couldn't figure out why Marla's younger brother, Lance was banging on the walls of William's college dorm room. Nafesa, Gee, Charmaine and Lenora were standing in the corner laughing at Lance. The more they laughed, the louder the banging became. The louder the banging became, the more distant the faces became. The banging got louder and louder and louder. Suddenly, William realized that the banging was coming his from his bedroom door. A voice accompanied the banging. It was his younger sister, Lenora giving a steady knock on the door.

"William! William! William! I know that you're in there William. William, there's a Mr. Basil on the phone for you. William, are you taking any calls?"

"Mr. Basil? What time is it? I didn't hear the phone. What time is it?"

Lenora opened the door and stepped into William's room. The room looked exactly as it did the day William left for college. The novels he read in twelfth grade were still resting on the bookshelf over his city issued desk. The city was going to put his uncle's desk out to pasture when his uncle stepped in and rescued it. It was reassigned to William's bedroom. Even the posters of the Godfather were still fastened to the wall. Once he left for college, he had never really returned. His room was now a layover between his flight from yesterday and his journey into his tomorrow. His room was a snap shot of Master Jennings. It was no longer relevant.

"William, it's ten-forty-seven. Are you taking the call or not?"

"Oh no! I can't believe I over slept. Why didn't anyone wake me? I'll take the call. Tell him to hold on for a second." His mind was in a state of panic. This was only his second week at work and the senior attorney of his division was calling to wake him because he had overslept. He looked around, trying to figure out what to do. There was a sock sitting on the floor next to his bed. He grabbed the sock and stuck it in his mouth. Lenora's mouth fell open. He reached over and removed the receiver from the cradle.

"'ell-o," he garbled.

"Hello. I'm holding for a William Jennings. Look, I've been holding for at least three minutes and unless you immediately put William on the phone I will hang up and you can tell William to look elsewhere for employment. Do I make myself perfectly clear?" vented Richard.

"'ichard. Iss is illiam at you are speaking ith. I'm aving an allergic e-action to omefing I ate ast ight. My face is the size of a asket-all. My muffer is making a-range- ments for me to go to a doc-ter." His sister was against the wall laughing.

"Well, when were you going to let us know? Half the day has gone by and not a peep from you or any of your family members. I am not in the habit of calling employees, especially not new employees. Is this the way you people do business?"

William challenged himself to believe that Richard had just refereed to his family as "you people" He snatched the sock from his mouth. His light face turned beet red.

"Excuse me Richard, did you just say you people? Did you just refer to my family as you people?" His sister was still against the wall, but her laughter stopped.

"I most certainly did. Why? Do you have a problem with what I just said?"

"Richard, for as long as you live, don't you ever make a disparaging remark about my family. Who do you think you are? I can tell you what you are. You're nothing but a cheap insecure nobody who walks around trying to make everyone's life miserable. Why? Because misery loves company. But let me let you in on a little secret, you are the joke of the office. Everyone hates you. And, your name is Dick. In fact, your name is Isa Dick. So, having said all of that, Isa Dick, you can find someone else to bother because I quit!" William slammed the receiver down. Lenora pushed herself from the wall, shook her head and walked out of the room. William was still swirling with anger. He felt that he had over-reacted, but he knew that he had to stand up for his family. He could not let Richard Basil, poor white trash who had connived his way to the top belittle his family. The Jennings had achieved their status a hundred years before Richard's family ever passed through Ellis Island. The Jennings had landed in this part of the world as servants. They were never slaves. They had worked as dock workers, preachers, schoolteachers, abolitionist, publishers, doctors, lawyers, judges, and politicians. Richard Basil was a first generation college grad. How dare he refer to William's family as "you people"? The surge of anger that had rushed to the top of his head began to simmer. Soon the anger subsided and the reality of what he had just done began to fill the space that had previously been occupied by the anger. He sat on the side of the bed and rested his head between his hands. *I must have lost my damn mind. I just quit an eighty-five thousand dollars a year job,"* he murmured to himself. But somehow, he felt good about it. It was an inner feeling of relief. It was like the feeling he got after he finished a final exam that he knew he aced. His Uncle Jesse strolled into his head. His Uncle had won the race for the District Attorney's Office two years ago. He promised William that as soon as William graduated from law school, he could come and work for him. Judge Jennings, William's father disagreed with that decision. The Judge wanted William to climb the corporate ladder. William obliged his father and never sought employment with his uncle. Deep within him, William wanted to work as a prosecutor. He wanted to get enthralled in the fast paced world of criminal law. It was where the action was, if not the money. When people picked up the morning papers, they wanted to read about the grime in the city. They could care less about large settlements. They wanted criminals to be settled with. That's where he wanted to be. Judge Jennings disagreed with that decision. William leaned over and picked up the receiver that he had just slammed down. He pressed the buttons on the receiver that coincided with 555-6000. An automated voice answered the phone.

"Hello. You have reached the Philadelphia District Attorney's Office. If you know the extension of the party you are seeking, you may dial it at anytime during this message." William pressed the buttons that coincided with 6001. A real voice answered the phone.

"Hello, Mr. Jennings' office. May I help you?"

"Hello Karen. This is William. Is my Uncle available?"

"How are you William?"

"I'm OK. How about yourself?"

"I'm blessed. Jesus is my guiding light. Hold on while I get your Uncle for you."

William could hear a click over the phone followed by a booming voice. It was Uncle Jesse.

"Well, well! What is this call going to cost me?"

"Just a job. I just quit my job with the firm. I wasn't going to make it there. I was destined to be a library specialist if I had stayed there. I was probably just a token."

"Well William, token or not, it's very important that blacks get into top positions at the top tier law firms. For you to just blow it off is unacceptable. You were the first black to ever work there as an attorney. It's the second largest firm in the city. What kind of an effect do think this is going to have on their future recruiting decisions pertaining to minorities? And, what has your father said about this? You know how he feels about you working over here."

"Unc, I don't mean to cut you off, but I only want to know if you can bring me on with you. I'll deal with my father later. I would really like to work in your office. I know the pay is only half of what I was scheduled to make once I passed the bar. I can't worry about if the firm will ever hire another minority. I made my decision and now I'm ready to live with it. Now, can you, or can't you bring me on board with you?"

His uncle was taken aback by his straight forwardness. He realized that he little nephew was now a man.

"Sure William. I think I can bring you on board with my office. Hell, if I can't then who can?" he chuckled.

"Thanks Unc. When do you want me to start?"

"Let's say the first of the month. I'll have Karen call down to personnel and they'll have you come in and fill out the necessary paperwork. Is that OK?"

"Sure. The first of the month is good. Thanks a lot Unc. I knew I could count on you. And by the way, I understood everything you said. It's just that right now I can't worry about it. Thanks again. I'll stop by the house and talk to you about everything in the next couple of weeks. Take care Unc." William hung up the phone feeling a lot better than he did when he picked it up. The first of the month was good. It gave him a couple of weeks to get his head together and, it freed him up to spend some additional time with Nafesa. Hopefully, she would call him today. It was time for him to get his day started.

William took a shower and threw on some street clothes. He was hungry and he needed a shave. He went down stairs to the kitchen to check out the fridge. He heard his mother talking on the phone.

"Oh my goodness," his mother gasped. "I think I see the ghost of my long lost son William. Can it be that he lives?"

"Ha. Ha. Aren't we the funny one." William was the only one of her three children who looked like her. Vanessa and Lenora were spitting images of their father. But, there was no mistaking whose child William was. William's maternal grandfather, William O'Leary was an Irishman who operated a small grocery store in the heart of an all black neighborhood. He soon fell in love with the people and more importantly, he fell in love with Mildred Grayson. The couple married and bore four children. William's mother, Lucille was the eldest. When she was young, Lucille was always told that she was stupid for identifying with her blackness when she could pass for an Italian. But, in the eyes of everyone who looked down on her and who looked up to her, she was black. And so, she stayed that which she was. She was tall, taller than her husband. She had emerald green eyes that lit up her face when she smiled. She had worn her hair in the same shoulder length hairstyle for the past fifteen years. She had been the same sweet, easy going woman all of her life. Rarely did she get excited about anything. But, William knew that quitting his job would be an exception. And, there was no doubt in his mind that Nafesa was going to make the hair that she had worn in the same shoulder length hairstyle for the past fifteen years, stand up on her head.

"Did I get any messages?" he asked.

"I didn't take any messages for you. The phone rang a couple of times and Lenora answered it so, you might want to check with her. By the way, what are you doing home today?"

"I quit my job today." William waited for the onslaught.

"You did what? William, have you lost your mind? What are you going to do now? That was an excellent job."

"Slow down Mom. I'm quite sure I did the right thing. I wasn't going to make it there in the long run. I was only kidding myself when I took that job. I should have gone with Uncle Jesse from the start. I called him and he said I could still come on board with him at the beginning of the month."

"Oh my goodness, wait until your father hears about this! He is going to have a fit. You know that you should have talked to him about this before you just upped and quit that job."

"Mom, I'm not a child who has to consult with Dad before I make a decision about my life. It is my life."

"Well, what about Marla? Did you speak with her before you made your decision? She is going to be a part of that "*my !ife*" you spoke about."

"Mom, right now, I'm not sure who is going to be a part of my life. The only thing that I do know right now is, I'm the only part of my life that I should have to worry about. If Marla doesn't like my decision, then she can move on. The decision has been made and I can't take it back."

"If I am correctly reading between the lines of what you're saying, you better be sure you know what you're saying. Because, you are about to turn some lives upside down, yours included. So you better think long and hard before you make any major decisions on your own. William, I know how you are. Once something new gets into your head you can't get it out until you're done with it or, it's done with you. Now I'm telling you, Marla is the best thing that ever happened to you. You would be a fool to let her slip through your fingers. Don't be like your sister Vanessa, she can't keep anything she's so wishy-washy. I know you don't want to hear me preach to you, but that's one of the reasons why I'm here. And you know you haven't heard the half of it yet. Wait until your father hears about this. Heaven only knows how he's going to take all of this mess. He is going to hit the ceiling."

"Thanks for your words of wisdom Mom. And by the way, Marla's not the best thing that has ever happened to me." William knew that this conversation would continue infinitum. He would have to leave the kitchen for it to end. He could feel his mother staring at his back as he walked out. It was time to move on. He was in a Nafesa mood; she was his shield of steel. He called up the stairs for his sister, Lenora.

"Lenora, did I get any messages?"

"Marla called. She said she called your office, but of course you weren't in. She said she was just calling to see if you were alright. Oh yeah, she told me to remind you to turn your cell phone on."

"I can't find my cell phone. Did anyone else call?"

"Anyone else like who?"

"Just anyone. And don't be so nosey." Lenora was twenty-two and without a man. She was an intellectual. She had an I.Q. of one hundred and thirty-eight. She majored in Anthropology and Archeology. She was currently attending a Doctorate program at the University of Pennsylvania. She was an adjunct professor at Temple University. She was scheduled to go to Egypt in December to join in on an archeological dig of an ancient ruin that was just uncovered. She was one of only seventeen people in the world who could decipher the ancient writings. Needless to say, Lenora was a heavy. She detested the fact that her womanhood was constantly being equated with her lack of a man. She did not need a man to define who she was. She was certain that one of these days the right man would come along with the right credentials and they would combine. But, until that day, she was perfectly happy sitting in the library or scanning the web for information on ancient Egypt and Babylonia. But, she was beautiful and it exuded itself despite her attempts at hiding it. It was almost as though she was ashamed of it. As though it got in the way of her being an intellectual. She had long straight black hair that she always wore in a ponytail. Her light caramel color made her the darkest of the children. She looked North African. She was five-feet, eight inches and never weighed an ounce over one hundred and twenty pounds. She could have made it to the top on her looks alone, but, she was a square. She was also William's best friend. Whenever he needed someone to talk to, he knew that he could count on her to give him the right answers.

"I'm going to the store to get some razors. I'm in desperate need of a shave. Does anyone want anything while I'm out?" There was no response to his inquiry. "If a person by the name of Nafesa calls while I'm out, ask her to leave a number where I can reach her."

"Nafesa? What kind of a name is that? Especially for a woman. It sounds like an inscription I would expect to find chiseled into a mummy's coffin. I hope she doesn't look like a Nafesa."

"And what does a Nafesa look like?"

"You know," she rubbed the back of her hand.

"You mean black and ghetto," he responded.

"I told you, you knew," she laughed.

"There is nothing ghetto about Nafesa," he retorted.

"But what about black?" she asked.

"I'm sick and tired of this family putting down dark skin people. We go around acting as though we're not black. The funny thing is, white people look at us the same way they do dark skin people. To them, we're all the same. We're the only ones running around separating ourselves based on skin color. Today, my boss called and referred to us as *you people*".

"Look William, do not take an attitude with me. You know how mom and dad feel about this issue. And to be truthful about it, I agree with them. Before this Nafesa came on the scene you were all in love with Marla. Remember her? The girl with the perfect skin. Isn't that how you described her just three weeks ago? Now, black is beautiful. I just think you should get your priorities together."

William could hear Lenora laughing at him as she went back up the stairs. He knew this was not going to be easy. He knew that his family would never accept Nafesa. Like Marla and her family, his family prided themselves on having maintained their light skin. His older sister, Vanessa was on her third marriage, all to white men. William knew Nafesa would never be welcomed in his house.

William decided to go to the firm to pick up his belongings. He walked into the lobby and smiled at Levi. Levi smiled back and gave a half wave. William caught the middle elevator to the fourteenth floor. The office was at its usual pace. He walked through the corridors, no one gave him a smile, or a nod, or any semblance that he had ever been a colleague or co-worker of theirs. He packed his belongings, the most prize worthy of which was a picture of himself and President Bush on a quail-hunting trip in West Virginia. William gave his office a farewell going over, turned towards the door and left the firm of Hitower, Viscomb, Palmer and Detmer. It felt just as good as it did on the day when he first walked into it.

The rest of the day seemed like an eternity. He hung around the house waiting for Nafesa to call. He checked his voice box every ten minutes hoping to hear her voice. There were no messages. He allowed his mind, his thought pattern, and his logic to be askewed by thinking nightmarish harm had come to her. He had to justify her not calling him. Then, he silently asked his God to forgive him even having such damned thoughts. It was seven o'clock and he had not heard from her. He decided to go down to the club just to sneak a glimpse of her. This way he could tranquilize his mind. He waited until eight o'clock before he left the house. He just wanted to make sure that she was OK. The air was free of the heavy humidity that had dominated for the past week. It was still a hot August night, but it wasn't a hot and heavy August night. Traffic was flowing. He made it to the club in less than twenty-five minutes. William pulled up directly outside of the club. A valet dressed in all black was standing on the curb outside of the club. William handed him the key and informed him that he would only be a few minutes. The valet gave him a green ticket stub and told William that he would keep the car curb side for the first fifteen minutes. William paused before he started up the stairs of the club. An older couple stood in line ahead of him. The maitre de greeted them as a party. The older couple requested a dining table for two. William disregarded whatever the maitre de was attempting to say to him and walked over to the bar. The music was jumping. The band was in the middle of an instrumental piece. He worked his way up to the bar counter. Then, he heard her voice. No, he felt her voice. He turned around to see her. Through the haze of smoke that blanketed the air, he could see her. She was wearing pants and a sleeveless blouse. The smoke and the colored lights disallowed him the ability to discern the colors of her out fit. But, the smoke and colored lights did not disallow him the ability to discern her beauty. He wondered if he was just too caught up with her or, was she truly that beautiful. It was probably some of both he compromised. The bartender pointed at him.

"Becks in a bottle," he replied.

William was certain that he was too far away for her to see him. The atmosphere at the bar was totally different from the atmosphere at the tables. The bar was busy, a lot of different things were going on at the same time. Money was being made and singles were on the make. The bar was for pick-ups. The tables were for couples. He tried to position himself so that she could see him. The club was too crowded for that to happen. William decided to leave, this was not the way he wanted to enjoy her. She was too afar from him.

William got back into his car and tried to figure out what had gone wrong. *"Why hadn't she called him? What had he done that had turned her off?"* He parked his car in the driveway and went immediately to his room. William searched through his CD collection for something to fit his mood. He wanted to hear her or something that resembled her. There was nothing in his collection that fit the mood. He remembered his father had an extensive CD collection. He ran down stairs to the den and searched through his father's collection. *The Best of Areatha Franklin.* "*Perfect.*" He ran back up the stairs and put the CD into the player. He flopped down onto his bed and closed his eyes. He must have dozed off because he did not hear the phone ring. Lenora woke him.

"Hey, wake up. It's your Nafesa." William sprang to his feet. He searched around the floor trying to find the phone.

"Hello. This is William."

"Hello, William? William?"

"Hey Nafesa, can you hear me?"

"Now I can. I'm on my cell. What's going on?"

"I was just reading," he lied.

"Yeah? What are you reading?"

"OK, I lied. I was sleeping?"

"Yeah? What were you dreaming?"

"I was dreaming that a beautiful woman was serenading me."

"I'm jealous."

"Don't be. You know the singer."

"Cool. I called you at your office morning. They told me you weren't in. My day just got crazy after that. We had a long rehearsal. Flavor, my key board player and manager wanted to try out some new material. It was hectic. After rehearsal I had a ton of personal stuff I had to take care of. I was hoping that you would stop in the club tonight. I thought I saw you standing at the bar, but I knew that you wouldn't just blow in and not stick around to say hello. You wouldn't do that now would you?" She was certain that it was him.

"It was me. The place was too crowded and the bar scene was killing the atmosphere so I decided to take off. It was hard leaving without speaking to you," he confessed.

"This is going to sound funny and I hope it doesn't scare you, but I miss you." She waited through the silence. "What are you doing right now?"

"Nothing. Like I said, I was sleeping. I quit my job today, so I have plenty of time to kill for the next few weeks. I'm supposed to start at the D.A.'s office at the beginning of the month. So, for the time being I'm free. Why? What's up?"

"Why did you quit your job? I thought you told me that you just started there a couple of weeks ago?"

"I did. I'll tell you about it some other time. I'm not in the mood to talk about it right now. Besides, it's a good thing; take my word for it."

"Then let's move on. I called to see if you could meet me outside of the club. I'd like to take you to my bat cave. You down?"

"A bat cave?"

"No, not a bat cave. Remember Batman and Robin and how their getaway was called the bat cave?" That's what I mean. My get away spot."

"Oh, OK. For a minute there, I thought you were into some kind of kinky vampire stuff. I was about to tell you that my mother was calling and hang up on you. Yeah, I'm down. Give me a half an hour."

"William, make it twenty. Like I said, I miss you. And, wear something that you don't mind getting dirty."

"I'll do it in fifteen. I miss you too."

William dugged through his dresser drawers and found an old pair of jeans and an old Princeton tee shirt. He put on his sneakers and ran down the stairs and out the door. He made it to the club in twenty-three minutes. He saw her standing on the sidewalk beside her car, she was talking to one of the band members. He recognized him as the keyboard player. He reasoned it was Flavor, her keyboard player and manager. He pulled up behind her and tapped his horn. Nafesa turned and looked. When she made out his face, she smiled. She walked over to his car, leaned in and gave him a soft kiss.

"Hey stranger, what took you so long?" William looked into her eyes and smiled. "I was low on jet fuel. Had to do an airborne fill-up."

"Let me tell Flav that he can leave. Then, I want you to follow me."

William watched her walk back over to Flavor. She had changed clothes. She had on a pair of skintight jeans. She wore them well. Extremely well. Her rear was full and round. He watched her give Flavor a tight hug and a polite kiss. Then, she walked over and got into her car. William caught Flavor starring at him. Nafesa's convertible top started to retract. She gave a forward wave and took off down Samsom Street. William raced off to catch up with her. He followed her for a half an hour. They were about twenty miles outside of the city, somewhere on a small narrow dark road when she stopped. It looked country. It was dark! Country dark! The night bugs danced in front of his headlights. He turned them off and walked over to Nafesa's car. She was fumbling around for something on her back seat. It was a blanket.

"Where are we?"

"In my bat cave," she laughed. "Now give me your hand and follow me." Nafesa turned on a small flashlight and led William down a small narrow dark road. A simple turn of his head to the right or the left produced nothing but a solid wall of darkness. The beam of brightness that shone from the flashlight cut an exact path for them to follow. It led them to a tree, the only tree in the middle of an open field. She opened the blanket and draped it across the grass beneath the tree.

"Where are we?" he asked.

"We're in Bucks County. This is my family's property. My mother's grandfather bought this property somewhere around the turn of the century. Last century of course. It's thirty acres. They used to farm it, but now they lease it out for hunting and camping. I used to come out here a lot when I was a little girl. When I wanted to be by myself I would come and sit under this tree and think my private thoughts. I used to call this my thinking tree. My mother always knew where to find me. There is a small pond over to the left. My brother, Rasheed and my cousins would always go swimming in it. I would just come over here and sit beneath this tree. My grandfather said he thought this tree is at least a thousand years old. Isn't that amazing. Trees are amazing. Just think about it; trees provide us with so many of the things that we need to live with. They give us wood, fruits, berries, nuts, sap and they help control the oxygen. Trees are the greatest living things on earth. Well, at least that's my opinion. What do you think is the greatest living thing on earth?"

"I guess I've never thought about it, but if I were to give an answer I would have to stick with man. The tree is a tree. It'll stay in the middle of this field and provide shelter to birds and squirrels, but that's it. Man has the power or should I say ability to change the tree, the soil that it is rooted in and the by-products that it produces. Man is a wondrous creature."

"Yeah, man is deep. But I'll stay with the tree. A tree doesn't destroy or kill but the opposite is true."

William felt the conversation getting a little too heavy. "This is getting a little too philo for me. I'll leave this discussion for the great thinkers."

"Besides my friend Jasmin, you are the only person that I've ever brought here. I've never brought a man out here. But for some reason, I wanted to share this place with you. Do you have a bat cave?"

"Yeah, I have a bat cave. My family has a little shore house in Cape May. I like to go down there a lot. I particularly like to go there in the winter. There is a certain solitude that the place has in the winter that's not there in the summer. What does this place look like in the day time?"

"You'll have to take me to your bat cave in the winter. In the day time, this area looks farmish. It's a lot nosier in the day. I-95 is over to the left. I like coming out here at night. Everything is so still. Look up at the sky. Look at all of those stars. You never get to see the sky like this in the city. My great grand father used to tell me that each one of those stars were my ancestors. He used to say that we are as old as the earth itself. Do you know that they say there are more stars in the sky than there are grains of sand on the beach? That's deep! When I come out here and sit beneath this big old tree and look up at all of my ancestors, I know that Allah exists. Allah has truly been good to me. Do you believe in God?"

"Yes, I believe in God. I'm a Christian. I go to church every Sunday. I agree with you, this place is proof that God does exists."

"I just heard a song by Natalie Cole that reminds me of this place. Part of the song talks about how many stars there are in the sky. It's a beautiful song. Maybe I'll ask Flavor to put it in the set. So many stars. So, so many stars. William, can you sing?"

"Not a bit."

"That's too bad. I think that there are only two true art forms. When I say true, I mean pure. One of them is singing and the other one is writing."

"Again, I've never thought about it. I'll have to reserve my comment until after I've given the subject more consideration."

"Wow, you sounded like a lawyer when you said that."

"Sorry."

The two of them sat on the blanket that she had draped beneath the old tree, that sat in the middle of a field, on her family's property, looking up at so many stars that could have been her ancestors. Nafesa hummed a song that he believed to be the song by Natalie Cole that talked about how many stars there are in the sky. Nafesa laid back. William formed a cross, resting his head against stomach. She let her hand maneuver through his hair. It was soft. She let her hand stroll down to his face. It was smooth. She raised up and leaned over to kiss him. He accepted her invitation. Her lips were full and warm. There was a fragrance that surrounded their kiss. It was human. He moved his hand across her face. It was silky. He let his hand play amongst the braids in her hair. She moved into him with a stronger kiss. They embraced each other with long passionate kisses. He placed his hands on her breast. Their moans and gestures spoke words too descriptive for speech. She placed her hand on his groin. His relaxation tensed. Her hand searched for him. She found him and began to massage him. He exhaled a long "ahhhh".

"Take off your shirt," she ordered. He tried to take off his shirt and hold her at the same time. She helped him. She folded his shirt and placed it on the blanket next to them. She caressed his chest and let her fingers fondle his chest hairs. He was hairy, but his hair was soft and silky. It was a different feel to her. It wasn't a good different or, a bad different, just different. Shamsadeen's hair was coarse. She removed her blouse and pressed her breast against his chest. Her breasts were warming. He massaged her breast and toyed with her erect nipples. Moans and gestures were continuously expressed. She rolled over and lay on top of him. Her hand wandered down to his zipper. He gave her staccato kisses across her neck. She unworked his zipper and let her hand find him. It was not a difficult task. He was hard. She measured him. She was satisfied. He closed his eyes and moved his lips around longing for hers. They resumed their long passionate kisses. Nafesa began a slow and methodical descent of his body. She stopped at the nape of his neck. She lingered there with strategic kisses. Her hands filled his hair. She lowered herself just a little, and began to flick at his nipples with her tongue. He *ohhh'ed*. Her tongue danced more fervently across his chest. She stopped and slid down, all the way down. She sat up enough to give herself room to bring him out of his pants. She exposed him. His moans filled the air. Nafesa smiled at his moans. She was enjoying pleasuring him. She placed soft warm kisses on the top of him. His head shook. He wanted her to stop. She would not. He realized that she was in control. She lowered down and engulfed him completely. Sweat ran down his body. She maneuvered him at her will. His hands pounded the soil. He wanted her to stop. She would not. She raised up and kissed him in the mouth. He could feel her starring at him.

"What's wrong?" he asked.

"Everything's right," she answered. He sat up and embraced her. They let their lips land where ever they chose. He leaned heavily into her, forcing her backwards. He unbuttoned her pants and let her zipper down. She searched for any part of his body to kiss. He moved his hand beneath her panties. From the feel, they were thongs. Whatever they were, they were wet. He let his middle finger run across her and tasted her wetness. He felt her shiver. He began to remove her pants. She complied. Then he removed her panties. She complied. He was right, they were thongs. He began to kiss her inner thighs. She jerked with each kiss. He let his tongue rub against her outer wall. She twitched. He parted her then entered her with his tongue. He began to lick her as if she were a cone of ice cream. Nafesa sat up.

"No baby, not like that. I'm not a cone of ice cream. Let me show you. Give me your finger. Now feel right here. Do you feel that?"

"Yes," he answered, like a school boy learning the first stage of a complicated lesson.

"That's what you want to stimulate. Now take your tongue and gently play with it. Then, put it between your lips and softly, very softly play with it."

William moved back into her. This time he did as he had been instructed. There was immediate gratification.

"Ohhh," she screamed aloud.

William closed his eyes and began to move her between his lips. He could feel her body jerking. This was different from anything he had ever experienced. She was different from anyone he had ever experienced. He found pleasure in pleasing her. He wanted to fulfill her. He wanted her to want his love. His own needs were being satisfied by her moans and movements. He felt himself wanting to explode.

"Come here William," she pleaded.

He stopped and with his tongue, he moved up her body. He took in the taste of her breast. She pushed them up for him to suck. She tasted of August heat.

"No, come here," she commanded.

He resumed his journey towards her lips. William wanted to kiss her, but was afraid that she would not want to taste herself.

"Kiss me," she demanded.

He took a deep breath. She was a leap into newness and he knew that once he leaped, he could never return. He leaped.

"Nafesa, I have never had anyone teach me how to please them, how to make love to them. I'm sorry if I disappointed you."

"Baby, you haven't disappointed me. It's about finding out each other's wants and desires, and trying to fulfill them. I'm quite sure you'll teach me how to make love to you."

"Nafesa, I don't think I can teach you anything."

"William, you're going to be surprised at what you're going to teach me."

They enveloped each other and let their lips finish their conversation. He felt her hand massaging his groin. He was amazed at the amount of heat his body was generating. He was sweating profusely. She pulled his pants and underwear down to his knees. Then she began to fumble through her handbag. By sheer feel alone, she pulled out a condom. He refused to ask any questions.

"Here William, put this on."

William fumbled with the packet. He was all thumbs. He could not believe how hard it was for him to get the wrapper off. Nafesa knew that he needed relaxing.

"Take your time baby. I'm not going anywhere."

The soothing of her voice relaxed him enough that he was able to get the wrapper undone.He placed the condom on with ease. She took over. He could feel himself slipping into her.

"Oh yes," she screamed.

"Oh my god," he moaned. He began to pump up and down on her. She wrapped her arms around him, halting his motion.

"William, slow down. You don't even have to move. Just lie here for a minute. Move only when you feel the need to. I just want to feel you inside me. I want to enjoy this for as long as possible. I want your love. Do you know what I mean?" she asked.

"Yes I do." William stopped his movements and just relaxed in the warmth of her body. It was beautiful. It was new. It was refreshing. It was way beyond anything he had ever experienced. He and Marla had made love making a physical act. Now, he was learning the spiritual side of love making. He rested his head against her breast. He listened to the steady thumbing of her heart. Nafesa began to make soft stirs with her hips. William joined her rhythm. It was a flowing motion. He felt her trembling. She began to speed up her movement. William followed. He felt a rush surging within him. He strained not to collapse onto of her. He wanted to stop but couldn't. Nafesa felt her body emanating small spasms. They began to grow. She could not control them. She pulled him deeper into her. He flowed and flowed. She gushed and gushed. His arms buckled. She received him and held him with all the love she could muster. Tears streamed down her face.

"Oh William, please tell me that you'll love me? Oh Allah, please let this be love?" she prayed.

"Oh God, can this really be happening to me?" he silently questioned.

CHAPTER EIGHT

William had barely slept. Nafesa filled his head. He had just dozed off when he felt the warmth of the morning sun rising across his bed. He adjusted his eyes to watch the sun push the darkness out of his room. The warmth felt good. It reminded him of the warmth he had experienced earlier while lying under a tree, in a field, somewhere in Bucks County. He rolled over and smelled his sheets. He wanted to smell her. He needed to sense something of her. He reached for the tee shirt he had worn. Certainly, it would smell of her. It did. He placed it over his face and let it rest there for awhile. He wondered what she was doing; what she was wearing and, if she was thinking of him. He was more than sure that she was. Last night was too special for her not to be thinking about him. He wished he had a picture of her. Anything of hers would suffice. He decided that he would go to Castle Records and buy the CD by Natalie Cole that had the song Nafesa had hummed. He had it bad, but it felt so damn good. He laid in bed until the darkness had totally surrendered. He rolled over and looked at the clock on his dresser. It was eight-forty. *"Time to get up."* He heard a child's laughter coming from downstairs. It sounded like his little nephew, Adam. William through on an old pair of jeans, a tee shirt and went down stairs to play with his nephew.

William's older sister, Vanessa was sitting at the kitchen table with her two sons, Adam and Jason. William's mother was making Adam a bowl of cereal. Adam was four and Jason was two. They were both a bundle of energy. As soon as Adam saw William, he ran and jumped into William's arms.

"It's Uncle William!" he exclaimed. Guess what Uncle William? Mommy and Daddy are taking me to school. I can go to school now cause I'm four. Jason can't go 'cause he only two. I used to be two, but now I'm four. When I was two, Mommy said I was this big." Adam parted his hands by about ten inches. "But now, I'm this big." This time he parted his hands by eighteen inches.

"Wow, you really are a big boy now. And you're going to school? I'm so proud of you." William put Adam down and walked over to Jason. Jason was clinging to his mother's leg. William leaned over and asked Jason to jump into his arms. Jason's arms flew up, but his legs never left the floor. William bent over and swooshed Jason up, lifting him straight up to the ceiling.

"Hey little man, how are you doing?"

"Stop," shouted Jason. Jason was old enough to realize that the word stop gave him some control over his interaction with other people. So he prefaced everything with stop. William paid no attention to Jason's command. William swung Jason around until Jason began to laugh.

"OK, Jay, time for you to get down."

"Don't call him Jay. His name is Jason," scolded William's mother.

"Oh mom, lighten up. You and your nick name phobia. What do you think, he'll grow up to be a schizophrenic or something?"

Both Vanessa and William laughed. Their mother failed to see the humor in his comment. Vanessa raced over and grabbed Jason who was trying to reach for a glass of juice that was on top of the kitchen table.

Vanessa was a pretty woman, not a beautiful woman, but a pretty woman. What she lacked in raw beauty, she made up for in perfected style. Everything about her was manicured. The way she walked, the way she talked, even the way she laughed was manicured. She had gone to finishing school to learn the correct ways of being a lady. Vanessa was spoiled. Their father had started it and a succession of men continued it. The strange thing was, they all misunderstood her. She hungered for a man to tell her no. Men who always told her yes were short-lived. Just ask her first two husbands and her soon to be third ex-husband. The only man who had total control over her was Sleepy, a droopy eyed, short, dark skin mail man who lived in West Philly. Sleepy was a hush, hush. Everyone knew about him, but it was forbidden to talk about him. Vanessa loved him. She had always loved him. He was the only man who truly loved her for who she was. When she was twenty, she brought him home, introduced him to her family and announced her plans to marry him. Her mother started to rapidly fan herself with the TV guide. Her father went ballistic. She was told that if she married Sleepy, she would be cut off from the family forever. Vanessa was not strong enough to survive an ex- communication from her family. So, she kept Sleepy and her love for him in the secret and private realms of her life. She married white men to both please and spite her father. It was obvious to everyone that she was miserable on the inside. She drank heavily and frequented with drugs. Her current husband wanted her to check into a rehab, but she would not consider such a thought. William watched her struggle through relationship after relationship with her unwanted lovers. Once, William saw her downtown with Sleepy and the two of them seemed to be so in love. It was the first time in years that he saw happiness on her face. She made him promise that he would never tell anyone that he had seen her with Sleepy. He never did. To hide her internal wreckage, Vanessa stayed immaculately dressed. There was nothing in her wardrobe that was not designer made, nothing. Her hair was Polynesian black. She wore it straight and shoulder length. She always wore sunglasses, usually Armani's. William knew that Nafesa was his Sleepy. He only hoped that he would be able to stand up to his family for her. He knew that it would be hard.

"What's going on little brother?"

"Nothing much big sis. What's going on with you?"

"You know, life is grand. Mom tells me that you quit that big-time job you had. She also told me that you're running the streets with a Nafesa. Now, don't you go up- setting the status quo."

"I'm just following in my big sister's footsteps."

"I hear she's a dark skin, jazz singer. What has dad said about all of this?"

"Nothing yet. I haven't been home long enough to talk to him about it."

"Well, you know the rules, it's all right to sleep with them as long as you don't bring them home for dinner."

"I can't worry about how anyone feels but me. The rest of the people can go f . . . , fly a kite."

"If it was only that easy," countered Vanessa.

Their mother was standing right there, but refused to participate in the conversation. William looked in the refrigerator for some orange juice. His nephews were chasing the cat around the house. The phone rang. He made a quick dash for it. Someone beat him to it. He guessed it was Lenora. He was right.

"William, it's for you," she shouted down to him. His heart began to race. Nafesa's face instantly appeared within his mind. He anticipated her saying, "hi baby". He put the receiver to his ear.

"Hello," he answered. "Oh, it's you," he said in a disappointed tone of voice. His mother shook her head in disgust. Vanessa laughed. William forgot that he was not alone.

"Well, excuse me for calling," snubbed Marla.

"No, I didn't mean it like that. I thought you were someone else," he said, inserting his foot further into his mouth.

"It's obvious that you thought I was someone else. The question is who?"

"So, Marla how are you doing? I was just about to call you," he lied, trying to change the conversation. It didn't work.

"William you have not been acting normal lately. And I haven't seen nor heard from you over the past few days. You're turning into a ghost. I'm quite sure Lenora has told you that I've called numerous times and have left you several messages. I've been trying to reach you on your cell phone, but you never have it on. You haven't even explained to me why you quit your job. What's going on William? Are you going through something? I think we should have a talk right away. You know, this is not the time to be getting cold feet on me. Things are moving to smoothly for you to start acting like this. I'm coming over there right now. I'll be there in twenty minutes," she rambled. William removed the phone from his ear for half of her speech.

"Sure, Marla. I'll be here." William hung up the phone. His mother turned and looked at him.

"I don't care what you think or what you say, that girl is the best thing that ever happened to you. Now you're going to turn around and lose her over some nappy head, jazz singer. When will you children ever learn? Your father and I have tried to teach you certain lessons for certain reasons. But, as soon as y'all get all hot in the ass, you want to run around with the first thing that drops their pants or panties. The only one of you that has any sense is Lenora. The two of you always have to learn the hard way. Well, I hope you lose Marla and she makes you come back to her begging on your knees. If I were her, I still wouldn't take you back."

Both William and Vanessa stood there dumbfounded. Neither of them had ever heard their mother go off on a tirade like that. She even said *ass*! William realized what Vanessa already knew, bringing a Nafesa into their family would not be taken lightly. He had just experienced the first full round of attack. He was yet to feel the full bombardment from his father.

"Well William, here comes your first true test of love. I hope you're stronger than I was. Just remember, your life is about your happiness and not about mom's or dad's stupid rules."

CHAPTER NINE

Nafesa was barely asleep when she heard the front door of her apartment open. She looked over at the red neon glow from the clock radio on the nightstand. It was three- fifty. She sat up and listened. She assumed it was Shamsadeen. She waited for him to come into the bedroom. Whoever it was stayed in the living room. It wasn't Shamsadeen, he would have come into the bedroom to check on her. He always did. She reached under the bed and grabbed the black handle thirty-eight Shamsadeen had given her. She never carried it. It was always under the bed. She put on a sheer robe and crept up to her bedroom door. She slightly opened the door and peered out to see who it was. It was too dark for her to make out who was in her living room. She saw the silhoutte of a person, but couldn't make out who it was. She could see that they were doing something with a couple of duffle bags beside the closet, but couldn't make out if they were putting something in the duffle bags or, taking something out of the duffle bags. She strained her eyes trying to make out who was out there. She was certain that it wasn't Shamsadeen. She asked herself if she should shoot first and ask questions later or, should she ask questions first then shoot if she didn't get the right response. She really didn't want to pull the trigger. She had never shot a gun in her life. She always refused Shamsadeen's suggestion that she go to the shooting range with him. Now, she wished that she had. She had to do something. *"I'll hold them until the police come."* Nafesa sprang into the living room with the gun pointed at the perpetrator.

"Mother Fucker, put your hands up. That's right Mother Fucker, I said put your hands up. And, if you make a move I'll blow your ass away," she yelled, hoping to startle the intruder.

"Shit Fe, it's me, Lil' Larry. Turn on the damn light. Girl you scared the shit out of me. And put that fucking gun away. Besides, didn't Shamsadeen tell you to shoot first and ask questions later?"

Nafesa felt along the wall for the light switch. She flicked it on. "Lil' Larry, what in the hell are you doing in here? You scared the hell out of me. How did you get in here? And where is Shamsadeen?"

"He'll be here in a few minutes. He had to make a quick run. We kept calling you as soon as we hit Maryland. We called your cell phone all night long. You know Shamsadeen is pissed off at you. Where you been?"

"Don't worry where I've been. You just tell me what you're doing with these duffel bags? And what are you putting in my closet?"

"You gotta ask Shamsadeen all of that shit. I'm just doing what I was told to do. Girl, you look good standing there."

Nafesa looked down and saw that she had on a see-through robe with no under garments beneath it. She was totally embarrassed. She backed up into the bedroom.

"Wait until Shamsadeen gets here. I'm going to tell both of you what I think."

Lil' Larry was laughing. He was Shamsadeen's right hand man. Lil' Larry was proven, there was no question about loyalty. And, although they both knew that is was Shamsadeen's ship, they also knew that it was Lil' Larry who kept it afloat. Lil' Larry was the brains behind the organization. He understood money and knew how to make it work for them. Lil' Larry got his name not because he was a little guy, he stood six feet three inches and weighed two hundred and ten pounds. Lil' Larry was not little. He got his name because when he was a kid there were two Larrys on his block. The other Larry was a big fat kid who was always being chased. To distinguish them, they were called Big Larry and Little Larry. Over time, the Little was shortened to Lil'. He was never called Lil' or Larry, but always Lil' Larry. He graduated third in his class with a business degree from Georgetown. And, he studied one year at the University of Pennsylvania's prestigious, Wharton School of Business. But despite all of his education, he was street. Lil' Larry's mother always told him the he and Shamsadeen were "two peas in a pod". They were born to hustle. They were always looking for a new hustle. They were always trying a new scam. When Shamsadeen started to make moves, Lil' Larry was right there with him. They complimented each other's strengths and weaknesses. They met as little kids. Neither of them had any brothers or sisters, so a kindred bond formed between them. Shamsadeen moved into his grandmother's house when he was seven, after both of his parents were killed by the city in a bombing incident. Shamsadeen's father, Mustafa Baku was the founder of the radical group, the Bakus. There numbers fluctuated between thirty-five and fifty members. They wore their hair in long dread locks and shunned all material possessions. The ate only the food they grew within their own compound. They refused to pay any taxes to the government at any level. Needless to say, there was constant friction between them and the city. To call it friction was putting it mildly. The truth of the matter was both sides hated each other. The Bakus were constantly harassed by the police and other city officials. The Department of Children's Welfare incessantly monitored the way the Bakus raised their children. There was never any proof that their children fared any differently than the other kids on the block. None of the Baku children attended regular school. The group did not want their children contaminated by the poison that was dispersed by teachers in the public school system. Mustafa, his wife Agee, and three other members had Masters degrees. A new member who came into the compound was wanted by the police for allegedly shooting a police officer in a botched bank robbery. The incident happened five years before the new member entered the compound. A jail house snitch who couldn't do his time, gave the police the info on Jerry Murray. The police tracked his whereabouts to the compound. They came to the compound with an arrest warrant for Jerry Murray, a/k/a Ishmael Baku. The Bakus would not surrender him to the police. A standoff began. The Bakus barricaded themselves in their compound. Sporadic gunfire was exchanged. All of the police attempts to seize the compound failed. Police Commissioner, Arthur Butterworth petitioned Mayor James Krall for permission to detonate a controlled device that would allow them to enter and seize the compound. Mayor Krall gave the go-ahead. Commissioner Butterworth gave the order. A controlled device was dropped from a helicopter on to the roof of the compound. A massive explosion shook the compound. A massive explosion shook the homes adjoined to the compound. A massive explosion shook every home within a block of the compound. The compound collapsed. Homes adjoined to the compound collapsed. Homes within a block radius of the compound collapsed. Flames jumped from house to house. People were running for their lives. Some of them lost their lives. The adult members of the Baku family refused to surrender. They sent the children out. The police fired on the children. Two of the kids were killed by police gunfire. The police stopped firing when they realized that the people running from the compound were unarmed children. One of the kids who fought their way through the gunfire, and the smoke, and the leaping flames was a half-naked boy, about six years old with a sign around his neck that read "Shamsadeen". A police officer snatched Shamsadeen by the arm and rushed him over to a medical unit. Of the forty-three people who were living in the compound when the bomb dropped, only six survived; two adults and four children. The lawsuits stormed in against the city and the officials responsible for the murderous fiasco. A settlement was reached. The surviving adults would each get one-point five millions dollars, the surviving children would each get two million dollars once they reached the age of eighteen, and the estates of the dead would share a pot of six million dollars.

On September 17, 1996 Shamsadeen Baku became a millionaire. His maternal grandmother, Mildred Johnson called the Yellow Cab Company and asked to have a cab come to the address of 1745 Caleb Street. Shamsadeen's grandmother lived two doors down from Larry Milboure. The cab came and took her and her grandson to the First Commerce Bank. A financial consultant met with them. He attempted to give Shamsadeen money management advice. Shamsadeen had his mind made up as to what he was going to do with his money. He asked the consultant to open an account for his grandmother and put five hundred thousand dollars in it for her. Next, he wanted an account to be started for Larry Milbourne. He instructed the consultant to contact Georgetown University and determine how much it would take to pay for Lil' Larry's education. The answer was one hundred and ten thousand dollars. A cashiers check was sent to the registrars office in the amount of one hundred and ten thousand dollars. Then, he bought the rights to own and operate ten street corners at thirty thousand dollars a piece. He put seventy-five thousand in his pockets and the rest, he let sit. Shamsadeen was in business. No one could question him about the source of his money. But, it took more than just money to run a drug operation the size of Shamsadeen and Lil' Larry's. They needed muscle, contacts, street corner hustlers, shooters, brokers, banks, off shore accounts, on shore accounts, hidden accounts, weasels, weapons, lawyers, customers, snitches, ruthlessness, callousness, liquidity, and coldness. Between the two of them, they were able to cover all of their needs. Once the money started to roll in, it was Lil' Larry who plotted how to make it untraceable. He followed the stock market and was in constant contact with the brokers. Once the money started to roll in, it was Shamsadeen who made sure that none of the workers stepped out of line, or came up short, or used the product, or switched the product. Shamsadeen and Lil' Larry were a two headed coin.

Nafesa genuinely liked Lil' Larry. He was fun and carefree. Shamsadeen stressed out over things that Lil' Larry would let roll off of his back. Lil' Larry would never let the thought of getting killed or going to jail worry him. "Just part of the business," he would say. That's not to say that he wasn't careful, Lil' Larry always planned every move. He had seen to many hustlers go down or go out because they didn't pay attention to the details.

Shamsadeen came into the apartment. Nafesa could hear the two of them talking. Shamsadeen seemed to be in a rush to take care of whatever needed to be taken care of. He strolled into the bedroom.

"What's up baby? Where you been? I was calling and calling and ain't nobody answered. I left a bunch of messages on your cell. What's up with that?"

"I stayed around with Flavor and the band to talk about what we're going to do after this gig ends," she fabricated.

"Oh yeah, I forgot about that. This is your last week at the OFFBEAT. Damn, what y'all gonna do? Check it out, I don't have time to talk right now, I gotta make a run with Lil' Larry. After that, I have to drop him off. I probably won't see you until this afternoon. You all right with that?"

"Sure baby, it's cool. I'll be all right. Just don't have anybody sneaking in here giving me a damn heart attack. I almost killed Lil' Larry."

"You ain't almost kill nobody. Besides, didn't I tell you to shoot first and ask questions later? I'll talk to you later. Let's roll Lil' Larry. It's going on five o'clock. We gotta handle by seven."

"Talk to you Fe. It was good seeing you. It was real good seeing you," laughed Lil' Larry.

"What's that all about?" asked Shamsadeen.

"Damn Shamsadeen, why you gotta know about everything? Can't Fe and me have our own little thing going on?" joked Lil' Larry.

"Shamsadeen let out a big laugh. "Don't make me hurt nothing in here."

Nafesa went back into the bedroom and got back into bed. She hoped that she would be able to go to sleep after all of the excitement. She closed her eyes. William drifted back into her thoughts. Her whole body felt as if it were smiling. She tingled. She could still feel his tongue exploring her body. She rubbed her fingers together as if she had his hair in her hand. William was a sign from Allah that it was time for her to move on and get away from Shamsadeen. But how? She knew that Shamsadeen would not let her pack up and leave. A sudden chill raced through her body. She thought about what Shamsadeen would do to William if he ever found out about him. The thought made her head swim. She closed her eyes and wished all of the bad would go away and the good would stay.

Nafesa was jolted out of her sleep by a loud banging noise. She looked over at the clock. It was eight-twenty-three. The banging became thunderous. She jumped out of bed and ran into the living room. As she entered the living room, the front door of the apartment burst open. Men in black jump suits with yellow D.E.A. lettering across their chest, stormed into her living room. They were shouting for everyone to get down. The more they shouted, the louder she screamed. The louder she screamed, the more they shouted. The situation was out of control. Chaos reigned. A medium height white man with salt and pepper hair, three stripes on his shoulder, and the name Shelmire stitched on his jump suit began to take control.

"SHUT UP! SHUT UP! SHUT UP!" he screamed. Everyone followed his instructions. The room became quiet. The agents began to move throughout the apartment with their guns drawn. For the most part they ignored Nafesa. Sergeant Shelmire took her to the side.

"Ma'am, my name is Shelmire. Is there anyone else in here with you?"

Nafesa shook her head, "no".

"Ma'am, we have a search warrant for this apartment. The first thing I want you to do is go and put on some clothing."

Nafesa realized that she was nude. She was so startled by the booming noise that she had forgotten to get dressed. She ran into her bedroom. A female agent followed her. Male agents exited the bedroom, but not before giving her a good look over. They smiled. Nafesa slipped into a pair of jeans and a tee shirt. The female agent instructed her to return to the living room. Sergeant Shelmire resumed his questioning of her.

"What's your name?"

"Nafesa."

"Nafesa what?"

"Am I under arrest or anything? Shouldn't I have a lawyer here?"

"Ma'am, you can have your lawyer here, your preacher here or, your second grade teacher here. It doesn't matter who is here. The situation as it stands is that you are not under arrest, so just tell me your name.

"Nafesa Islam."

Shelmire looked down at a notebook he had. "Confirmed. Ms. Islam, we're looking for your beau, Shamsadeen Baku. We have reason to believe that he transported two duffle bags full of cocaine here in the early morning hours. You can make it easy for yourself and just tell us where the drugs are. If you don't, we're going to take this place a part until we find what we're looking for. So what's it gonna be?"

"I don't know about any drugs."

"Look, quit the shit! You live in this fancy apartment, your sweetheart drives a big ass Mercedes, and you drive a BMW convertible. Neither of you work for a living. So don't tell me that you don't know about any drugs. Now I'm telling you, if you don't help us and we find the drugs, your pretty black ass is going down!"

"I sing for a living. I don't know anything about any drugs."

"Then start singing and tell me where the drugs are. I'm getting tired of playing this stupid ass game with you. Your black ass is going to jail."

Nafesa watched an agent move towards the closet in the living room. She remembered Lil' Larry was at that closet earlier in the morning. Her eyes followed the agent. Sergeant Shelmire eyes followed her eyes. He ordered the agent to hit the closet. The agent tried to open the door but it was locked. Nafesa felt her knees buckle. The door to that closet was never locked. The agent brought a dog over. The dog sniffed around the door and began to bark wildly. Other agents poured into the living room. A heavy set agent with an ill-fitted toupee walked over to the door carrying a sledgehammer. With one strong swing he knocked the knob out of the door. The door swung open. The agent shouted "bingo". Nafesa thought she was going to faint when the agent brought two duffle bags from out of the closet. The dog began to bark frantically. The bags had locks on them. Another agent walked over with a pair of lock cutters. He cut the locks. The agents all gathered around the bags with a look of excitement on their faces. Nafesa wanted to throw up. The agent picked up one of the duffel bags and began to dump out its contents. Nafesa watched as the items fell out of the bag. The bag was full of old shoes and old sneakers. The agents were dumbfounded. The agent quickly grabbed the second duffel bag and dumped it. Old shoes and old sneakers. Nafesa broke the silence with laughter.

"Are you sure you have the right house?" she asked.

"Don't be smart you little cunt," one of the agents shouted.

"Tear this place apart," shouted Sergeant Shelmire. Nafesa watched as the agents systematically destroyed the apartment. Everything was destroyed. The dishes, the art work, the TV, the stereo system, they even destroyed the goldfish bowl. After they were through, the Sergeant told her to tell Shamsadeen that this was just a friendly house call. The next time Shamsadeen would not be so lucky.

"Have a nice life Sergeant," Nafesa screamed, as they marched out of the apartment. Then, she sat on the floor and looked around. Her designer apartment looked like a war zone. The whole thing was too close for comfort. She could hear the murmurs of her neighbors out in the hall. The neighbors were in agreement that the apartment was a drug den. "Why would the D.E.A. raid the place if it wasn't?" Nafesa started to cry. Things had gone too far. She had stayed too long. She never expected to stay this long. She was only supposed to stay until she got back on her feet. That was over four years ago. As she sat there, she hated Shamsadeen for what he had just put her through. Even worst, she hated herself for being there. If

Shamsadeen was what he was, what did that say about her? And, was the Sergeant correct? Was she sticking her head in the sand? Had she kept her head in the sand too long? *"That's it, it's time to go."* Her mind flipped from the "what if" to "what now". She remembered that Shamsadeen had told her that if an emergency were ever to happen she was to call his cell and put in the code 9911. She went back into the bedroom and dug through the piles of clothing on the floor to find a better outfit. She threw on some jeans and a top, grabbed her bag and keys and ran out of the apartment. She felt the stares from her neighbors as she ran down the hallway. She suspected that the D.E.A. was probably watching her. She did not care. She had to make contact with Shamsadeen. She hopped into her car and raced out of the garage. She was too paranoid to use her cell phone; the D.E.A. could have bugged it. She needed to find a safe place so that she could get her head together. She made a hard u-turn and headed towards Germantown Avenue. Nafesa made a right hand turn off of Germantown Avenue onto a narrow street of neatly kept rowhomes. Flowers and plants adorned most of the enclosed porched fronts. Nafesa pulled up to the curb of a light green front that was decorated with orange Mums and a smiling ceramic frog that held a sign that read "3927 Powell Street". Nafesa parked the car and raced up to the front door. She rang the bell until Jasmin came to the door.

"Damn Fe, what's wrong? Why you ringing my bell like a wild woman? You look like somebody just tried to kill you or something." Nafesa rushed into Jasmin's living room and flopped on the couch. "Girl, the fucking D.E.A. just tore my apartment up looking for drugs. They had me stand there while they were looking around. They said they were looking for two duffel bags of coke. When they found the two bags in the closet of my living room, I thought I was going to die."

"Wait a minute. You trying to tell me that they found two duffel bags full of coke and they let you go?"

"They found the bags, but there wasn't any coke in them. The only thing they found was Shamsadeen's old shoes and sneakers. Jas, they had one of those drug sniffing dogs in there and that dog was going crazy. I just knew I was going to jail. They kept threatening that if I didn't tell them where the drugs were they were going to put me under the jail. I was scared as shit! Then when they didn't find any drugs, they tore my apartment to pieces. Everything is fucked up, everything. I mean everything. That's it. I can't take this stuff any more." Nafesa felt the tears starting to well up in her eyes. She broke down and started sobbing. Jasmin held her in her arms.

"It's going to be all right," she comforted.

"I need to use your phone. I got to call that damn Shamsadeen and tell him I'm done with him and his little drug kingdom. Next time I might not be so lucky. Who in the fuck knows, next time I might end up dead. I've got to call William."

"Who in the hell is William?"

"Remember the guy from the club that I was telling you about the other day? I finally met with him and the two of us really hit it off."

"Fe, how much hitting did the two of you do?"

"Let's just say we hit it!" Nafesa walked over to Jasmin's coffee table and picked up the phone. She dialed Shamsadeen's cell phone and entered the code 9911, followed by Jasmin's number. The phone rang within twenty seconds.

"Shamsadeen? It's me, Nafesa."

"What's up baby? Why you use the code?"

"Shamsadeen, I can't live like this anymore. I can't take this shit. I've got to get away. I can't live like this!"

""Slow down Nafesa. What in the fuck are you talking about? You used 9911 to tell me this shit?"

"No. I used 9911 to tell you the fucking D.E.A. came and raided our apartment. Now that damn place looks like a fucking bomb went off in it. That's what I called to tell you. I'm never going back there."

"My hunch was right about those dudes down in Atlanta. Just be cool Fe, everything is going to be alright. I know they didn't find anything. I wouldn't stash anything where I live. I ain't crazy. Besides, fuck that apartment. We'll buy a house and have an interior decorator hook it up. Check it out, you said you wanted to go to New York for a minute. Why don't you do that? It'll be good for you. Let things cool off around here. For now, I want you to check into the Center City Hilton. I'll take care of everything. Don't stay at Jasmin's. They'll add her spot as a place to hit. I can't stand her fat ass, but I don't want them raining on her for nothing. So, do like I say, go to the Hilton. I'll stop by later today to check on you. DO NOT GO BACK TO THE APARTMENT! I'll send a couple of smokers around there to get us some clothes. Better yet, we'll do a shopping run. You understand me right?"

"Shamsadeen, you don't understand me. I want out!"

"Fe you ain't going nowhere! Besides, now is not the time to be talking about that kind of shit. Just do like I said and we'll talk about the other shit later. I gotta take care of some business. I'll talk to you later. Bye."

"Shamsadeen, don't you hang . . . He hung up on me."

"What did he say?"

"He told me check into a hotel."

"You don't have to check into a hotel. You can stay here."

"No. He said he didn't want the Feds to raid your spot for nothing."

"You mean Shamsadeen was thinking about me like that?"

"I gotta call William and have him meet me somewhere."

William was sitting at the desk in his room, searching through the internet for information on jazz and jazz singers when heard a car pull into his driveway. He walked over to the window to confirm that it was Marla. His hunch was correct. She looked up at him and gave him a worried smile. He had seen that smile on her face before. Whenever she was felt troubled about the course of their relationship, that smile appeared. He'd seen it many times during the course of their college years. What usually followed the smile was a lengthy dialogue on the need to strengthen their relationship. Really, it wasn't much of a dialogue. Marla usually did all of the talking and, it was usually Marla who made all of the suggestions, and, it was usually Marla who decided how they were going to remedy their problems. William usually just sat and listened. He was the prop. Today, he was not in the mind-set for a unilateral dialogue. He had to figure out a way to handle her; properly of course. He walked over to his door and listened. He could hear Marla having a conversation with his sister and mother. There were polite chuckles exchanged amongst them. He decided to stay in his room until he had to go downstairs. He sat on the side of his bed and waited for someone to summon him. His mother summoned him.

"William! William, Marla is here for you."

"OK. I'll be right down." William put on his game face and went downstairs. Marla was sitting at the kitchen table with Vanessa. Between Marla and Vanessa, William was unsure who the better dresser was. Whoever was the better dresser, the other was a close second. Marla was wearing an airy canary yellow dress with a matching scarf around her neck. Her legs were long and slender and she was slender and long. Marla looked splendid. As he stared at her, he realized why he had spent the last ten years of his life dating her. She was beautiful. If she wasn't the best thing that ever happened to him, she was definitely the second best thing that had ever happened to him. He was anticipating a call from the best thing that ever happened to him. He walked into the kitchen and smiled at Marla. She returned the smile. Vanessa smirked. His mother shook her head.

"Hey stranger, long time no see," said William.

"It's not my fault," replied Marla.

"Vanessa, don't you and I have something we need to discuss upstairs?" interrupted Mrs. Jennings.

"No, not really. But, I can take a hint," responded Vanessa. Vanessa and Mrs. Jennings left the kitchen and went upstairs. William sat down beside Marla and then stood back up.

"Is there something I can get you while I'm up?" he asked.

"Yes, there are a few things that you can get me. I would really like a glass of orange juice. I'll tell you about the rest of what I want when you come back." William knew he was in for an ear full.

"Is that all you want while I'm up?"

"William, just hurry up with the juice so that we can talk."

William poured her a glass of orange juice, sat it down in front her, then sat himself down.

"OK Marla, tell me what is so imperative that you had to rush over here? I really don't see the need for a special conversation. It's not like anything is wrong with us. I mean, I'm just trying to get my head straight. I just went through it with my job. There really isn't anything else to it. I know I probably should have spoken with you about quitting my job, but my head was spinning. Like I said, I just have to get my head together. Besides, I knew that it would have upset you," he lied.

"That's what you say William. But why do I feel like something else is going on? I've been with you for ten years. I can tell when you're going through something major. Like when you're trying to make a significant change in your life. What's scaring me is, I feel as though you no longer want me in your life."

"Marla, how can you say that? It's not as though I've been ducking you or ignoring you. I still feel the same way about you. I've been busy. We just had dinner together and made love last Sunday. So, how can you say something is wrong?"

"I don't know William. Maybe I'm wrong, but my intuition is telling me that something is going on that will destroy our relationship. Now, if you tell me that I'm wrong, then I'll believe you, but tell me the truth."

Before William could tell her what she wanted to hear, the phone rang. He felt his pulse race. He hoped it Nafesa, but prayed that is wasn't. He let the phone ring. When he did not want Lenora to answer the phone, she always beat him to it. Now that he wanted her to answer the phone, she wouldn't pick it up.

"Well, aren't you going to answer the phone?" she asked.

"Let Lenora answer it, that seems to be the only thing she does around here except read. Right now, I think it's more important that we finish this conversation."

Lenora came to the top of the stairs and announced that the call was for William. She deliberately did not say who it was. She knew that he was talking with Marla. William was confident that she would not have him take a call from Nafesa while he was speaking with Marla.

"Excuse me." William walked over to the phone that hung on the kitchen wall. "Hello . . . Oh hi. How are you doing? . . . You do?. When? . . . Where? . . . Yeah, I remember how to get there. How could I forget? . . . Is everything OK? . . . Sure. I'll see you in a few. Let me get myself together and I'll be there . . . Ditto." William hung up the phone and turned around to see if Marla had read between the lines of his sterile conversation. The expression of hurt of her face told him that she had.

"William, what was that all about? Who were you speaking with? Tell me the truth. Are you seeing someone else? Tell me the truth. Are you sleeping with her?"

William knew that this was not the time for true confessions. "Marla, why are you accusing me of something like that? You should know me better than that. I don't have to sit here and listen to you make stupid accusations against me. If that's all you have to say, then I think it's time we say good-bye. I can't deal with you right now."

"William, why are you side-stepping my questions? Tell me the truth. Are you seeing someone else?"

"Damn it Marla, no! I am not seeing anyone else," he cowered.

"Then who was that on the phone?"

"It was a head hunter. A head hunter! She was giving me some information on where I have to go for an interview. I quit my job the other day. Remember? I knew that in the long run, I wasn't going to fit in there. So, I quit before things got too far out of hand. OK? Now are you satisfied? Maybe I should give this marriage stuff a little more thought. If I have to explain myself every time the phone rings, I better start to rethink what I'm getting myself into."

Marla became quiet. She began to second guess herself. Maybe she was over-reacting. He was correct; they had just spent a full Sunday together. "I'm so sorry William. Maybe it's just that I've been handling all of the wedding arrangements by myself. You know I love you. I'm sorry."

William stood up and walked over to her. He put his arms around her and kissed her on the top of her head.

"It's alright Marla, it's alright. Now let me get dressed for my interview."

Marla stood up and gave William a soft kiss on the lips. William could tell that she was one second from crying, but he didn't have an extra second to give.

"Do you want me to ask Vanessa to come down? I'm quite sure the two of you can make some of the wedding arrangements together."

"That sounds good," she whispered.

"So, I'll call you when I get back from my interview and let you know how it went." William dashed upstairs and left her waiting in the kitchen. He looked for Vanessa and asked her to keep Marla company until he was able to get out of the house. Vanessa complied. William gave Marla a quick smile as he ran out the front door. Mrs. Jennings joined Marla and Vanessa in the kitchen.

"I hope you can get him together because he's going through it now. But, I have plenty of faith in you Marla," confided Mrs. Jennings.

"Well, I wish him luck with his interview today. Maybe if he can get this job it'll take a lot of pressure off of him," defended Marla.

"What interview? I thought he was supposed to start at the Prosecutor's office with his uncle. Maybe I'm wrong," responded Mrs. Jennings.

Shock and hurt filled Marla's face.

"He told me that he wasn't certain if he was going to work with Uncle Jesse. He said that he would continue to interview until he was certain about what he was going to do," lied Vanessa. Her lie was more for Marla than it was for William.

Although Nafesa had brought him to her bat cave when it was pitch black, William was certain that he could find his way back. He was low on gas and had to stop at a station to get gas. A little boy ran over to his car and asked if he could pump the gas for William. Although he was usually hesitant about pan-handlers and beggars, William let the kid pump his gas. This would give him more time to think about Nafesa. She sounded as though something was wrong. He wondered if she was OK. William became upset with the kid because it seemed the kid was taking too long to pump ten dollars worth of gas. Finally, the kid walked over to William's window and told him that he was finished. William gave the kid sixty-eight cents; that was all of he change that he had on his center console. The ride seemed as though it took forever. When he finally arrived, he saw Nafesa standing beside her car. She looked good, but something was missing. She didn't have her glow. Now, he was certain that something was wrong. He drove up and parked behind her car. She didn't greet him with a smile. He smiled at her hoping that would cheer her up. It didn't. He moved towards her. She held her hand out for him to hold. He grasped her hand and pulled her into him. He felt a slight resistance from her. He tried to lean into her and give her a kiss. She turned her head away from him. A slight pain began to develop in his chest; right around the heart area.

"What's wrong Nafesa?"

"I wish I could say everything was right, but I can't."

"Look, just tell me what's wrong. You're not in any trouble are you? Do you need money or anything?"

"William, I don't think that we should see each other anymore. I think that we should stop this train before it picks up too much steam."

"What are you talking about? Last night we were under that tree, that tree right there making love. It was love, I don't care what you say, I know that it was love. How can you tell me today that we shouldn't see each other anymore? It's that Sham-sardine guy isn't it?" William was shaking his head in disbelieve. The slight pain that had developed in his chest; right around the heart area was now throbbing.

"William, there's more to it than Shamsadeen. It's about me bringing closure to some old things before I begin something new."

"But how can you bring closure to something as new as us? You're not telling me the truth. Tell me what's really going on. You can't tell me that you don't have feelings for me."

"Look William, just believe me when I say that it's best that we stop seeing each other. I'm in a situation that could ruin your life. I have to separate myself from something before I can bring you into my life. I'm not saying that I don't have feelings for you, it's just that it's not safe to have those feelings right now."

From the tone of her voice over the telephone, William knew that something was wrong, but he had not expected this kind of wrong. "Nafesa, please, tell me what's wrong? You're talking in circles. Tell me everything that's going on. Let me be a part of this decision." The throbbing in his chest; right around the heart area was now pounding.

"William, why are you doing this to me? Just take my word for it. We can't be together at this time!" She tried to steel her disposition, but her words were like the rain drops from a quick summer shower that fell onto hardened earth, they lack the power to saturate.

"Nafesa, why are you doing this to me? Please, please, please just tell me everything and let me in on what's going on? Please, that's all I'm asking."

Nafesa inhaled a deep breath and closed her eyes. "William, I'm involved with one of the biggest drug dealers in the city. He has a whole organization under him. He's making unbelievable money. He has money spread throughout the stock market, he has property in the islands, he has a race horse in Kentucky and he has several offshore accounts. And that's just the tip of the iceberg. I know he has a lot more than that. This morning the D.E.A. broke into our apartment looking for drugs. I was in the apartment all by myself. I was terrified. Praise be to Allah, that they didn't find anything. They tore up the apartment and promised that they would return," she exhaled.

"Let me ask you one question and I need a truthful answer. Are you a part of his organization? To get to the point, do you deal drugs?"

"Hell no! William, I have nothing to do with drugs. I wouldn't even know what the shit looks like. I must give Shamsadeen credit; he has never brought the actual stuff home. At least not that I'm aware of."

"Well, you do realize that you could get implicated in all of this under a conspiracy theory. If you know he's a drug dealer and you accept his money, and his gifts, and live the life of a drug dealer's girlfriend, then a jury could find that you were intimately involved in the whole thing. My uncle is the District Attorney. I can talk to him for you."

"William, why are you scaring me? I don't need to hear that shit right now. I'm trying to free myself from all of that shit and here you come putting me square deal in the middle of it. I don't need to hear that right now."

She was confusing William. Last night she was perfect. Now, here she stood telling him that she was an accomplice to a drug organization. And, that she was the girlfriend of the top man in the organization. Last night she perfect. Today, she was far from it. Even her language was different. She was not pure. She was a Nafesa. His family was right. He should have never allowed himself to slip into this mess. He had left the woman he had loved for ten years at home with her eyes about to burst with tears for a stranger. All the years of trust that the two of them had built, he destroyed for a Nafesa. But, for as much as his mind was telling him to run as fast and as far as he could from this Nafesa, this girlfriend of a drug lord, that pounding in his chest; right around the heart area would not let him leave her.

"I don't know what to tell you. All that I can do is offer you my help. Like I said, my uncle is the District Attorney. I'm quite sure that I can make arrangements for you to talk to him if you're willing to cooperate against this Sham-sardine."

"Damn it William, his name is Shamsadeen. Sham-sa-deen. I can't snitch on him. I could never do anything like that. I'm just going to go away. Saturday is my last day at the OFFBEAT. When the last set is over, I'm going to jump in my car and drive up to New York for a couple of weeks. I need to get my head together. I need to be alone. I'm sorry for starting something that I know I'm not in a position to finish at this time. I'm so, so sorry William. Can you forgive me?"

Her words had not saturated him. He refused to hear that she was walking out of his life. He had to hold on to her. Her newness meant too much to him. She had released him from himself and now he knew that he could never go back to the old William. She had opened him up. He was no longer afraid of the uncertain; he wanted it. He wanted her.

"Maybe it is a good idea for you to go up to New York. Can I come up there with you? I don't have to start my new job until the first of the month. We could spend time together; get to learn more about each other. I don't even know your last name. We could have some fun. Maybe I could help you figure out the best way to handle this situation without running away from it or, from me. So how does that sound?"

"Islam."

"Islam, what?"

"That's my last name. Islam. Nafesa Islam."

"Isn't that the name of your religion?"

"William, I'm not here to discuss religion with you. I wish the two of us could hang out in New York, but it wouldn't work. I'm going up there for a week or two to stay with my brother. He's an Orthodox Muslim. I could never bring you into his house and sleep in the same bed with you. To make matters worst, you're a Christian. Believe me, it would never work."

"I'll stay at a hotel. Or, I could stay with my cousin Mark. He has an apartment up there. You could stay with me if you wanted to. Or, you could stay with your brother and I'll meet you whenever and wherever you say. Nafesa, I'm trying to hold on to you. Help me out. I don't know what else to do or say. I can't let you just walk out of my life."

Nafesa looked into his eyes and knew that he was right. She knew that she could not walk away from him. She wanted him and, she needed him. But, she did not want to ruin him or, get him hurt over her stupid decisions. "William, let me think about this. I need some time. The gig is over on Saturday. Come to the Saturday show and I'll let you know what I'm going to do. Please, don't come to tonight's show or tomorrow's show. I need to keep my head clear. Seeing you will only cloud it up."

"I can work with that. It'll be hard staying away from you, but if that's what you want, I can handle that. Now, can I handle you for a moment?" William tried to hold her. Nafesa stepped back.

"Not today William, at least not right now."

They both looked at each other. William moved away from her and started back towards his car. He turned and looked at her before he entered it. With a half-hearted smile, she blew him a kiss. Happy to receive any token of her affection, he snatched it out of the air.

"Oh Allah, please do not let any harm come to him."

CHAPTER TEN

William zoombied home. He had been wounded and the pain was new to him. It pounded again and again, and again in his chest; right around the heart area. The pain reverberated up and into his head. It made him dizzy or, as his nephew Adam would say, it made him "zizzy". Plain and simple, it hurt like hell. He had no idea how long it took him to get home or the route that he took to get home. But, before he knew it, he was in the driveway of his family's two story colonial with the manicured lawn. Somehow, he felt as though he had aged during the car ride home. He pondered the powers of Nafesa. How had she gained so much control over him in so short a period of time? He'd known Marla for over ten years and she didn't have a fraction of the control over him that Nafesa had. Was she a voodoo priestess? He parked his car and went into the house. His parents were sitting in the family room. He barely gave them a greeting as he rushed up the stairs. His mother shook her head. His father called for him to come back down, but William ignored him and continued up the stairs to his bedroom. He could hear his father stomping up the stairs. Judge William Jennings was a small man; he stood five-feet-six-inches and weighed one hundred and thirty-three pounds on his heaviest day. He was born small and he stayed small. He was the smallest and the youngest of the six boys in his family. His mother was overly protective of him. His brothers always picked on him. In fact, everybody always picked on him. He never won a fist fight with any of his brothers. In fact, he never won a fist fight with anybody. He dreaded his size. His mother constantly reminded him that size only mattered amongst children. In the real world, it was the size of a man's intelligence that determined whether he was big or small. So, little Billy took to the books. He couldn't do

anything about the size of his body, but he could do something about
the size of his intellect. He was determined to be the smartest kid his
mother had. He studied and studied and studied. He established a
work ethic that was both impressive and relentless. He graduated
from high school at the age of fifteen. He completed college at the
age of eighteen. At the age of twenty-one, he was practicing law. Ten
years later, he was on the Bench. He was a "my way or the highway"
man. And he ran his courtroom like he ran his home. "Discipline
was paramount for the success of a family and for the success of a
people" was his motto. He loathed the blacks who appeared before
him in court. They all had the same excuse as to why they were the
dredge of society; they came from a broken home; they were raised
in public housing; they were exposed to drugs and alcohol at an
early age. The excuses were a thousand fold. Prison terms of thirty
and forty years were not uncommon in his courtroom. "They are the
ball and chain of the black race. They are dead weight on a ship
barely afloat. We must purge ourselves of these people if we are ever
to move ahead as a people." Judge Jennings was a small man. He
was born small and he stayed small.

Judge Jennings knocked on William's door. "William, I need to
speak to you. Open the door. I want to speak to you immediately!"

"Dad, I'm not in the mood to be bothered by you or anyone else
right now. Let's try talking a little later."

"I'm not asking you William, I'm telling you!"

"Dad, stop trying to order me around. It hasn't worked since I
was in high school and it's definitely not going to work now. I said I
don't feel like talking to you now, so please leave me alone."

"Well, I think it's about time that you find a place to live. If you
can't do as I say do in my house, where I pay the bills, then it's time
for you to leave."

"Fine dad, I'll leave. Just do me a favor and leave me alone for
right now? I need to be by myself."

Mr. Jennings stood out side of William's door not knowing
what to say next. He knew William would not have spoken to
him in that tone of voice unless something was really bothering
him. He wanted to apologize and speak to his son as a friend
instead of a father, but he knew that it was too late for that. He
walked away from the door and left William to deal with whatever

was on his mind. There would be another time to let William know how he truly felt.

William sat backwards in the chair that faced the window in his room. He stared out into his neighbor's driveway. Their property was dotted with the largest tree on the block. As a kid, William had marveled at the size of the tree. He was told that the trees were federally protected. The neighbors couldn't cut them down if they wanted to. They wanted to! The roots constantly broke through the cement, large branches were always falling on their cars or on their roof, and one of the trees had a hard lean towards their house. It was just a matter of time before it toppled over. The Federal government would periodically send crews around to prune the trees. William's neighbors, the Feltons wanted them to be gone. Their homeowner's policy was the highest on the block. Today, as he sat in his room peering out of the window, William wished he were a tree. Life was too complicated and carried too many problems. *"Maybe Nafesa was right about trees."* But he didn't want to think about her, or how she looked, or how she walked, or how she sang, or how she smiled or how she smelled, or how they had made love, or how they watched the stars beneath the old tree on her family's property. He wanted to purge himself of her. He wanted to be free of this beautiful dark brown girl who was juxtaposed to everything that he had been taught about beauty. He wanted her out of his heart and out of his head. He wanted the pounding pain in his chest; right around the heart area to go away. But, he knew that she wouldn't go away. Better yet, he couldn't let her go away. Maybe, if he was able to rid her of this Shamsadeen character, she would be free to be his. His mind began to spin. Shamsadeen was the sourse of their distress. If he were able to eliminate Shamsadeen, Nafesa would be his. He jumped up from the chair and raced over to the phone that was sitting on top of his bed. He dialed his uncle's phone number. Karen answered the phone. William asked her to put him through to his uncle. Karen oblige.

"Hey Unc, I need your help."

"Don't I even get a hello or, how are you doing?"

"Unc, I'm serious, I need your help. What do you know about a big time drug dealer named Shamsadeen?" There was a long pause of silence.

"William, what do you know about Shamsadeen Baku?"

"Unc, that was my question to you. Remember?"

"William, now I'm serious, what do you know about Shamsadeen Baku?"

"I know a close friend of his who might be in trouble."

"William, the last thing you want or need is to be involved with a close friend of Shamsadeen Baku. That's a recipe for disaster."

"Unc, please tell me what's up with this guy?"

"William, between my office and all of the Federal agencies that are investigating Shamsadeen Baku, we could probably write a book about the guy. The problem is, we haven't been able to throw the book at him. What we know is, he's the only surviving child of Mustafa and Agee Baku. His parents and practically all of their followers were killed in the bombing incident that happened back in the eighties. There was a big lawsuit that stemmed from the incident. The settlement from the lawsuit gave Shamsadeen two million dollars when he turned eighteen. That's part of the problem with us being able to catch the prick. He's been able to hide all of his illegal money behind the money from his settlement. He has a money wizard by the name of Larry Milbourne who handles all of the money that the organization makes. They call him Lil' Larry. The guy is a money guru. He could be a millionaire if he worked on Wall Street. Hell, he's probably a millionaire now, we just can't locate all of his money. We know that Shamsadeen bought about a dozen street corners when he first collected his settlement money. When I say bought a street corner, I mean he purchased the rights to be the exclusive drug dealer for that particular corner. From there, his organization has grown tenfold. Some of his growth has been by financial acquisitions and some of it has been by muscle. Whenever we dismantle an organization, he seems to be able to slide in and set up shop. He and his side kick seem to be naturals at the business. They've managed to keep their organization running smoothly. And, they've prospered into the millions. They run a tight ship. They reward loyalty and they punish disloyalty. We think that he's killed at least five people in the last year alone. But, they always seem to stay one step ahead of us. The most recent murder that we think he's responsible for is a character who went by the name of PeeWee. His real name was Calif Bryan. We have a couple of leads on the murder, but they'll probably end up going south on us. When I say south, I mean the witnesses will change their statements or, they won't show up or, they'll simply disappear. Shamsadeen dates two women. One is a jazz singer who he likes to parade around, kinda like a trophy piece. The other one is just as ruthless as he is. The word is, she could probably run the organization as effectively as he does. I think her name is Lorean. No, I'm wrong, her name is Lorraine. Yeah, that's it, her name is Lorraine. Lorraine has a twin brother who is a homosexual. He or she, depending on the view you take, calls himself LaShonda. Believe it or not, we're pretty sure LaShonda is the enforcer for the organization. I still find it amazing that a blatant, cross dressing homosexual is the enforcer for one, if not the biggest drug organizations in the city. I've seen Shamsadeen's other girlfriend perform. She sings with a band that calls themselves Na . . . something. I can't remember right off hand, but I have it written down. She's hell of a talent. And, she's a beautiful girl. It only begs the question as to why she's with him. Unless, she's a part of the organization. And, I have to believe that she is. She can't enjoy the fruits without working the field. You know, I just thought of something. Maybe they use the band to launder some of their money. I'm going to make a note of that and have her checked out. There is a light at the end of the tunnel for us. The word that we're starting to hear is that Shamsadeen is starting to spread himself a little too thin. He has a couple of underlings, Raoul and Rockman who have big eyes and little brains. Our intelligence reports is starting to learn that these two guys are trying find some corners where they can set up their own business. Only time will tell if they survive their ambitious endeavors. Well, nephew, that's a lot of information. As you can tell I've been studying this guy. We want him! Now, what information do you have that could be helpful to this investigation? Do you know anything that might save someone from getting killed?"

"Not just yet Unc, but I'm working on it. Do you think I could help work the file when I come on board?"

"I don't think so William. Files like these are years in the making. There are too many lives at stake. Now again, I don't know who you know that's affiliated with Shamsadeen and his organization, but I'm warning you, leave that person alone. By the way, the information that I just gave you stays between us. If I find out that you leaked this info out to anyone, I mean anyone, our relationship will change. Do you read me?"

"Don't worry Unc, I'll never mention this information to anyone. And, I do plan to leave that person alone. See you on the first." William hung up the phone and tried to digest all of the information his uncle related to him. He was scared. He was scared for both himself and for Nafesa. If the police could not stop this guy, how could he? He could hear his mother's voice in the back of his head, "I told you so". He wanted to speak to Nafesa, but he knew that was an impossibility. He needed to be with someone. He picked up the phone and dialed 215-555-6079.

"Hello, Mrs. Bertrem, is Marla there?"

CHAPTER ELEVEN

Nafesa gave Jasmin a big hug and without words, walked out of the door. She drove around the city trying to figure out what she should do. She knew she was too upset to make it through a rehearsal. She needed to get away without running out on the band. Nafesa decided to call Flavor and tell him what was going on. She reached over to the passenger seat and groped through her bag, trying to find her cell phone. She found it and dialed Flavor's number. His answering machine came on. Nafesa left him a message telling him that she would not be at rehearsal, but she would be at the club on time. She needed to be with someone. She thought about her mother and tears streamed down her face. The loneliness was too hard. She wanted to contact her father, but she was certain that the two of them could not make it through five words with each other. They hadn't had a meaningful conversation since the death of her mother. She still blamed him for mother's death. He had robbed her of the only person who had ever loved her unconditionally.

Dr. Amin Abdul Islam was a philosophy professor at Williamson University, on the outskirts of Philadelphia. He was a chain smoker who smoked at least two and a half packs of Pall Malls a day. He was seldom seen without a cigarette dangling between his fingers. His finger tips were stained brown. Nafesa and her brother, Rasheed had grown up in a haze of smoke. Nafesa hated being with him or, going anywhere with him. She hated car rides with her father. She was trapped in a mobile box filled with a steady stream of yellowish smoke. The longer the car ride, the heavier the yellow smoke. Nafesa begged him to stop. Either he couldn't or, just wouldn't listen to her. Nafesa could never remember him making one attempt at quitting. Her mother Melissa Islam, a registered nurse kept quiet about his smoking. She was a passive woman. Even with all of the information about second hand smoke, she remained silent about his smoking. Nafesa's only real show of defiance against her father was in regards to his smoking. It was at her high school graduation party. They were all having a good time. Her father came home and tried to join the party. He filled the house with cigarette smoke. She pleaded with her father to stop smoking while the party was going on. He refused to stop smoking in his own home. Her friends began to filter out. Within an hour and a half, the party was over. Nafesa left with her friends and stayed with Jasmin for two weeks. She refused to set foot back in the house. She only returned at the plea of her mother. Six years ago, her mother was diagnosed with lung cancer. Her mother never smoked a day in her life. The doctors attributed it to second hand smoke. They told her that her lungs looked like the lungs of a person who smoked a pack a day for ten years. Nafesa watched her mother go from a healthy, happy, vibrant woman to a shell of a human. She suffered. The cancer ate away at her slowly. The doctors gave her eight months to live. She prolonged for twenty-one months. Nafesa's disdain for her father grew with each month that she watched her mother agonize. She went to the hospital with him on the day her mother died. He had to have a cigarette before he went into the hospital. Nafesa left him standing outside of the hospital smoking a cigarette. She wondered how the two of them ever met each other. They were extremes.

The two met at Duke University when Amin Islam was in the Philosophy Department's doctorate program, and Melissa Thorton was a senior in the School of Nursing. The both loved jazz. They saw each other at a jazz session in a local college jazz hole. Their smiles attracted each other. She was brown skin with coiffured black hair. She had narrow squinting eyes that strained through heavy glasses. Her breast were big, real big and dominated her petite frame. But her smile . . . it was full and outreaching. It spoke to you. It told you of the warmth of the person who harbored it. Melissa looked to her right and saw a tall lean man who was totally absorbed in the music. The music seemed to be his catharsis. He wasn't enjoying the music, it was his refuge. He turned to his left and noticed a beautiful smile hello-ing him. He returned the smile with a toothy grin. He looked away, picked up a cigarette and blow out a heavy stream of smoke. It was jazz. It was expected. He was only smoking a few cigarettes a day. She kept a vigilant gaze on him. He accepted her unspoken invitation and worked his way over to her table. Their conversations were opposite. She was close; he was aloof. She wanted to have six children; he wanted to destroy any life that impeded the progress of the Blackman. She was small town Pennsylvania; he was public housing Detroit. She was a devoted Christian, he was a non-committed Muslim. She was innocent, refined, honest and clean; he was tainted, harsh, untrue, and tarred. They fell in love. Within a year, they were married. He was only smoking a half a pack a day. Two years later, Rasheed Ibrahim Islam was born. He was only smoking a pack a day. Three years later Nafesa Amira Islam was born. He was only smoking a pack and a half a day. Five years later, Dr. Islam was hired as an assistant professor at Temple University. Melissa Islam took a job as a nurse at Eisenhower Hospital. Three years later, Dr. Islam became a full professor at Williamson University. He was only smoking two packs a day. Eleven years later, his wife lay dying in a hospital bed with lung cancer. He was only smoking three packs a day. The doctors all but told him that he had sentenced her to death. On the day that she died, he went to the hospital with his daughter. He could not bare to look at the mass of humanity who lay in the bed in room 2209, knowing that the mass of humanity was once a loving woman whose humanity was beyond mass. He wanted to cry, but could not let his daughter see him cry. He knew that his daughter detested his smoking. He deliberately lit up a cigarette just so he could be alone and weep in his guilt. His daughter left him. He extinguished his cigarette and wept, wondering what the beautiful brown girl with the outreaching smile ever saw in him.

Even in her dire state, Nafesa was not ready to forgive her father. Besides, she did not want him to think that she was coming back with her tail between her legs. She wanted to call William and tell him to forget everything she had just told him and come be with her. She knew that she couldn't do that either. She thought about calling her brother, but Rasheed was too righteous. If he even thought that she was dating a purveyor of poison, he would disown her. So, she did as Shamsadeen had told her to do. She checked into the Center City Hilton. She stayed in her room waiting for Shamsadeen to call her or come to the room. He was the only person she could talk to about what was happening. She would never, ever tell him about William. She could never, ever tell him about William. The day passed and Shamsadeen never called her nor did he come to the room. She felt deserted. She tried to focus her attention on tonight's show. She couldn't. She didn't even have anything to wear. She thought about going back to the apartment to get an outfit, but she remembered how emphatic Shamsadeen was about not going back there. It was the perfect excuse, at the perfect time to go shopping. She was certain that her rock, Jasmin would go shopping with her. She called Jasmin and asked her to take a ride to the mall with her. Jasmin agreed. The rock held firm. Nafesa went back to the street with the neat row of houses and picked up Jasmin. She hoped that Jasmin would help settle the confusion that was swirling out of control in her mind.

"Girl, you still look a wreck! In fact, you look worst now than you did a couple of hours ago. Fe, I don't think you should go to the club tonight. The band can cover for you. Don't they have a backup for you? You just don't look good to me. This shit has got you stressed out of your damn mind."

"I'm OK. I'll be alright by tonight. I just need to take a ride and clear my head. Going to the mall to buy an outfit will relax me. I was hoping that Shamsadeen would come by. He never showed up. I did a lot of thinking about my mother today. You know, it's funny, you never realize how much you miss your mother until something like this happens. My mother would tell me exactly how to handle this situation."

"Fe, I don't wanna sound cold or nothing, but your mom isn't here to help you. Whenever you get stressed, you tend to do nothing and use your mother as an excuse for doing nothing. Your mom spent a lot of time with you before she died trying to get you to understand that you're going to have to make it on your own. I'm not telling you to forget your mom or nothing like that, but what I am saying is you have to be responsible for yourself. You have to be ready to make the hard decisions. I remember your mom and even if she was still here, she wouldn't make your decisions for you. She'd give you advice, but you'd still have to make the decisions. Hell, I give you advice and have told you what to do a thousand times. You won't listen to me. Look at me, I don't own shit. I still live with my mother. The one thing that I do own is me. Now you, you have everything. You got a funky apartment. Well, at least you had a funky apartment. You drive a brand new convertible BMW. And, you wear nothing but designer clothes. But what you don't own is yourself. Shamsadeen owns that just like he owns everything else that you think is yours. That's why he don't like me, he knows that he can't own me.

Nafesa knew that Jasmin was right on both matters. Nafesa's mother wasn't here to help her. And, if she were here, Nafesa would still have to make her own choices. And, Jasmin had told her a thousand times to leave Shamsadeen and she hadn't listened. She just could not or, would not do it. For the first time she was beginning to realize that she was an accomplice to Shamsadeen's drug dealings. She spent the money he gave her; she drove the car he bought her; she lived in the fancy apartment he furnished for her; and she wore the clothing he purchased for her. She was an accomplice, a silent accomplice, but an accomplice just the same. She had sold herself for the material bull shit. She could make it without him. She was a jazz singer with a promising career and making decent money. She didn't have to have a brand new car; she just needed basic transportation. She didn't need a fancy apartment to live in; she just needed a roof over her head. She didn't need designer clothing to wear; she just needed good quality clothes. One thing her mother had always preached to her was "anything over the basics was ego". She wanted to pull over and leave the car and everything else that Shamsadeen had given her on the side of the road. Then, she began to reason that she had earned everything he had given her. And, with the raid on the apartment she was entitled to keep everything.

"Jas, I've earned all of this shit for putting up with his ass."

"Fe, if that's what you want to believe, then who am I to tell you other wise. But you and I both know the truth, you can't let go. Oh yeah girl, you hear about PeeWee?"

"No. What about PeeWee?" Nafesa almost slammed on her brakes.

"Damn Fe, you ain't hear? They found his ass stuffed in a trash bag in the bathroom of Gretta's Sweet Spot. But check this out, he had his dick stuffed in his mouth. Now, you tell me whoever did that shit ain't cold?"

A hugh portion of Nafesa's stomach knotted. She had to vomit.

CHAPTER TWELVE

Saturday came with less excitement than William had expected. The past few days had allowed him time to return to the life he had known before Nafesa. And, the past few days had not brought him any clarity to the situation. In fact, the past few days only brought him more confusion. Regardless of Nafesa's decision, personal questions were surfacing within him. He had spent a considerable amount of time with Marla over the past few days. Good times, enjoyable times, romantic times. He was surprised at how much he enjoyed her company. They had gone to the movies; they had gone out to dinner; they had spent some time at the pool house; they had tried out his new love making techniques with surprising satisfaction; and more importantly, they had good conversations together. He learned things about Marla he never knew before. He learned she did not want a large family, two kids at the most. He learned that she hated cold weather and wanted to live in a warm climate. He learned that she was afraid of his father. He learned that she was pro-abortion. He learned that she was contemplating going to medical school. He learned that she believed in a God and really didn't care about organized religion. He learned that she first fell in love with him on April 17, 1994 when he paid another student five dollars for an umbrella so that she wouldn't get wet in the rain. What he really learned about her was that she thought like a woman and not like a big girl. She told him that she was the same person, it's just that it's taken him all of these years to really listen to her. He was beginning to remember why he had fallen in love with her back in tenth grade. But, right beneath his layer of happiness with Marla, was his desire to be with Nafesa. Despite the confusion that was swarming in his head, his heart ached for her. He missed her. He needed her. That was the difference between his feelings for Marla and his feelings for Nafesa. He had Marla, he longed for Nafesa. It was hard not seeing her over the past few days. He wanted to go down to the club to see her, but he knew that it would probably do more harm than good. So, he waited. In anticipation of Nafesa wanting to spend time with him, he told Marla that his cousin, Mark had invited him up to New York to hang out for a couple of days. She offered no resistance.

At four o'clock, William began to study the clock. The hours moved like days; the minutes moved like hours; and the seconds moved liked minutes. When the hands on the clock met at the six, he decided to get ready. He took a quick shower, dried and lotioned his body, sprayed on some Arrid deodorant, and oiled his hair. He searched through the bottles of cologne on his dresser and settled on Halstons. It was his favorite. He always received compliments when he wore it. He decided to wear his seldom worn, but best dressy outfit. It was his emerald green Versace jacket, with a pair of light green Perry Ellis pants, and a short sleeve silk, egg shell white shirt. He even polished his brown Lamberti shoes. He looked in the mirror for a final check. William convinced himself that no woman on this planet could resist him. He just hoped that Nafesa wasn't an alien. He had his car washed earlier in the day. He was too clean to be clean! He looked at his watch, it was seven-twenty. It was time to go. He stepped out into the night air. He could smell the fragrance from the lilac trees that dotted the front of the house.

The heaviness of the August air from the humidity had slackened. The air was still heated, but without the soupiness. He flopped down into his car and searched through his CD collection. He settled on the "Love Jones" CD. It offered a good mix for a mixed up heart.

William arrived at the club fifteen minutes before the show started. He wanted to make sure he got a good seat. He walked into the club and surveyed the floor to see where he would sit. The seat that he sat in when he first saw Nafesa was available. *"Why not?"* He made his way over to the table and sat down. He looked around to see who was waiting on his section of the club. He saw Charmaine. She saw him and put up a finger to indicate that she would be with him in a moment. He acknowledged her with a smile. Two attractive women were sitting at the table next to his. One of the women with big breasts and a short clinging dress went out of her way to make contact with him. She got up from her table and squeezed past him. She accidentally touched him with her butt.

"Excuse me. I'm so sorry. They put these tables too close together. It's hard to maneuver," she said with a polite smile on her face. William tried not to show her any interest. He kept the conversation short. "Don't worry about it. These tables are kinda close."

When she returned, William pulled his chair in, allowing her extra space to pass by. He never looked at her. Throughout the night, she kept her voice up loud enough for him to hear her conversation. *"Maybe some other night, but not tonight."* This was going to be a special night, he was sure of that. Charmaine came over to his table.

"Hey guy. How have you been? Nafesa put your name on her guest list, so you cool. Becks in a bottle?"

"Hey Charmaine. I've been doing great. Thanks for asking. Yeah, I'll have a Becks in a bottle." William watched as Charmaine disappeared into the swelling crowd. The electricity in the air had been amped up. Charmaine returned with his beer as Brother Haki took the stage. William watched as Brother Haki unraveled the microphone cord. He pushed a slight puff of air into the mic to test it. It worked. The lights dimmed. William felt his body starting to rush.

"Good evening ladies and gentlemen. For those of you who don't know me, my name is Brother Haki and I am your host. Tonight is a sad night for us here at the OFFBEAT. It's the final night for the band. I want to tell you that for the past three weeks they have kicked it out. This place has been packed every night I'm willing to bet that most of you have already heard them and couldn't get enough. Am I right or what?"

"You right about that Bro," someone shouted.

"Brother man, that was a rhetorical question. I really didn't expect an answer," joked Brother Haki. The crowd laughed.

"As I was saying, this band has been everything we thought they would be and more. I hope we can get them to sign an extension and stick around for another week or two. I know we're going to have to vie with the big clubs up in New York, but so what, it's only money. Your money I might add. So drink up and eat up. Are you tired of me talking? Rhetorical question. Well ladies and gentlemen, without further adieu, please give a big hand for the band, Nafesa!" As always, the crowd exploded. The band came out onto the stage and Flavor walked over to the microphone.

"Hello, my name is Flavor and since this is our last night here, I just want to express our appreciation for your support over the past three weeks. You people have made us feel so welcomed each and every night. You don't know how much that means to us. I hope that we've returned a fraction of the love that you've shown us. And since this is our last performance at the OFFBEAT, we really want to tear it up for you tonight. So, sit back and enjoy the groove."

The band opened with an original instrumental. Then, they moved into "Jesus Children". William watched as Nafesa moved onto the stage. Just looking at her let him know that she was into this show. She was into a groove. Tonight, she didn't search the crowd for him. She turned and looked directly at him. Somehow, she knew where he was sitting. Unlike the other nights, she didn't ignore the crowd for him. She felt him and gave him some of her, but she stayed with the crowd. The crowd was feeding on it. *"She's a professional. Let her do what she does best."* William sat back and enjoyed watching the crowd enjoying her. This was the first time he ever watched her as an entertainer. On the other nights, he was too mesmerized by her to sit back and listen to her. Tonight, he wanted to groove with her and the band. From time to time, she would throw him an occasional smile.

The entire band was into a groove. Everyone maxed their solo. They were tight. William watched as Flavor surveyed the crowd with a smile on his face. The band moved from song to song with singular ease. The audience responded after each number. Nafesa worked the crowd like a pro. William marveled at her as she moved through the crowd. She worked her way towards William. She stopped next to him and held out her hand for him to touch. William embraced her hand. They stared at each other for a few seconds. It was obvious to everyone that they were a couple. The big breasted woman with the short clinging dress rolled her eyes at Nafesa. Men wanted to touch her, women wanted to be her. She moved back to the center of the stage. It was time for the band to do their finale. Nafesa pulled up her stool and sat down with the mic in her hand.

"Y'all have been so good to us over the past three weeks. Every night we've performed at the OFFBEAT, you've shown us nothing but love. I hope that we were able to return some of that love to you."

"I'll take some of your love, baby," someone shouted. The crowd laughed. Nafesa smiled.

"I'll bet you would. No, but in all seriousness, we would like to thank you from the bottom of our hearts. Some of you have been here more than once or twice to show us your support. Thank-you. However, like the old saying goes, all good things must eventually come to an end. We're going to end our stay with a special number. Well, at least I think it's special. This song was written for me by a couple of the band members, Flavor and Mel. Stand up guys." Flavor and Mel stood up. The crowd gave them a complimentary applause.

"They wrote this song for me at a time when I needed some newness in my life. And, if by magic, newness came to me. I say magic because you can't be in love and not believe in magic. Love, real love is magic. The first time I ever sang this song, I fell in love with it. The next time I sang this song, I fell in love with someone I didn't even know. So I guess this song has magical qualities. As such, I would like to dedicate this song to all of the people sitting out there who are looking for a little magic in their lives; who are looking for some newness in their lives. This song is for you." There was a quiet excitement in the club. Expectations of magic filled the air. Lovers held hands. Singles longed for a hand to hold. A soft mood began to vibrate within the club. The piano cleared the air. The guitar refilled the air. The rest of the band followed suit. William closed his eyes. Nafesa began to breathe lyrical magic. It was a good song that she made beautiful. She made the song provoke feelings. Or, maybe her feelings were provoked by the song. Either way, the audience was the recipient of its beauty. The entire club swayed with the song and followed it. There was a momentary period of silence when the song ended. It took a second or two to for the crowd to come down. Then, they began to applaud. It was a rolling applause. Nafesa wiped the tears from her eyes, looked up and smiled. They band stood up and moved to the front of the stage. They took a bow. The crowd's applause continued, but now they were standing. Nafesa picked up the mic and concluded the show with a "thank-you".

Nafesa and the rest of the band were back stage celebrating. The owner of the club sent back five bottles of champagne. There was word that a record scout was in the audience. Flavor was searching for her. This was the break the band was looking for. Nafesa tried to make her way out into the club. There were a lot of people trying to congratulate her. She finally broke away and went out to the front of the club. She saw William off to the side, standing against the wall. She quickened her pace. When she was close enough to him, William extended his arms towards her. She moved into them. They stared at each other. She closed her eyes and extended her lips towards his. He lowered his head and pressed his lips against hers. It was there. Everything he remembered about her reappeared. He missed her. She backed away from him with a glow on her face.

"Hi baby," she smiled.

"Hey beautiful," he replied.

"How did you like the show?"

"You were the show. What more can I say?"

"You look good. That's a real nice outfit you have on. And, you smell fantastic. What is the fragrance that you're wearing?"

"It's Halstons. I was always told to wear my best when I intend to meet the best."

"Oh, is that right?"

"That's right."

"So, did you miss me?" she asked

""I hope you give me a chance to show just how much." William grabbed her by the hand and pulled her towards him. She stopped him.

"Not now. I have to go back. Hamid, the club's owner is throwing a party for us tonight. Family and friends only."

"Who gets to go as your guest, me or Shamsadeen?"

"William, you don't have to compete for me. Please, I'm really, really pumped right now. Don't bring me down. You know what I mean? I'm too high on goodness tonight. So, let me ride my cloud. Deal?"

"Deal."

"William, you won't believe what else is going on."

"You have your next gig already lined up?" he guessed.

"No, even better. There's a rep from a record company here who's real serious about getting us into the studio for a recording session. You don't know how long we've waited for this. Allah is so good to me."

"Congratulations. Just remember me when you blow up. Send me some free back stage passes and an autographed copy of your cd when you come to town," he joked.

"I don't know, you might have to get in line with the rest of my groupies."

They both laughed. Then they stared at each other again. William knew he could never love Marla the way he loved Nafesa. And, although he had been with Marla for over ten years, he knew Nafesa was his soul mate.

"Nafesa, I was really afraid to come here tonight. After our last conversation I thought you didn't want to be involved with me anymore. I was hoping, no, I prayed that wasn't the case. When you took the stage tonight, and I watched you perform, I knew you still wanted me just as much as I want you. I wish I could tell how different my life has been since I've met you."

"William, it's not that I didn't or don't want to become involved with you, it's just that I'm afraid of what could happen to you if we do become involved. Shamsadeen is not just a person who talks just to hear himself talk. If he makes a threat, he's the type of person who will carry out that threat. I don't want anything to happen to you. I don't want to be the cause of your getting hurt."

"I'm a big boy. I can take care of myself. And, I can take care of you. Guys like Shamsadeen thrive on fear. They love to instill fear into a person then use that fear to bring the person down. I'm not going to let him or anyone else ever put fear into me. I wasn't raised that way."

"I pray that you're right."

"I thought that you said there was a party going on backstage?" asked William, trying to change the mood.

"There is. Come on back and let me introduce you to some friends of mine."

The rear of the club was packed with people. Nafesa was the star amongst them. Everyone was congratulating her, no, everyone was showing her love. She soaked it up like a sponge. She moved effortlessly through the crowd. She was a natural. When she saw Flavor, she walked William over to him.

"Flav, this is William, a friend of mine. William this is Flavor, my bestest friend, my big brother, my mentor, and my strong shoulder."

Flavor's grin stretched a mile across his face. He exchanged hand shakes with William. "Nice to meet you Black."

"It's nice to meet you Flavor."

"Fe baby, you were on tonight. Girl you brought the house down. And that intro into our new number was perfect. You had the crowd eating out of your hands. I almost dropped a tear my damn self. You have got to add that to the act! I'm telling you Fe, you da man."

"Flav, you know it's not about me, it's about us. What about the record promoter? Did you speak to her? What did she say?"

"Now Fe, you know Flavor is about taking care of business. We're supposed to go up to New York next Wednesday and meet with her and her people. She wants to get us into a studio so we can lay our new song down. But first, we have to get together on the paper."

"Damn Flav, I can't believe that this is finally happening for us. All the hard work is finally paying off. We're about to make it to the top."

"Don't count your eggs before they come out of the chicken," advised Flavor.

"You know what? William's a lawyer. Maybe he can look over the contracts for us?"

"I'm not a lawyer yet. I just took the bar exam. I'm just a law school grad for right now."

"Man, to hell with the technicalities. You got a J.D. right? Besides, I don't think you have to be a lawyer to review contracts."

"Yeah, I do have a J.D."

"That's all we need to know. If Fe is down, then I'm down," said Flavor as he stuck out his hand to seal the deal. "By the way Fe, that record company lady wants to meet you. She's over there in the light blue outfit. Her name is Theresa Muntz. Make sure you talk to her tonight."

"Hell, the way I feel I'd dance with her tonight. Let's go baby." Nafesa worked her way over to Theresa Muntz, the record company lady.

"Theresa. Hi, I'm Nafesa."

"Nafesa, I'm so glad to meet you. And please, call me Terri. Girl, you have so much talent. I've been hearing about you. Your name is starting to buzz throughout the industry. I figured that I better get down her and meet you before someone else does. And believe you me, you're everything that I've been hearing. Your show tonight was fantastic. And, the way you closed your act was out of this world. I was definitely feeling you. I've already given Flavor my business card, but here, let me give you one also. He and I scheduled a date for next Wednesday to have you guys come up to New York to get things rolling. And I should tell you, it may be best for you to think about yourself as a solo act. But don't worry about that right now. I just wanted to put that little bug in your ear."

"Wow, that's a lot to think about now or later."

"Look, never talk shop when you can talk fun. So how about if we wait until Wednesday to talk shop? I'll see you then."

"That sounds good. I'll see you on Wednesday."

Nafesa took William by the arm and led him out the side door of the club. The coolness of the early morning air felt refreshing. The cigarette smoke from inside of the club had scented their clothes and filmed their eyes. William's eyes teared when the new air rushed into them.

"William, are you crying over me?"

William laughed. "These are tears of joy."

"That's some deep stuff that Terri was talking. I've been with Flavor and the band too long to just drop them like a hot potato. Either they take us as a group or they don't take us at all."

"I think you should wait and see what the record company has to say before you come to any conclusions. If it appears that they want you as a solo act then you should talk it over with Flavor and the rest of the band. That's probably the best way to handle that situation. Hell, if one of you can get in, then it seems that would make it easier for the rest of you to get into the business."

"I don't know. Maybe you're right. I'll just wait and see what happens next Wednesday. So, what about us right now? You know that I'm going up to New York as soon as the party is over. I'm leaving straight from the club."

"I was hoping you would invite me along."

"William, I told you before, I'm staying at my brother's house. He'll never let you and me sleep in his house. He's an Orthodox Muslim. I have to dress differently when I stay with him. He'd have a hard time with a Christian staying in his house. And I'm pretty sure you can't afford to stay in a hotel for a week. So, how are we going to make it work?"

"Like I told you before, I have a cousin who lives in New York. His name is Mark and he's an intern at Manhattan General. I called him the other day and asked him if we could stay with him for the week. He said it would be OK. He's working sixteen to eighteen hour shifts, so he probably won't be home that much. He said if he needs a place to crash, he'll stay at his girlfriend, Marci's apartment."

"That's cold William. How could you ask your cousin to give up his apartment like that?"

"It's OK. Mark and I use to hang out together. We grew up like brothers. We went to college together. I always go up to New York and stay with him. He's the one who showed me where all of the clubs are in New York. I promise you, it's OK."

"Are you sure?"

"I'm more than sure. Like I said, don't worry about it."

"OK. If you say so. So how are we going to do this? Do we take my car, your car, or both cars?"

"I have to honest about this, your car looks a little more cosmopolitan than does mine. It's not that my Grand Am doesn't make it, it's just that a convertible BMW looks like New York."

"I agree," said Nafesa.

"I need to stop by my house and let my folks know where I'm going to be, drop my car off, and get some clothes and stuff to take with me. What about you? Do you need to stop and get some clothes and stuff?"

"No, I've already put everything I need in the trunk of my car."

"Good. When we leave you can follow me to my place. From there, we can get on the road." William moved towards Nafesa like a puppy in need of a head rub. She smiled at his cuteness and brought him into her arms. William began to give her small kisses on the top of her forehead. She raised her head so he could kiss her on the lips. Nafesa closed her eyes and took in the warmth of his lips.

"Oh Allah, please let all of this be true."

CHAPTER THIRTEEN

The ride to New York was long and tiresome. William offered to drive, but Nafesa thought it best if she drove. They stopped once at the Turnpike Rest and Go to get gas and coffee. The cd player pumped out a steady medley of easy going jazz tunes. William called Mark to let him know that he and Nafesa would be there sometime between five and five-thirty. Mark had to report to the hospital by five, so he would probably be leaving no later than four-fifteen, but he would leave the door unlocked for them and, he would leave them a spare key in the top dresser drawer. Nafesa followed William's directions and meandered through the streets of the Bronx until she reached a brown-stone front with the address 238W. Peacock on the front of the door.

"That's it, right there. Mark's apartment is on the second floor." Nafesa parked the car and gave the street a once over to determine how safe her car would be. It looked OK. There were other high end cars on the block. But, hers was the only one with out-of-state tags on it. There wasn't much she could do about it and, she was too tired to worry about it. She and William grabbed their bags from out of the trunk and climbed up to the second floor. The door to Mark's apartment surrendered on the first try. William looked at his watch as they walked into the apartment, it was five-twenty five. The apartment was small and cluttered. It had a tiny kitchen, a small middle room, a little bedroom that was just large enough for the bed and the dresser, it had a cramped bathroom on one side and a small closet on the other. There were medical books and charts and periodicals and magazines lying everywhere. The walls were bare. It was definitely temporary housing. The only decoration in the apartment were pictures. There were pictures everywhere.

They appeared to be a chronicle of Mark's life. There was even a picture on Mark and William when they were little boys. Nafesa picked up pictured and studied it. William came over and smiled at it.

"Is this you she asked?"

"Yep. That's Mark and me playing on the beach at Martha's Vineyard when we were eight."

"He look's a little older than you."

"Really, we're the same age. In fact, he's only twenty-seven days older than me. His birthday is May the second, and mine is May the twenty-ninth."

"Is everyone in your family light?"

"Yep."

"He sure does have a lot of pictures of this white girl. I guess that must be his girl friend? Half the pictures in here are of her."

"Yeah, that's Marci. She's from Paris. Mark's crazy about her. He met her in med-school. They're supposed to be at my house in a couple of weeks for dinner. Mark wants my family to meet her. I've met her once, she's good people. We had a good time together. The next time they go to Paris I might go with them."

"Do you think that your family is going to approve of him dating a white woman? My family would hit the ceiling. Hell, they might hit the ceiling over me dating you. But once they saw that you were black, they'd be cool. When I say my family, I mean my brother. My mother passed a few years ago and my father and I don't speak. Are both your parents black?"

"Yes, both of my parents are black. My mother's father was white and my father's maternal grandmother was white. How come you and your father are estranged?"

"I'm not strange, he's strange," joked Nafesa.

"You know what I mean."

"It's a long story that I would rather not go into right now. I'm too tired."

"My parents won't have a hard time with Mark bringing Marci to our house. Really, they probably won't give it a second thought. To be honest with you, they'll have a harder time with you than they would with her."

A sharp pain of insult ran through Nafesa's body. "With me? Why with me? Because I'm black?"

"No, not because you're black, but because of your dark skin. I don't know of any dark skin people in my family. Look at all of the pictures in here. Do you see any dark skin people? We were always taught that we'd be better off if we stayed in our own color line. Dark skin people would only bring you down."

"You have got to be kidding me. You mean your family who are black, actually taught you that racist bullshit? William, if I wasn't so damn tired I go off. But right now, I'm just too tired to care."

"Hey, I'm not saying that's the way I feel. That's how my family feels about the issue. I'm here with you aren't I?"

"But now I have to ask myself why are you here with me. Are you using me to rebel against your family? Or, are you just experimenting and when you're through, you're going to return to your nice light-bright world? That's what's wrong with us as a people. We bring too much of the white-man's bullshit to the table with us. The same issues we have with the white-man, we have with each other. Internal racism is a secret within our own. Like I said, I'm too tired to take this any further. I'm going to bed. I have to make my prayer by ten o'clock. Please wake me? Promise?"

"I promise." Nafesa went into the bathroom to wash off her makeup. She came out, took off her clothes and put on a sleeping gown. William was struggling with the linen that Mark had left out for them. She smiled at him and gave him a hand. It was a truce token. She was tired and the bed looked inviting. She lay across the bed. William watched as sleep over took her. He watched as the emerging sunlight that stole into the bedroom and danced across her African evening skin. It seemed to accent her highlights. William thanked Mother Nature for the splendor of her beauty. He laid down beside her and draped one arm over her. For today; for that minute; for that moment, she belonged to him.

Nafesa thought she heard someone knocking at the door. She jumped up and, for a second, she had to remember were she was. She listened to see if someone was at the door. It was people from the neighboring apartments either coming or going. She looked around for a clock, but couldn't find one. *How in the world does he function without a clock?* she asked herself. She tried to remember where she left her watch. She back traced her thoughts from earlier in the morning and remembered that she had left it in the bathroom. She got out of bed and went into the bathroom to get her watch. She looked at the time. It was ten-twenty-five. "You promised," she said aloud. But, she knew that William was just as tired as she was. She used the toilet and rinsed out her mouth. Then, she left the bathroom and walked around the tiny apartment to acclimate herself. The pictures of Marci reminded her of the conversation that she and William had before she went to sleep. *"Who cares how his parents think as long as he's not like that,"* she reconciled. She went into the kitchen area to check out what kind of foods were in the refrigerator. Old lunch meats and juice was all that she found in the fridge. She wondered how anyone could live like that. She found where Mark kept his glasses and poured herself a glass of grape juice. She sat down on the floor and started to plan her day. First, she would take a shower, then, she would pray. After that, she would call her brother and let him know where she was. Finally, she would wake William so that the two of them could plan their week together. She would keep today's plans simple. She walked over to her carry bag and searched through it looking for a towel and other sundries that she needed to get herself started.

She felt refreshed after the shower. William was still dead asleep. After she was dressed, she reached in her purse for her tiny compass. She kept the compass so that no matter where she was, she would always be able to tell which way was east for the purpose of prayer. The compass pointed towards the middle room. She began her prayer.

William reached over and felt for her. She was not there. He stood up and wiped the sleep from his eyes. He got out of bed and looked around for her. He thought he heard movement in the middle room. He walked to the middle room and saw Nafesa doing some kind of a strange ritual. He thought she was performing a yoga exercise.

"Good morning. What are you doing?" he asked. Nafesa did not answer him.

"Nafesa, what's going on?" Again, she did not answer him. He sat on the floor and watched her. She would stand, she would bow, she would kneel, and she would chant. *"This is some weird stuff."* When she was done, she turned and looked at him.

"I'm sorry that I didn't answer you, but I was in the middle of my prayer. I couldn't interrupt it to answer you."

"So that's what you call that stuff. Boy, praying my way sure looks a lot easier."

"William, it's not stuff, it's my prayer. It's a personal time spent with Allah. If you really put your heart into it, you can feel his presence."

"I guess it's like feeling the holy ghost or something."

"I think it's time we change this conversation. So far we're zero for two on the conversation chart. We better start to find something we have in common or this is going to be a long week," she stated half jokingly and half seriously.

"You're right about that," responded William.

"I have to call my brother to let him know where I am. What's the address and phone number here?"

"238 W. Peacock Avenue, apartment 2-A. The phone number is 555-7810."

Nafesa picked up the phone and dialed her brother's number. William walked over to the bathroom.

"Alsalamu 'alaykum, Rasheed . . . I'm doing fine . . . How's the family? . . . Good . . . I was . . . No, I'm with a friend . . . No, I'm in New York. Over in the Bronx. Do you have a pen? . . . Ok, I'll hold on . . . Ready? . . . The address is 238 W. Peacock Avenue, apartment 2-A. The phone number is 555-7810 . . . Yeah, I plan on stopping by . . . Shamsadeen is still in Philly. I need you to do me a favor, if he calls tell him that I just stepped out and give me a call. You have my cell number don't you? . . . A friend of mine . . . William . . . No, he lives in Philly . . . We're staying at his cousin's apartment . . . Stop it . . . Maybe around eight . . . Just be relaxed when you meet him . . . You'll see . . . No . . . Look. I'll see y'all around eight . . . Wa 'alaykum al salamu." Nafesa hung up the phone and walked back into the bedroom. William was standing there putting on fresh underwear.

"Boy, Mark must have a five gallon water tank. The water was ice cold. I hate a cold shower," he complained.

This was the first chance she had to really look at him and his body. He was handsome. Not gorgeous, but handsome. He was about the same height as Shamsadeen, but much thinner. Not skinny thin, just thinner. He was hairy. His body was a lot lighter than his face. His face and arms were tanned. His chest area was very light. He could almost pass for white. There was that small amount of pigmentation in his skin color that prohibited him from being able to pass for white without a doubt. He reminded her of an olive complexioned Italian. He was the type of man who would get better looking with age. He would never get old rather, he would become distinguished looking. He was handsome. Not gorgeous, but handsome.

William looked into the mirror that was attached to the dresser and saw her starring at him. He smiled at her. "I can take these underwear off and we can make love."

"You must have read my mind."

"I meant to tell you that I'm a psychic."

"Ok Mr. Psychic, tell me what I'm thinking right now?"

"You're thinking that I'm full of crap!" They both laughed. William took off his underwear and moved towards Nafesa. She began to take off her clothes. William sat on the side of the bed and watched her undress. She deliberately took her time. It was for his enjoyment. William enjoyed every second of it. Her watched as her panties glided down her legs and land on the floor. She was smooth. Her skin glistened. He guessed she was a size four or five. How stupid he was to believe that beauty could not reside in darkness. She shattered that myth. When she was completely undressed, she knelt down between his legs. His penis stiffened. She began to pattern soft kisses between his thighs. Small red circles would linger after the kisses. With each kiss, she came closer and closer to his penis. Finally, she began to kiss the top of his penis. Each kiss raised his temperature. She let her mouth taste a little more of him with each kiss. Soon, she had all of him in her mouth. Her head began to bob back and forth. His toes curled. He had to hold and squeeze something. He fell back and reached for the pillow. It helped. Her head continued to move back and forth at a steady pace. His body was boiling. He felt his body surging. Just when he thought he was about to explode, she stopped. He sighed and continued to squeeze the pillow. She raised up and began to kiss him on the chest. His nipples were ripe for the taking. The surge began again. He tried to push her away to stop the flow of pleasure. She resisted.

"Please stop Nafesa? Please stop?" he begged. She ignored his pleas. He began to sweat. She stopped. He could feel her looking at him. He opened his eyes and saw her hunched over him with a big smile on her face.

"So you like?" she asked in a weird accent.

"I love," he replied, trying to mimic the accent. Nafesa rolled over and lay on the bed beside him. William knew this was his invitation. He rolled over and pushed himself off of the bed. He fingered her toes then, he began to kiss them. The kisses turned into rapid sucking. Her legs began to vibrate. He stopped and moved up her legs with his tongue, halting at her pubic hair. Her hair was different from Marla's. Nafesa's hair was short and coarse; Marla's hair was soft and silky. Neither better, just different. He touched her moist vagina with his finger and tasted her wetness. He felt her twitching as he moved across her. He wanted to show the teacher how well the student had learned his lesson. He kissed her exactly where she had shown him. She jerked. He kissed her there again. She jerked again. He stuck out his tongue and began to play with her. She moaned aloud. Her hands were racing across his head. She called his name over, and over, and over. The more she called out, the faster he moved. The faster he moved, the more she called out. He could feel her body trembling. He could taste her body arriving. It was thick, and warm, and flowing. She pushed his head away and pulled him up on top of her.

"William, look in my bag and get a condom. Hurry up. Damn it William, hurry up," she ordered.

"I'm moving as fast as I can." William searched through her pocketbook and found a two inch by two inch silver packet, with a circular insert. He removed the rubber insert and unrolled it onto his penis. "It's on," he announced.

"Good. Now come here and lay on top of me. I want to look into your face while we're making love."

William sprawled himself on top of her. He felt her searching for him. She found him and guided him inside of her. He felt himself sinking inside of her. She squeezed his shoulder blades and started a heavy thrusting motion.

"Slow down. Or, has the teacher forgotten the lesson?"

"No baby. I haven't forgotten."

"Nafesa, I've never had someone take me where you've taken me."

"William, I want to hear the sounds of our love making; just our bodies and our moans."

They quieted their words and listened to their sweaty bodies stick then separate. They took in the sounds of their sighs and their moans. They moved from position to position. The sweat raced down their bodies like freed river water running from a busted dam. His head was swimming in euphoria. She was drowning in ecstasy. He wanted to come so he stroked harder and harder. She wanted him to come so she pushed harder and harder. She felt the wholeness of his muscle inside of her. He felt her warmness surrounding him. He was about to erupt.

"Nafesa. Oh god. Nafesa!" She listened to his call and added more movement with her hips. He collapsed inside of her, letting out a breathless moan.

"Call my name! Call my name!" she ordered.

"Nafesa! Nafesa! Nafesa! Nafesa! Nafesa!" he surrendered. The two of them fell to the bed soak and wet. They were breathing as though they had just completed a marathon. They parted themselves. Then they turned and looked at each other. Smiles filled their faces. Nafesa's cell phone rang She ignored it. They curled up into each other like twin fetuses trapped in a womb of love.

"Oh Allah, thank-you and forgive me," she silently prayed.

The remainder of the day was a restful waste. They called and had Chinese food delivered to the apartment. Nafesa exercised her voice while William read. She wanted to go to her brother's house, but could not muster up the strength to leave the apartment. William was content having her completely to himself.

Monday did not start off any differently. Their love making was draining. Nafesa was determined to get out of the apartment and do some shopping. There was no way she was going to stay in New York and not do any shopping. And, she had to see her brother. They decided they would go out for lunch; go to the shopping district; take in a movie; go see her brother; and come back to the apartment for a little love making night-cap.

For the most part, their day had gone as planned. The lunch was good, the shopping was ok, and the movie stunk. During the ride to her brother's house, Nafesa became disturbingly quiet.

"What's up?" You seem to have become withdrawn since we've gotten back in the car. What's wrong?"

"I really don't feel like going to my brother's house with you. I know how he's going to act. He's on this self righteous trip right now. Anyone who's not a devout Muslim is a wrong-doer, destined to burn in the fires of hell. He's over the top with the religion. A fanatic or something. Sometimes I think he thinks that he's holier than Mohammed himself. I'm going to have to cover my head before I go inside his house. You don't have to go inside if you don't want to. I'll understand."

"I don't have a problem meeting your brother. If he doesn't want me in his house then I won't go in. What more can he say or do?"

"I guess you're right. If he acts up, we'll just leave. Let's play it by ear and see what happens," she suggested.

William pulled up outside of Rasheed's house. They got out of the car and walked up the pathway that led to the front door. Nafesa put her headdress on. William rang the bell. Within a minute, a young voice came from behind the door.

"Al salamu 'alaykum. Who is it?"

"Wa 'alaykum al salamu. It's your aunt Nafesa."

The door opened. It was Mohammed, Rasheed's oldest son. A heavy fragrance of incense streamed out of the house and filled their nostrils.

"Daddy, it's aunt Nafesa and some white man."

Within seconds, the hall leading to the front door was crowed with bodies. Rasheed had nine children. They were stair steps in age. Rasheed came to the door. His wife, Ameenah was not allowed to come to the front door. Rasheed gave Nafesa the Islamic greeting to which she returned. All of the kids gave her the greeting in chorus form. Nafesa could feel the tension as Rasheed studied William. William stared directly into Rasheed's eyes, determined to hold fast. Rasheed was a male version of Nafesa. They could have passed for twins. Usually, Nafesa would have been in the front room by now. Rasheed did not invite them in.

"Rasheed, this is my friend, William. William, this is my brother, Rasheed."

William extended his hand towards Rasheed. Rasheed simply nodded his head. Nafesa knew that this was not going to work.

"William and I were on our way to dinner. I told him I wanted to stop by and say hello to you and the kids. By the way, tell Ameenah

I said hello. I'll be here until Saturday or Sunday. If I get a chance, I'll stop by later and talk to you about what is going on. We have to run or we'll lose our dinner reservations," lied Nafesa.

"No problem Nafesa. That'll be good if you stopped by later. Al salamu 'alaykum."

"Wa 'alaykum al salamu," parted Nafesa as she backed out of the doorway.

William left the house not knowing what had gone wrong. Although Nafesa had warned him about her brother, he never expected Rasheed to be that cold towards him. William could tell from Nafesa's face that she didn't want to talk about what had just happened. The two of them walked back to the car and drove back to the apartment without ever speaking a word about the incident.

When they got back to the apartment, William sensed that Nafesa needed some cheering up. He tried toying with her, making stupid jokes, and singing to her. Nothing he did or said took her out of her somber mood. He was surprised at the amount of influence her brother had over her. He wanted to talk to her about it, but he didn't want this to become another one of their ill-fated discussions. So, he just left it alone. There was no love making, just quiet thoughts.

In the morning, William awoke to Nafesa talking on her cell phone. She appeared to be back to her old self. From the gist of the conversation, she was talking to Flavor. William went into the bathroom and took a shower. When he came out of the bathroom she was sitting on the side of the bed with a big smile on her face.

"Well, tomorrow is the big day. Flavor and the rest of the guys are so pumped up. They can't wait. After talking to Flavor, I'm starting to get a rush from it all."

William was happy to see her smiling again. "I was wondering when it was going to hit you. You seemed so cool about it all."

"Not really. I've been excited. It's just that I've been enjoying the newness of you since we've gotten here. I want to go back in town and do some more shopping. I want to buy an outfit for tomorrow. Flavor said that the band was dressing in yellow as a theme. I want to match the guys."

"You don't think that's a bit too much? I mean everyone dressed in yellow. Grown men wearing yellow! You'll have to change the name of the band from Nafesa to Nafesa and the Lemonades."

"William you need to stop. It's a show biz thing. Nobody intends to walk around New York as a group wearing yellow. We're just going to meet the record company execs all wearing a common color. It shows solidarity."

"If you say so. Did you talk to Flavor about what Terri had mentioned to you?"

"You mean about me going solo? No way! I would never speak to him about that until after they approached me. That's if they even approach me."

"Yeah, that's probably the best way to handle that situation. Just let that one play itself out. No need for you dropping a bomb prematurely."

For the rest of the day, Nafesa could not stop dreaming about making it big. She dreamt about the places she wanted to visit, the halls she wanted to sing in, and the personal parties she wanted to be invited to. The more William listened to her dreams, the more he became afraid that her stardom, her fame and her fortune did not include him.

Nafesa did not let William see her in her new yellow outfit until she was completely dressed; makeup and all. His mouth fell open when she walked into the bedroom. She looked marvelous in her yellow skirt suit. She was radiantly beautiful. William kissed her on the forehead and wished her good luck. He had learned from Marla that you never kiss on the lips when the makeup and lipstick are fresh. Nafesa forbade William from coming along with her. She told him to have a cold bottle of sparkling apple cider waiting for her when she returned. William wanted champagne, but Nafesa did not drink alcohol.

Nafesa practiced her business demeanor during the car ride to the meeting. She decided that she would let Flavor do all of the talking. She would use her smile to the maximum. Traffic was a nightmare. It took her fifty-three minutes to travel a couple of miles to the office building. She prayed everyone would get there on time. She finally made it to the Wilson Plaza. It was a huge building with an underground parking lot. She entered the garage and wound her way down deep into the sub-terrain garage. She found a space and parked the car, got out, and walked towards the elevators. She looked around to find which level she was parked on. It was level H-RED. She looked at her watch, it was ten-forty-five. She had fifteen minutes to spare. She took the glass elevators to the lobby. As the doors opened, she saw a human mosaic of yellow standing by the front desk. She thought about what William had called them, Nafesa and the Lemonades, and laughed to herself.

"Well, if y'all ain't too yellow to be yellow," laughed Nafesa.

"Well look at you; looking like a yellow rose," greeted Flavor. The rest of the band greeted her. It felt good to be with them again. She had missed them over the past few days. They were truly her family. In fact, they were her only family at this point in her life. Then, her mind strayed to Shamsadeen. She had not called him in three days. And, she had not accepted any of his calls. She knew that as soon as this meeting was over, she had better call him to ease his mind. Flavor and Mel took her by her hands and walked her over to the elevators. The rest of the band followed them. They rode up to the twentieth floor. When they stepped off the elevator, there was a large sign welcoming them to New Heat Records. Their confidence soared. A smiling young redhead greeted then as they walked through the large glass doors.

"Well, you must be the band, Nafesa. Welcome to New Heat Records. Ms. Muntz is expecting you. I'll let her know that you are here. There's some coffee and danishes on the table for you. Feel free to help yourselves."

With the exception of Greg, the lead guitarist no one touched the food. They were all too nervous. They waited for about ten minutes before Terri appeared. She was wearing a yellow pants suit.

"Well, I see that yellow is the flavor for the day. I'm glad to see you all. Is everyone here?"

"Yep, we're all here," answered Flavor.

"Good. Follow me and let's get this party started. I want everyone to relax and feel comfortable. This meeting is about you and for you. My people are dying to meet you. I've told them nothing but good things about you."

They followed Teri through a maze of corridors until them came to a large glass conference room filled with people in suits. Nafesa was surprised at the stuffiness of the surroundings. She counted eleven suits. Their average age seemed to be around forty. She had anticipated a meeting of young, laid back, MTV executives. Terri introduced everyone to everyone. Nafesa knew that she would never remember any of the names. She was too amped up, but she smiled as they were introduced. There was someone there for every aspect of the business; marketing, legal, production, and several others that Nafesa had never even thought of. A slight sense of intimidation began to creep into her. She was glad that Flavor was there. He exuded a strong air of confidence throughout the meeting. He listened to them, took notes, and responded with well thought out questions. But, Nafesa also knew that Flavor was way over his head. He was no match for the business entourage that surrounded the conference room table. She was thankful that he had gotten them this far. Getting someone to take them to the next level wouldn't be that much of a problem. She was certain that Flavor had already recognized their need for someone who was much more familiar with the high end business aspects of getting a record contract. Flavor was holding his own, but it was a Custer's stand.

"So, when do we get to cut our record?" he asked.

The suits all turned and looked at the suited man sitting at the head of the table. Marvin Greenstein was the first suit that Terri had introduced.

"Well Mr. Johnson, as soon as we can come to an understanding about the financial end and other minor matters. And I really do not foresee any obstacles appearing in any of those areas."

"Well, if everything does go as expected, when do we get into the studio," asked Flavor, trying to pin the suit down to a specific time.

"I would guess that if everything goes as expected, you'll be in the studio in a month or two. Of course, this is just a guestamation."

"That's cool," said Flavor.

"How soon do we get to review the contract?" asked Nafesa.

"As soon as it's prepared," answered Terri. "I would think you guys should have a contract for review within the next week. What we want to establish here is that you guys will not deal with any other company in the mean time. If the contract comes down and we cannot come to terms, then everything is back to square one. I'm quite sure once you review the contract with your attorney or agent, you'll find New Heat Records to be one of the fairest companies in the business. So we're not concerned about the contract. What we want is exclusivity until then."

"Well Terri, as the manger of the group, I don't think any of us will have a problem with that. As long as it's understood that if the contract is not to our liking, we can move on without any hard feelings," responded Flavor. There was a murmur of consensus from the rest of the group.

"Then I think we have a tentative arrangement," smiled Terri. Everyone stood up with big smiles on their faces. Handshakes were flowing. Terri escorted them back to the front of the suite. She gave Nafesa a hidden wink. Nafesa understood its meaning. The band remained composed until the elevator stopped at the lobby. When the doors opened, they bounced into the lobby. They were floating. All of their hard work had finally paid off.

"Oh Allah, thank-you. Thank-you."

CHAPTER FOURTEEN

S hamsadeen and Lorraine were cruising around in the V12 listening to an old Biggie CD. Lorraine wanted a pair of those Timberland high heeled boots that all the hip- hop queens were wearing in their videos. One of the shops on Walnut Street carried them. She called ahead and had the sales lady set a pair on the side for her. They wanted eleven hundred for them. Lorraine was a slum plum turned ghetto queen. She was a red-bone with deep auburn hair that she wore to the middle of her back. And by the way, it was her hair. She even had freckles on her cheeks. She wore a size ten and loved every inch of her body. Her legs were perfect. Her breasts were large, full and up-right. Her ass was a show stopper. She wore her nails long and colored. She wore only designer clothes. She had two carats in each ear. She had seven tattoos. Her favorite one was on her right shoulder and showed two nine millimeters pistols crossing each other with GANGSTA BITCH written underneath in bright red lettering. Lorraine was a bomb shell and, a shelled bomb.

"Damn Lorraine, I ain't feeling no boots that cost over a stack. It ain't the money or nothing, it's just I ain't feeling no eleven hundred dollar Tim's."

"Look whose talking. You just dropped four ones on that fucking hat. And to be for real about it, it's ugly as shit!"

"Fuck you, don't be calling my piece ugly. I didn't say anything when you came home with that fucked up pants set. That has to be the ugliest piece you have in your closet." They both began to laugh. Lorraine and Shamsadeen had spent a lot of time together over the past few days. It felt good to be with him like this. It reminded her of the old days before Miss Black Beauty popped the fuck up. She and Shamsadeen had history; they had been together for over eleven years.

They had met at a basement party when she was only fourteen and he was sixteen. She had heard that he was going to be there and she was hot-to-trot for him. She'd been watching him in the neighborhood for the past three months. She went to the party with her best friend Vonnie. All night she had refused to dance with anyone, waiting for Shamsadeen to ask her for a dance. She kept her eyes on him. Soon, she saw him walking her way. Her heart began to race. He walked past her and asked Vonnie for a dance. To make matters worst, Vonnie accepted his offer. This was too much for Lorraine to take. Vonnie knew how she felt about him. There was no way in the world Vonnie was going to have him. If it meant having her brother kick Vonnie's ass, she would never have him. Rage filled her eyes. She looked over and Vonnie was waving at her; inviting her to cut-in. They were friends again. Lorraine worked her way over to the dance area and casually cut-in. Shamsadeen didn't seem to mind. When the song was over, she tried to start up a conversation with him, but he seemed non-chalant to her. He just walked away. By the end of the party, she was the only one who he hadn't asked to dance. She decided she would wait for him after the dance. He brushed her off. That was too hurtful. She wanted to return the hurt. There was a stick lying on the curb. She picked it up and swung it at Shamsadeen. He ducked and Lil' Larry pushed her to the ground. She just laid there crying. Shamsadeen walked over to her and helped her up. He smiled at her and walked her home. They've been a couple ever since. Needless to say, she hated Nafesa. Nafesa was an intruder into her world. Miss Blackie was a trophy, a prized piece who was just along for the ride. She was convinced that Nafesa could never understand Shamsadeen. She didn't deserve him. All she did was beg and bitch. But what really hurt was that he had the audacity to flaunt the bitch around town and, in her face. Who in the fuck did he think he was? Did he really expect her to just take this hurt without any paybacks? No soon as he wanted some real loving, he always ended up in her bed. So, what did the black bitch have to offer? Or, was Shamsadeen just too fucking stupid to see that Miss Blackie was just taking him for a ride? If anything ever happened to Shamsadeen, Ms. Bitch was a goner. She would be raped and then shot once in the head. Lorraine had already given LaShonda the order to make it happen if Shamsadeen was ever out of the picture.

Lorraine was certain that there was no one, no one that Shamsadeen trusted more than her. Not even Lil' Larry. And, she was more than certain that there was no one, no one who he loved more than her. Not even Miss Blackie. Lorraine had his front, his side, and his back. When word leaked out that Fat Felix and his crew were going to make a move against Shamsadeen, Lorraine put out the order to snuff Fat Felix. And when the Dominican and his crew robbed Shamsadeen's stash house, Lorraine personally put a bullet in the Dominican's right ear. She kept her eyes fixed and her ears tuned. She reached over and turned down the radio.

"Shamsadeen, what you been hearing about Raoul and Rockman?" she asked.

"Nothing. Why? What you been hearing?"

"Nothing really. But they been acting real strange and shit. Like last night when they stopped in with the money, they were acting strange. I can't put my finger on it, but it was like they were trying me or something. You know how negroes get when they start to feel themselves; they want to stick out the chest. That's how Fat Felix was acting just before him and his crew tried to make a move. Raoul was talking to me with bass in his voice and Rockman kept flashing his Glock. I was like, what the fuck is this all about? If I were you, I'd keep an eye on those little faggots."

"I hear you, but it don't make any sense. I don't know why they would want to try some dumb-shit. They don't even have a crew to be making a big move. They'd have to have somebody backing them. That's the only way those two knuckle heads would try to make a move on me. But that still doesn't make any sense; I gave them my three best corners to run. As long as they come through with the money, all the rest of the bullshit don't matter. I don't give a rat's ass about them beating their chest and shit. I'll bury those punks before they knew what hit 'em." They both smiled. Shamsadeen's cell phone began to play a salsa beat.

"Talk to me," answered Shamsadeen.

"Shamsadeen, this is Gee. Got a minute?"

"Yo, talk. What's up Gee?"

"I want to thank you for putting Nafesa and her band in touch with me. They went over real big. They showed a lot of love and the crowd gave them a lot of love. It was all a good thing. But check it out; I didn't know that you and Nafesa weren't together anymore."

"What the fuck you talking about Gee? Who told you that shit?"

"It ain't what somebody told me, it's what I've been seeing. You know me and you go back years. I mean, we were on the streets together. I don't want to start something; it's just that I thought that the two of you were over. By the way, you wouldn't have something to keep a brother rolling would you?"

"Look Gee, you know I'll take care of you if the info is real. So tell me what you know. Now if your shit is bust, you know the deal, right?"

"Like I said, this is what I saw with my own eyes. Nafesa's been hanging out with some real light skin dude. I've never seen him around before. From the looks of him, he probably works in one of the office buildings down town. A real buppie looking dude. I've been seeing the two of them in the club together. They be all hugged up and shit. Word is they went up to New York together. Now I can't vouch for that, but the rest of the stuff is what I actually saw. Man, she had this dude at the finale party that Hamid threw for them on Saturday. I let her know that I saw her, and what she was doing wasn't cool. You know, just a brother looking out for another brother."

"Look negro, squash that brother shit. You want payment. You earned it. Stop by and see Casino, he'll have something for you." Shamsadeen click off the phone. Lorraine could tell from the tone of the conversation and the look on Shamsadeen's face that something was wrong. Whenever Shamsadeen got really angry, the veins on his forehead looked like little muscles. His little muscles were flexing.

"What was that all about?" she asked.

"Gee was talking some shit about Fe being with some real light skin negro. If that mutha fucka is lying, I'll blow his ass away myself."

"Damn baby, why would Gee call with some shit like that just to get you mad? He knows that if he was fronting, you'd come after him. What's wrong, you can't take the fact that your sweet little chocolate girl is giving up the ass to Mr. Vanilla?" she teased.

"Shut the fuck up Lorraine."

"Negro, please. You know that I ain't afraid of nobody on this planet. So unless you a fucking Martian, you can drop all of that bass."

"Look Lorraine, now ain't the time for your shit. Ok?"

"If you want, I'll take care of Miss Goody Two Draws. It would be my pleasure; my fucking pleasure to do her for you."

No, I'll handle her and dude. You keep an eye on Raoul and Rockman for me. Yeah, I'll handle Nafesa's ass."

Shamsadeen knew that Lorraine would and could handle Raoul and Rockman. He also knew that she would take great delight in handling Nafesa. But this was a matter that required personal attention. He had to figure out a way to see if Nafesa was really swinging with someone else. He couldn't imagine her falling in love with someone else. He had given her everything she needed and wanted. He tried to show her how much he cared for her by showering her with gifts. Hell, how many sisters could say that their man gave them a 325i convertible? True, Lorraine drove a 430 C Mercedes, but Lorraine worked for her car. Nafesa never had to get involved with the business. Lorraine was an integral part of the business. She made deliveries, collected money, and made sure everything ran smoothly. Whenever he had to leave town, she ran the operation. She could even flex when she had to. And, with her brother LaShonda, they were a deadly force. The only thing he asked of Nafesa was to stay beautiful inside and outside. He even pulled some strings with Hamid, the owner of the OFFBEAT to get her in. True, once she was in, they loved her, but it was him who got her in. Now she wanted to insult him and, do it in public. She must be in love with this guy. Why else would she be seen with him in public? When did all of this happen? How did all of this happen? She always said that she could only sleep with a man if she was in love with him. A pain raced through his heart. The thought of Nafesa being in love with someone else made his stomach queasy. He wanted to hurt someone. He wanted to hurt Gee for telling him. But, he knew that he couldn't hurt the messenger. Besides, his business depended on street gossip. It kept him in tuned to what was happening. He could not and would not stand for it. Nafesa had to pay for this in a serious way. And the dude she was swinging with had to pay for this with his life. *That's it, I'll break her down by taking out dude.* He smiled at the thought.

"Lorraine, turn that up. That's my song." Lorraine stared absently out of the passenger side window. A slight smile trickled across her face.

CHAPTER FIFTEEN

Nafesa reminisced as she and William drove back to Philly. She laughed to herself at some of the stupid discussions that they had. She chuckled to herself at some of the private moments they had spent together. She smiled to herself at some of the intimate moments they shared together. It was one of the best weeks of her life. She was in love and she knew it. It felt good. The problem was, she wanted everyone to know it, but she knew how dangerous that would be. She had already overstepped her boundaries by being seen with him at the club. Gee had seen them, and he made it clear that she was overstepping her bounds. And, to make matters worst, Gee had a nose problem. If money was tight, he might barter her for a free high. She hoped that his money wasn't tight. She looked over at William who was gazing absently out of his window and rubbed the side of his face. She had prayed for him to love her as much as she loved him. She was fairly certain that he did, but only time would tell. But, she couldn't keep her mind from racing back to the downfall of their love; Shamsadeen. He would not just walk away from her. And she was more than certain that he would never allow her to walk away from him. She knew that she would have to deal with the situation if she and William were going to make it as a couple. She thought about never returning to Philly. She could always stay with her brother until she found herself an apartment. She had plenty of money saved up. But, staying in New York meant being away from Flavor, the band and William. She decided to let fate run its course. Allah would see her through any obstacles. Allah would not place her in a situation that she could not handle. Allah would not place more on her shoulders than she could bare. She would feel a lot more comfortable if William believed in Allah. She would continue to pray for him.

"Nafesa, I want you to meet my parents."

"Why?"

"Why not?"

"Don't try to get out of the question. Why do you want me to meet your parents especially if you know that they're not going to like me because of the color of my skin? That sounds so funny. I'm going to have a hard time with a black man's family because I'm black. That just doesn't make any sense to me."

"You're right, it doesn't make any sense, but I want you to meet them. Maybe after they meet you they'll change their minds. Or, maybe they won't. I want you to meet them because I love you. Besides, your brother didn't exactly make me feel at home. And you can't tell me that he didn't act that way because of the color of my complexion. He didn't know if I was a Muslim, Buddhist, Christian, or Atheist. As soon as he saw how light I was, he didn't want to have anything to do with me. So, before you go off on my family, think about your family's attitude."

"You're right. It's just that I don't feel like going through any unnecessary changes at this time. I have too many other things to deal with."

"Please Nafesa, all I'm asking is for you to meet my parents. It doesn't have to be today. Just do me a favor and think about it, ok?"

"Alright, I'll think about it. Just give me a little time. You know, something just occurred to me. I've never asked if you were seeing someone. I guess I just took it for granted that you weren't. So, are you seeing someone?"

"That's a long story."

"What do you mean by that?"

"I just mean that it's a long story."

"Well, we're in Passaic, New Jersey. We have another hour or so before we get to Philly. We have time."

William was not sure what to say or, how much to say. He wasn't sure if he should lay it all on the line or, should he play it safe and tell her half of the story. He decided to tell her the whole story.

"Believe it or not, I'm engaged." As soon as the words fell from his lips, William could feel the silence fill the car. He turned and looked at Nafesa. She was looking straight ahead. She deliberately would not look at him. "So now you don't have anything to say?" he asked.

"William what do you want me to say? I've just spent a week with you. You and I have made love and you never told me that you were engaged. How do you think that makes me feel? What was I, just a fling? Someone to get your shit off with?"

"Nafesa, that was something I was involved with before I met you. I never told you because I never had a chance to. If you know anything about me, you should know that I was going to tell you. You should also know that I would never play you like that. I love you. I thought I loved her. After meeting you, I realize I don't love her. Especially now that we've spent this week together, I know I'm not in love with her. What I know for sure is I'm in love with you. I'll take care of what I have to take care of."

"What's her name?"

"Marla."

"Is she pretty?"

"Yes."

"Is she light skin?"

"Yes, she's light skin."

"Have you set a date for the wedding?"

"Yep. Next year. June the twenty-ninth.

"Will you invite me?"

"Nafesa, stop this. Why are you interrogating me over this? Like I said, this is something that was put into motion way before I met you. Now that I've met you, I have no intention of marrying her."

"You won't feel bad dropping her?"

"I don't know how I'm going to feel. I'm quite sure I'm not going to feel good about it. I've dated her for over ten years. She was my high school sweetheart. Please, can we talk about something else?"

"Fine! Let's move on. I've stopped counting. What number is this on our unpleasant conversation list?"

"Who knows," he mumbled.

CHAPTER SIXTEEN

S hamsadeen picked up Lil' Larry and took him to the specialty shop to pick up Lil' Larry's new Lexus four by four. It looked good. Lil' Larry smiled as soon as he saw it. The windows were replaced with a special bullet proof tinted plastic, the sides were protected from armor piercing bullets and, he had a special plate placed along the bottom of the truck for protection against bombs. Lil' Larry always took things to the extreme. He and Shamsadeen decided that they would cruise around for the rest of the day in the four by four. Shamsadeen told Lil' Larry to follow him back to the hotel room so that he could get some clothes to take over to Lorraine's apartment. And, he wanted to leave the V12 in the hotel's indoor parking garage. Lil' Larry followed Shamsadeen back to the garage. He followed Shamsadeen into the garage and up the winding ramps. Shamsadeen parked his Benz in the upper level reserved for the hotel's long term patrons. Shamsadeen asked Lil' Larry to meet him down in the lobby level. Shamsadeen pulled into a spot marked L7. He turned off the car and reached into the glove compartment for his nine millimeter. He also carried a Glock, but his nine was his baby. He was superstitious about his pistols. He learned early to never rely on an untested weapon. His nine was with him when he first began to put his organization together. When Puerto Rican Hector made a move against him, his nine brought him through that battle. Puerto Rican Hector cried before the nine silenced his sobs. When he and Lil' Larry accidentally got caught in the crossfire of a gun battle, it was his nine that delivered. And, when Khalil decided he was going to make himself the number one man in the organization, it was the nine that squashed Khalil's future ambitions. In fact, the only time he ever relied on his Glock, he suffered three wounds, one to his left shoulder and two to the left leg. So, the Glock was relegated to back-up status. Shamsadeen put the nine in his waist band and began to walk towards the entrance of the hotel.

Lil' Larry was going down the ramp of the garage when he thought he saw Raoul and Rockman speeding up the ramp in a pearl white Buick LeSabre. He wasn't positive if it was them because he didn't recognize the car. But, his sixth sense told him that it was them and, that they were up to something. He stopped at the next level, made a u- turn and started back up the ramp. He saw Rockman getting out of the car in a crouched position. He saw the silhouette of a person that he knew was Shamsadeen. Raoul began to cruise real slowly towards Shamsadeen. Rockman began to cut through the parked cars as if he was trying to angle off on Shamsadeen. Lil' Larry reached over and opened the glove compartment and took out his forty-five automatic. He started to cruise as if he was looking for a parking spot. Rockman noticed the Lexus and looked in its direction. It was too far away for him to make out who the driver was. Raoul looked in his rear view mirror and saw the truck cruising around. He didn't recognize the Lexus. When Lil' Larry got twenty feet from he car, he sped up. Shamsadeen turned around when he heard the tires screeching. Lil' Larry rammed into the back rear of Raoul's car with full force. Raoul's head hit the windshield causing it to shatter. Rockman let off a volley of shots at the truck. The bullets entered the outer layer of the Lexus, but were stopped by the protective plate. Shamsadeen saw what was happening and began to fire at Rockman. Rockman returned the fire. Lil' Larry jumped out of the Lexus and ran to the front of Raoul's car. Raoul lay motionless against the steering wheel. Lil' Larry pressed the barrel of his forty-five against the left side of Raoul's temple and pulled the trigger. The interior of the car turned blood red with small fragments of head parts everywhere. Rockman fired a shot at Lil' Larry. Shamsadeen screamed for Lil' Larry to move around to the rear of Rockman and cut him off. Rockman fired two more shot at Lil' Larry. Shamsadeen walked straight towards Rockman, firing rapid shots. Lil' Larry did the same from the rear of Rockman. Rockman alternated shots between the two of them. Shamsadeen's nine clicked empty. He reached for his Glock and felt a heavy burning sensation fill his left forearm. He knew he was shot.

"Mutha fucka," he screamed. "Blow that punk ass faggot away." Rockman's gun clicked empty. He started to run. Lil' Larry cut him off. Rockman tried to make a quick dash towards Shamsadeen. Shamsadeen opened up with his Glock. He saw Rockman drop. He ran over to see if Rockman was still moving. He wasn't. The only sign of life that he showed was by way of heavy staccato breaths. He eyes were rolling in his head. He looked up at Shamsadeen with dying pity in his eyes.

"Who else is down with this? Tell me, who's backing you?" demanded Shamsadeen.

"Fuck you! If you only knew. Watch your back pussy."

"No, fuck you. And you betta watch your back in hell." Shamsadeen emptied his Glock into Rockman. His body jumped with each bullet. Lil' Larry gave him a send off with a final shot to the head. They could hear the sound of sirens coming up the ramp. They ran back to the Lexus and drove out of the garage. Lil' Larry was careful not to speed. Police car after police car came up the ramp as they drove down.

"Get me to the Medic. He'll take care of this." Blood was pulsing out of Shamsadeen's arm. Lil' Larry slowly picked up speed. He drove down to the North-Side Public Housing Development. He had to hurry and find the Medic.

The Medic was a heroin addict who served as a medic in Vietnam. He went to Nam wanting to be a doctor, he came home from Nam needing a fix of heroin. He was as good as any doctor for removing a bullet. Going to the hospital for a gun shot wound required the hospital to contact the police. Shamsadeen could not afford that. So, for an ounce of heroin and five hundred dollars, the Medic would repair him. Lil' Larry knew he had to keep Shamsadeen conscious.

"Damn Shamsadeen, look at my new truck. It's all messed up. The front is smashed, the side is full of bullet holes, and blood all over my interior. Next time we have to roll in your car," joked Lil' Larry.

"Shamsadeen tried to laugh. "Yeah, I guess I kinda turned your new truck into a used truck. Check it out, who do you think put them up to something like that? I don't think they were smart enough to plan a move like that by themselves."

"Shamsadeen, this wasn't no real thought out shit. Dig it, they're dead and we're still alive. Those fools were just trying to make a move. No one who's down with us would use those clowns to make a move against us. Didn't Lorraine tell you that she thought they were up to something?"

"I hope you're right. I don't feel like this shit anymore."

"Hey black, it's part of the trade."

"Now I have two things to worry about. My business and Nafesa."

"What's up with Nafesa?"

"Gee told me he saw her with a light skin dude. He said they were all hugged up and shit."

"That's fucked up. You have to lay low for a while. I'll find out what's up with that. Gee's probably lying."

"I don't think so. He's got nothing to gain from it. My arm is starting to feel numb. Speed it up."

Lil' Larry was careful not to drive too fast or too erratic. He made a final turn on to North Eighth Street. There were only two standing buildings on the entire block. The rest of the area looked like someone had dropped a bomb on it. There was nothing but rubble from burned out building after burned out building. The two standing buildings appeared to be one day from collapsing. There was trash and garbage piled everywhere.

"We're here. I see the Medic. He's sitting on the steps. Man, you must really trust that negro. He doesn't look like he could take a potato out of a sack."

"Don't worry about how he looks. He'll hook me up."

"While you're with him, I'm going to ditch this truck. I can't believe that I haven't had this thing for a whole day. I'm going to take it to those Irish boys so they can chop it up."

"Sorry about that. Just go and buy a new one tomorrow. I really can't feel my arm." Shamsadeen's voice was getting low and his speech was starting to slur. Lil' Larry pulled up to the steps and called for the Medic to come over. The Medic was a short stocky man who wore his hair in a nineteen-seventy afro. His beard was uneven and unruly. His army shirt was cut off at the sleeves. His plaid Bermuda shorts were dirty and faded. He had on high top Converse sneakers with black dress socks. A half smoked cigarette rested in his ear

"Medic, I need your help. Hurry up man," ordered Lil' Larry.

"Peace man. What you need?"

"Damn negro, I need you to perform a wedding. You know what I need so hurry up."

Medic hurried over to the truck and looked inside of it. He saw Shamsadeen laid out across the back seat.

"Holy shimoly, bring him in. We gotta hurry. We ain't gonna have time to get him to the room. I gotta take care of him right here or it might be too late. I gotta stop him from going into shock." Lil' Larry and the Medic helped Shamsadeen out of the Lexus, he was too weak to make it on his own. He was loosing consciousness. Lil' Larry did not want to take Shamsadeen into a shooting gallery, but he knew that it was here or nowhere for Shamsadeen. They struggled their way through the narrow opening of the building. The inside of the shell reeked of human squalor. It was dim inside. The Medic pulled a board from the window so that sun light could filter into the room. There were five or six mattresses strewn across the floor. A kerosene heater sat in the middle of the floor. Lil' Larry assumed that it served multiple functions; heat in the winter, a stove for heating up canned food and heroin, and light for visibility at night.

"Put him down right there."

"That mattress looks too damn nasty," complained Lil' Larry.

"It's the best we got in this hospital. Now you can take him to Downtown General where they have nice white sheets for him to lay on. And, where they have nice white policemen for him too."

Lil' Larry reluctantly laid Shamsadeen down on the mattress.

"Look Medic, I'm leaving him here with you. I'll be back in a few hours for him. When I get back, he better be alright. If he ain't, you'll be laid out right next to him. Do you understand me?"

"Look Lil' Larry, you can stop with the threats. I done been to hell and back. I did two tours in Vietnam. I done seen bodies piled ten feet high. I was shot four times and lived through all of 'em. So all that stuff you talking, don't scare me a bit. If he makes it, he makes it. If he don't, he don't. The best I can do is to try and save his ass. So why don't you get out and let me do what I have to do. When you come back, have my ounce and my five hundred dollars."

Lil' Larry knew that the Medic meant every word he said. Lil' Larry felt helpless. He left wondering who was really behind Raoul and Rockman's move. Although he told Shamsadeen that he thought they were acting alone, he knew that they had been backed by someone. Someone with a lot of ambition.

CHAPTER SEVENTEEN

It was eleven o'clock in the morning and it was already ninety-four degrees. They had left New York with the top of the convertible down. By the time they were half way to Philly, they had to raise the top to keep the sun from burning the heads. Nafesa pulled into the driveway that led to the front of the Jennings' residence. The house and surrounding property looked like where William would live. The West Mount Airy section of Philadelphia was where the social and political elites lived. The driveway was clean cut and well manicured. A woman who Nafesa guessed was William's mother, was on her knees working on her garden.

"Just pull up behind my mom's old 240D. That's my mom working in her garden."

Nafesa pulled up behind a nineteen-seventy 240D Mercedes Benz that was parked in the driveway and turned off her car. She stared at Mrs. Jennings who never took her eyes off of her tomato plants. William rubbed Nafesa's leg and exited the car. Nafesa pulled the trunk release lever so that he could get his luggage. William lifted his suit case from the trunk and sat it down on the pavement. Then, he walked around to Nafesa's side of the car. They stared at each other for a moment and exchanged quick smiles. William leaned into the car and gave her a soft kiss on her left cheek. She accepted it. Neither of them noticed that Mrs. Jennings had stopped her gardening and had her sights directly on them. When she saw her son kiss this unknown woman, she shook her head in disgust and walked towards her front door. William made Nafesa promised that she would call him as soon as she got to the hotel.

The last time Nafesa spoke to her brother, he gave her a message that Shamsadeen had called and said that he had found a new apartment for them, but it wouldn't be ready for two weeks. She dreaded going back to the hotel. It reminded her of her college days and living in the dormitory with her roommate, Melissa. She and Melissa hated each other from day one. Melissa was a light skin girl with emerald eyes, from Mississippi. Melissa was certain that the world revolved around her. Nafesa's world and her world collided with their first hello. And, the collision didn't stop until Nafesa moved into her own apartment. Her thoughts returned to her present situation. She definitely did not want to have to stay at the hotel for two more weeks. All she needed was a few days to get her head together. Once she had time to be alone and think, she was certain that she would come up with a solution to her problem. The drive back to the hotel was filled with memories of the week before; memories of her week with William. The expression on her face changed from melancholy to happiness. She pulled into the parking garage without ever noticing any of the surroundings. Then, flashing red lights snapped her out of her driver's trance. There were police cars everywhere. Out of the corner of her eye she saw Sergeant Shelmire. He signaled for the cop who was directing traffic to pull her over. She pulled over to the side of the street and watched him and his agents run towards her car. She knew this whole thing had Shamsadeen written all over it. Why else would the D.E.A. be here? And, why else were they pulling her over?

"Hello, Ms. Islam."

"Hello, Sergeant."

"I guess you heard there was a big shoot out in the parking lot an hour or so ago. We got two bodies up there."

Nafesa could feel her heart drop. She tried to keep her composure, but knew her nervousness showed.

"Don't worry, your sweetie pie isn't one of them. We're pretty sure he had something to do with this. Do you know where we can find him?"

"I haven't seen for over a week. I thought you guys would have been keeping an eye on him for me."

"Would you like to come down to headquarters to answer a few questions? I promise you it'll only take a few hours at the most."

"Sorry, I have plans for the rest of my day. So, unless I'm under arrest, I don't have plans on going anywhere with you. Like I told you, I've been in New York for the past week. I was with a very good friend of mine, so whatever happened here today, I wouldn't have any knowledge of it. And, I don't know where my sweetie pie is. Now, if you don't mind, I would like to go to my room and relax."

"It's just a matter of time before he goes down. And, you know what I think?"

"Not that I care what you think, but I'm sure you're going to tell me anyway."

"I think you're pretty little ass is going down with him. And I'm going to take great joy in squeezing those handcuffs around your tiny little wrists."

"Well Sergeant, if you were paid to think you'd be bankrupt."

"Time will tell. You take care Ms. Islam."

Nafesa raised her window and drove off. Her knees were shaking. She had to go to the bathroom. The parking lot was sealed off. She had to park on the street. She reached over to get her hand purse out of the glove compartment. She saw William's cell phone mixed between the paperwork that she kept stored in her glove compartment. *"He must have put it in there on our way up to New York. I'll have to call him as soon as I get my head together."* She was too afraid to go to her room, but she didn't have any other place to go. When she got there, four policemen were stationed outside of her door. The hotel manager looked at her with disdain. She felt like a criminal. She couldn't tell if the police had searched her room. Nothing looked at though it had been touched, but she was quite sure that they had looked around. This was becoming all too familiar. She decided to take what little belongings she needed and leave Shamsadeen and his madness forever. But, she knew that she still had to worry about William. She couldn't walk away from the newness that she had found in him. She needed his love too much to leave him. Then, a strange feeling of relief overcame her. She felt a certain sense of empowerment; a sense of freedom; a sense of direction. The final straw had been drawn. *"Oh Allah, please guide me and protect me,"* she prayed.

William was not in the house five minutes before he heard a knock at his door.

"Who is it?" he asked.

"It's me."

"Hold on for a second Lenora. Let me put on some pants." William reached over and grabbed a pair of Yale sweat pants that were lying on the bed. "Alright, you can come in now."

Lenora walked into the room with a serious look on her face. "How was New York?" she asked.

"It was great. I had a real nice time."

"Mark called to make sure that dinner was still on for next week. He said he didn't stay at the apartment with you last week. I guess he thought that everyone knew about Nafesa staying up there with you. And, mom said that she just saw the two of you in the car together."

"So, what's your point? Look, you get paid to decipher, I don't. If you have something you want to say to me or tell me, please do it and stop beating around the bush."

"There is a lot that I want to say to you. First, I think you're making a big mistake about this Nafesa. You're thinking with your penis and not with your brain. Secondly, you're going to destroy Marla all because you got the hots for a night club singer. For God's sake, have her on the side, but don't blow your wedding over her. I had to lie to Marla about your car being parked in the driveway, when you were supposed to have driven to New York. I told her that you took the train because your car was acting up. I didn't lie for you, I lied for her. And lastly, Uncle Jesse stopped by and was talking to dad. He told dad that you were asking about some big time drug dealer named Shamsadeen. He mentioned the name Nafesa as being a part of this drug dealer's organization. I definitely heard him and I'm quite sure mom heard him. Dad didn't put one and one together. Mom is destroyed by all of this. And to tell you the truth, I was also hurt hearing that. If Uncle Jesse knew that you were running around with a drug dealer's whore I seriously doubt if he would be able to give you a job at the D.A.'s office. Just think of the headlines, "**D.A.'s Nephew Linked To Drug Dealer's Mistress**". I know you think that I'm against her because she's just a dark skin jazz singer, but it's more to it than that. She smells of trouble. The type of trouble that it takes years to recover from. I don't think that you have that to give right now. You're a young man with a lot going for yourself. Hell, you're my big brother. I love you. I don't want to see you make a mistake of that magnitude."

"You're wrong. She's not a part of a drug organization. She was dating a guy who turned out to be a drug dealer. Now, she's with me, and he's just a part of her past. Everybody thinks they know what's best for me. I'm a grown man. I can think for myself. And I definitely don't need advice from my little sister about how to run my personal life."

"Run or ruin your personal life?" William, you can raise your voice at me all you want. You know what I'm saying is the truth. If you're not going to think about yourself, then the least you can do is think about the rest of the family. We do care about our name. Besides, although you can't see it, you're playing with fire. Have you ever thought about how dangerous it could be to date a drug dealer's girlfriend? I'm quite sure this Shamsadeen fellow didn't get his reputation by helping little old ladies cross the street. Uncle Jesse said he's the biggest drug dealer in the city. He said this guy is ruthless. So do you really think that he's going to sit back and let you take his girl? You better start to open your eyes. You could be putting us all in danger."

"I think you've been watching too many gangster movies. These guys can't afford to have the police and other authorities tracking them down for messing with law abiding people like us. They only go after each other. Besides, I'm not afraid to stand up to him. He's where he is today because no one has ever stood up to him."

"Now I think you've been watching too many gangster movies. He's where he is today because he's probably murdered everyone who stood up to him. He killed his way to the top. No one gave him the key to the throne. William, promise me that you won't do anything stupid. Or, should I ask you to stop all of this stupidity?"

"You can say or ask anything you want, but I'll handle this my own way. Now I'm tired, I want to take a nap."

Lenora looked at him and shook her head. She knew he was bitten, and there was nothing that she or anyone else could say to him. He had to play this out on his own. Her concern was William's inability to see how dangerous this situation actually was. He was on the path to getting himself or someone else hurt, or even worst, killed.

William felt a wet warmness move across his neck. It stopped and rested on his left ear lope. He tried to shake it off. It was pleasurable.

"Nafesa, you're trying to wear me out," he mumbled. The next thing he felt was a hard sting race across his face. He jumped up. It was Marla.

"Marla, why did you slap me?"

"Who is Nafesa?" she screamed.

William was silent. He tried to figure out how Marla knew about Nafesa. "What are you talking about?" he stalled.

"I'm talking about you saying Nafesa's name when I'm kissing you on your ear."

William knew that he was busted. I guess I must have been dreaming. You know how dreams are. You can't control what you dream about."

"William, like I told you before, you are starting to act out of character. There is something going on. Don't tell me that I'm wrong. You weren't dreaming. That's the name of that black jazz singer you were so interested in. Is that where you've been for the past week? Tell me the truth, you were with her weren't you? I hate you William, I hate you!"

"Marla, stop talking like that. Like I told you, I must have been dreaming. You're making nothing into something major. Stop it. I stayed at Mark's for the whole week. If you don't believe me ask him for yourself. He'll tell you that I was at his apartment."

"I don't know William, something is wrong and it hurts. I love you. I want to spend the rest of my life with you. Please don't do this to me. Don't walk out of my life like this. I can feel you slipping away. I know there is someone else. The way you make love to me tells me there's someone else. Tell me you don't love her. Tell me that."

William couldn't believe that he was going through this with Marla. He had just finished with Lenora. It was as if Lenora had cursed him. He didn't want to hurt Marla. She did not deserve to be hurt like this.

"Marla, there isn't anyone else. I love you. We are going to get married next June. We are going to spend the rest of our lives together. Now come here and let me show you how much I love you and only you." He reached for her and brought her into him. She rested her head on his shoulder. He could feel the wetness of her tears. He turned her face towards his and began to kiss her tears. There was a steady flow of tears for him to kiss. The phone rang. He heard Lenora answer it. Then, he heard her walking towards his room. He hoped that she would spare Marla any unnecessary pain.

"William, it's for you. I tried to take a message, but he said it was an emergency."

"Tell them I just walked out the door and you couldn't catch me." He could feel Marla hold him tighter. He let his fingers run through her hair. He put his head on top of hers and closed his eyes. He wanted to cry. He was hurting someone whose only wrong was loving him. Marla deserved better.

CHAPTER EIGHTEEN

Shamsadeen woke up wanting to vomit. His stomach felt like it was being turned inside out. He looked around to get his bearings together. It all started to come back to him. He had been shot in the arm. He felt a heavy throbbing in his left arm. He looked down at it. It was wrapped in thick white gauze. The Medic had done his job well. Lorraine was sitting in a chair in front of the TV playing Assassin on the Play Station.

"Lorraine. Lorraine," he called.

She turned around and gave him a pearly white smile. "Hey baby, you looking a lot better. How you feeling? You looked like shit when Lil' Larry brought you here."

"I feel fucked up. My stomach feels worst than my arm. How long have I been here?"

"It's Tuesday. You've been here since Sunday. You're lucky you're alive. All that blood you lost, you should be dead."

"It ain't got anything to do with luck. The people who should be dead are dead. You were right about those two faggots. They tried to take me out. Lil' Larry spotted them before they knew what was happening. I gotta clean house now. I gotta clean up my house and my business. I need someone to get me some pain killers. Medic probably used heroin to knock me out. That's what's wrong with my stomach. I need some real strong shit that won't put me to sleep. I gotta get back on my feet. There's a lot of things that I have to take care of. Where's Lil' Larry? Call him and tell him that I need him."

"He just left. He said he'd be back in an hour. I doubled up on the Medic. He did such a good job, I felt that he deserved more. The cops have been kicking ass about that hotel shit. It's been all over the news. You know they don't like it when bodies start to turn up in their back yard. Negroes can kill each other all they want as long as they keep it in the hood. You know they're looking for you. On TV, they said they're looking for you for questioning. I think you should get the fuck out of here for a while. Maybe go out west and get healed up. They can't prove that you had anything to do with that shit. They stopped by my other spot to ask me some questions. I told them hear no evil; speak no evil; see no evil."

Shamsadeen mustered out a slight laugh. Lorraine was too smooth. This apartment was her little hide away. No one knew about this place but him, Lil' Larry and her. They kept it that way. If the place was ever hit, they knew the leak had to have come from one of the three of them. Not even Nafesa knew about this place. It was not necessary for her to know about it.

"You're probably right about getting out of here for a while. I gotta let things cool off around here for a minute. And, I need to get my body back in order. I'll take Lil' Larry with me. You and your crazy ass brother, LaShonda can hold down the fort. But I have to take care of some stuff before I leave. I gotta find out who else was in on this. I can't believe that they made a move against me on their own. Somebody had to hype them up. And, that shit with Nafesa has to be taken care of."

"Look, let me handle all of that shit. You get out of here for a while. I especially want to handle little Miss Black Beauty. Lil' Larry said she's been over Jasmin house since Sunday. He said the word is that the light-bright dude she's been banging is a lawyer from uptown. Dude is supposed to be connected. Word is they went to New York together for a week. I guess Mr. Light-Bright has been banging out Little Miss Darkie's walls."

"Look, we've been through this conversation before. I'll handle Nafesa myself. Call Lil' Larry, I need to talk to him right away. I gotta get this whole mess straightened out. I want you to think about who might have been down with those two fuck-ups." Lorraine smiled. "I've been thinking about that already. I think I know. I can't be one hundred percent certain, but I'm about seventy-five percent sure."

"Hell, that's good enough for me. If we're wrong, then fuck it. Better them than us. Who do you think it is?" he asked.

"I don't think it was any of our people. I think it was Mohammed."

"Mohammed? Why would he want to start a war with us? He's rolling on his own. He already owns Camden."

"I paid some people to keep their ears open. The word is Rockman and Raoul went to Atlantic City with Mohammed the day before they let loose on you. Think about it, if you could have Philly or Camden, which one would you want? Now think about this, if you could have Philly and Camden, would you turn it down? See, Mohammed could move into Philly and give Camden to Rockman and Raoul to run."

Shamsadeen was shaking his head in agreement. "You're right. Mohammed has always been nipping at my heels. I never paid much attention to him 'cause he was all talk and no action. I could have taken over Camden anytime I wanted to. But, Camden is a headache waiting to happen. Mohammed can barely keep those country fools from killing each other. I do as I was taught, stay in your own hood. So, that corn eating sissy tried to take me out. Cool. You know what I'm gonna do? I'm gonna blow his fucking head off. He's gonna have to have a closed coffin funeral. That way, everybody who sees him will know what'll happen to them if they fuck with Shamsadeen Baku. First though, I want a couple of his people killed just to let him know that I'm coming after his ass."

Lorraine smiled with excitement. She loved the action. "I'll call LaShonda and tell him to take care of that."

"Cool. Now call Lil' Larry. I want to know everything about Nafesa and dude." Lorraine picked up the phone and called Lil' Larry on his cell phone. He picked it up on the second ring.

"Hey Lil' Larry, wa'zup? . . . Shamsadeen is awake . . . Yeah . . . Hold on. Lorraine passed the phone to Shamsadeen. He raised up on the bed and tried to position himself so that he could hold the phone with as little pain as possible.

""Thanks for looking out black . . . I'll be feeling better once I get some real pain killers . . . That's what I told Lorraine. That heroin ain't no joke . . . Yeah, I have to start exercising . . . Don't worry about that . . . How long is it gonna take for you to get back here? . . . Lorraine told me that they're everywhere trying to get information . . . Look, hurry up back here so that we can take care of business . . . Cool . . . Yeah, I need you to bring me a few bottles of Pedialyte . . .

Yeah, that stuff they give to babies when their system is all messed up . . . Cool. See ya." He handed the phone back to Lorraine. "He should be here in an half an hour. You know what? I'm horny as all hell. Come 'ere."

"Negro, you must be crazy. You ain't giving me no bum shot. When you hit these walls, you gotta come correct. I ain't accepting nothing half ass from you."

"Come 'ere and knock a brother off. I can't take care of you right now. I'm too weak. Your ruby red lips look real sexy."

"Oh, so you want me to go down on you? What's in it for me?"

"I'll give you a Shamsadeen IOU. Redeemable anytime, anywhere."

"Alright, I don't want to hear any shit when I cash it in."

"Girl, my IOU is better than gold." Lorraine laughed. She looked at him and gave him a sensuous smile. She knew Nafesa was on borrowed time. She was here to stay. Shamsadeen had tried to leave, but he always came back. She walked over and sat on the side of the bed. She saw him whence as she lowered her weight onto the bed. She gently rubbed his head to sooth him. She felt his tenseness began to relax. She worked her hands down to his groin. She began to fondle him with both hands. His tenseness was gone, or at least, it had shifted. She got straight to the point; there was no time for foreplay. She heard him moan. Before she was done, he would be hollering.

Lorraine was rinsing out her mouth when the doorbell rang. She peered through the peep hole. As she expected, it was Lil' Larry. She opened the door. Shamsadeen had fallen back to sleep.

"Hey, what happened? Did the medicine knock him out again?"

"Yeah, you could say that. The medicine knocked him out again," laughed Lorraine.

Lil' Larry looked at her and joined in on the laughter. He knew exactly what she meant.

"Well, wake him up. I don't have time to sit around and watch his ass sleep for another day. I have things to do; places to go; people to see; and a world to discover."

Lorraine walked into the bedroom and carefully shook Shamsadeen. "Baby, Lil' Larry is here. Wake up. Shamsadeen, Lil' Larry is here."

Shamsadeen began to come around. When his eyes focused on Lil' Larry, he strained to maneuver himself into a comfortable position. He tried to smile, but the pain vanquished his attempt.

"Brother love. Thanks."

"Brother love. You look a little better. Make sure I get some of that medicine Lorraine gave you if I ever get shot."

Shamsadeen tried to laugh, but the pain was in full force. "Look man, we gotta take care of some business real quick. Lorraine solved our mystery for us. It was Mohammed who had me set up. I told her what I want to happen to him. Rap with her and make it happen. She said you got some word on Nafesa and her sidekick. Let me hear it."

"Man, you sure you want to go through this right now?"

"Lil' Larry, talk to me."

"Alright. She's running around with this dude who could pass for white. He looks like an Italian. His name is William Jennings. Remember the judge who gave Frankie fifteen to thirty on that bullshit drug case? Judge Jennings; that's dude's father. Check this out; dude is real linked. His uncle is the fucking D.A.! Dude lives in West Mount Airy. He's surrounded too strong for us right now. He's bad news for us to mess with. That's too much heat. If we even thought about hitting dude, they would rain down on our asses like white on rice. I know how you are Shamsadeen, but I'm telling you, we can't afford to mess with white boy. But check this out. We can send him a second hand message. He has a sister who is fucking around with Sleepy. You remember Sleepy from high school don't you? Dark skin boy with real droopy eyes. Well anyway, he's a mailman now and he lives in West Philly."

"Yeah, I remember him. He use to play ball all the time. Quiet guy. Never hung out much. Yeah, I remember him. It's a small world isn't it?"

"That it is. The word is, Sleepy and dude's sister hook up about three times a week over at his spot in West Philly. They say she blows into the hood like she's some kind of a goddess and shit. Mother fuckers be drooling all over her. She's been rolling with Sleepy for years. Of course, Sleepy is just a shot on the side, she's married to a white man. They say the bitch is a bad piece."

"That's some good info. You know what I'm gonna do? I'm gonna send Mr. Jennings a little message about stepping into places where he don't belong. Get me two crazies from West Philly. I want them to do me a favor."

CHAPTER NINETEEN

Lurch and Jay were working the four to midnight shift on Mohammed's busiest corner in Camden. Jay was talking to a young girl who was trying to look ten years older than she actually was. Her weave fell down to her shoulders, her daisy dukes stopped slightly above the base of her ass, her wife beater barely covered her thirty-six-C's, and her nails were too long for her to be employed. Lurch was keeping an eye on the traffic. A fire engine red Hyundai pulled up to the corner. Lurch walked over to the car. A big- boned woman with platinum blonde hair was driving.

"Z'up baby? What you need, ready rock or powder?" asked Lurch.

"Oh no, I don't do no crack. Give me some powder."

"Whatever. How many you want? All I got is dimes."

"Give me two dimes," she said as she passed him a twenty-dollar bill through her window. Lurch took the twenty-dollar bill and called for Jay to come over. Jay walked over to the car and reached into his pocket and retrieved a small brown paper bag.

"How many she get?" asked Jay.

"Two," answered Lurch.

As Jay reached into the bag to get the two dime bags of cocaine, he saw the nose of a Mac Ten pointed at him. "Oh shit," he hollered, as he tried to run away. The big-boned woman with platinum blonde hair, sprayed him down. Lurch turned around and saw Jay falling to the ground. Shock and fright filled his face. He reached for his gun. He was too late. Another volley of bullets spewed out of the Mac Ten cutting him down. The young girl, trying to look older stood frozen against the wall. Then she fell to her knees and started to beg.

"Please, I don't sell for them. I was just talking to him to see if I could get a couple of dollars. Please. I won't say anything. Oh God, please don't kill me?" she begged, with tears storming down her face.

"Sorry sweetie, you saw too much. You'll be talking like you Oprah when they get through with your fat ass." A small squirt of bullets flashed from the gun. The girl's body slumped against the wall. "Nothing worst than a fat ass, begging bitch," laughed LaShonda as she slowly drove away.

Mohammed and Lela came out of the Step'n Out night club. Mohammed looked around to make sure nothing unusual was going on. He walked over to the valet and gave him the bright yellow parking ticket. The young faced kid, dressed in black looked at the number and ran around to the back of the club. Mohammed held Lela's hand. Her blonde hair swayed with the gentle summer breeze. She saw a couple of black women starring at her. She smiled at them. She was use to it. Black women always sneered at her when she was with Mohammed. The valet pulled up in front of them in a white Jaguar XJ. Mohammed walked around to the driver's side of the car. Lela waited for the valet to come around and open the door for her. Mohammed tipped the valet five dollars and drove off. As he was driving away, he remembered that the valet who brought him his car was not the same person who he had given his bright yellow parking ticket to. He brushed it off. Lela put in a CD of the Whispers.

"Baby, why do sisters always sweat me when I'm with you? They act like they own every black man just because they black. I don't get upset when I see a white man with a sister. To each his own is what I always say."

"You know how black women are, they don't know how to treat a man, then they get mad when you find a white woman who does. They all fucked up in the head. You always got to do battle with them. I ain't got time to be fighting with my woman about who supposed to be wearing the pants in the house. You know what I mean? If I want to fight, I go out and take another player's corner. That's the type of shit that you fight over. All the rest of this stuff is for the birds."

"You are so right about that. I know you're the man and I'm not trying to be a man. You treat me like a woman and I treat you like a

man. In fact, let me take care of my little man while you're driving."
Lela reached over and began to tug on his zipper.

"That's what I'm talking about. Sisters don't want to do right,
but they always want you to be there for them at the drop of a dime."
Lela had him in her mouth and was issuing full and heavy strokes.
Mohammed's stomach was tightening. They stopped for a street light.
A young white girl in a fire engine red Mustang 5.0, pulled up next
to him. She smiled at Mohammed. Mohammed nodded at her. He
was too consumed to engage her at that moment. She raced her engine.
Lela's head was racing too fast for him to get caught up in a street
race. Mohammed waved her off. She was mouthing something at
him. He couldn't make out what she was saying. She motioned for
him to roll down his window. His window slowly slid down. She let
down her passenger side window.

"What's up?" he asked.

"Shamsadeen told me to tell you hello." Mohammed's face was
caught between fear and puzzlement. He knew that he had left himself
exposed, but he couldn't figure why Shamsadeen was coming after
him. He had always respected Shamsadeen's power and was grateful
that Shamsadeen had never tried to take over Camden. Lela's head
rose up to see what was going on. A big-boned woman with platinum
blonde hair, rose up from the passenger's seat in the 5.0 with a sawed
off, single barrel shotgun in her hand. There was a loud boom. Where
just a moment ago there was a head with a face caught between fear
and puzzlement, there was now only a torso wriggling out of control.
The Jaguar rolled to the side of the curb and stopped. Lela was
screaming hysterically. She was cover with blood, brains, and other
human body parts. Her door opened. LaShonda stood beside her
with the shotgun in his hands.

"Shut the fuck up bitch before I blow your fucking ass away."
Lela continued to scream.

"I'm warning you bitch, shut the fuck up."

Lela's screams got louder. LaShonda grabbed Lela by the hair
and flipped her over. He pulled up her dress and pulled down her
panties. Lela was still screaming and trembling. She felt cold steel
enter her ass. That was the last thing she felt.

"I told you I was going to blow your ass away." LaShonda walked
over to the Mustang. He and his boyfriend slowly drove off.

CHAPTER TWENTY

Vanessa looked at Sleepy as he slept. Then, she looked up at the clock on the wall. She remembered when she gave him that clock. She was tired of asking him "what time is it?" and watching him fumble around for his watch. It was probably the most expensive piece of furniture that he had in his apartment. The big hand was on the four and the little hand was on the seven. The sun was just past sunset. It was time for her to leave. She hated leaving him. Outside of Adam and Jason, he was the only thing that gave her life meaning. Sleepy had called in sick so that they could spend the entire day with each other. They had a good day together that culminated in passionate love making. She watched as his chest heaved back and forth, pushing out a full snore. She loved him, even the way that he snored. She got out of bed and stood in front of the mirror to brush her hair. *"When is he ever going to stop putting Royal Crown grease in his hair? I know, I'll buy him some hair oil tomorrow when Marla and I go shopping,"* She had the routine down. She could shower, dress and make it to her family's house to pick up the kids before eight-thirty. She walked to the bathroom and started the shower. She thought she heard a thump at the front door. She paid it no attention. Sleepy's apartment complex was full of children who were always running up and down the hallway. She was about to step into the tub when she heard the front door crash open. She ran to the door of the bathroom to see what was going on. She couldn't see anything, but she could hear Sleepy arguing with someone. Then, she heard footsteps coming towards her. She shut the bathroom door, grabbed a towel to wrap around herself and hid behind the shower curtain. There was no place else to go. She heard the door open and saw an outstretched had with a shiny silver gun in it. The shower curtain was suddenly ripped from the pole and she was face to face with a filthy looking man with most of his front teeth missing. He was smiling at her.

"All lookey, lookey. If it ain't Miss High and Mighty. Now I want you to come out of dis batfroom. C'mon now. Don't make me kill your pretty lil' ass. Jis do like I tells you to do."

"What do you want? I have a little bit of money in my purse. You can have it and, you can take my credit cards. I won't tell the police," she begged with a slight edge of sternness.

"Naw pretty girl, I want more than your money and yo credit cards. Don't git me wrong, I'm gonna take dem too. But first, we gonna have a lil' fun. Me and you; then you and Jimmie; then me and you; then you and Jimmy, until we all gits tired." Vanessa started to cry. "Please don't hurt me like that. I have two sons. I'll give you anything you want, but please don't hurt me like that."

"You gimme anythang I want?"

"Yes, I'll give you anything you want."

"Promise?"

"Yes, I promise. Anything."

"Good. I want some pussy. Now you promised you'd gimme anythang I wanted. So take dat fuck'n towel off bitch. Who knows, maybe afta tonight, you'll have three sons," he laughed.

"Sleepy! Sleepy! Sleepy!" she screamed.

"Bitch shut the fuck up 'n take yo red ass out dar. And didn't you hear me tell you to take dat towel off your ass?" He raised the gun to the side of Vanessa's head. Vanessa was trembling. She untied the knot of the towel. It fell to the floor. She watched as his toothless smile re-emerged on his face. He stuck out his hand and fondled her pubic hairs.

"I ain't never fucked a bitch who had soft pussy hairs." He forced her into the bedroom where another man was holding a gun on Sleepy.

"Goddamn, she fine," shouted Jimmy. "How you git a piece of pussy like dat man? Dat's dat uptown pussy. What in da fuck she doing down here wit a broke ass muffa fucka like you?"

"I guess da bitch is slumming," joked the man with the toothless smile. They both started to laugh. Sleepy knew what was going to happen next. What he wasn't sure of was if they were going to allow him and Vanessa to live after they were finished with her. His bet was that they weren't.

"Hey, why don't y'all just take what you want and leave her alone. It don't make any sense to mess with her like that," pleaded Sleepy.

"Shut da fuck up. We tell y'all what to do. And we is gonna take what we want. We wants her. Now go lay da fuck down bitch and open up doe's legs. You betta not make me fight yo ass e'fer," ordered the man with the silver hand gun.

Vanessa froze with fright. She felt a heavy blow smash against her left temple. She fell to the bed. She began to scream hysterically. Blood was trickling down her face.

"Bitch, if you don't shut up all dat noise I'm gonna blow Sleepy's balls off. Now do like Memphis told you to do and open up dem dar legs of yourn," demanded Jimmy as he pointed the gun at Sleepy's testicles.

Vanessa closed her eyes and slowly opened her legs. She could feel Memphis forcing her legs apart. There was talk and laughter going on, but the voices started to blur in her head. She felt him push his fingers into her.

"Dis bitch is as dry as saw dust. Gimme some of dat grease over dar so I can lube her da fuck up. I wanna slip right into this pussy. I ain't gonna be bruising my dick up."

"Why are you doing this to us?" asked Sleepy.

"Cause we got paid to, dat's why. Shamsadeen told us to have some fun wit y'all and he paid us to do it," answered Jimmy.

"Shamsadeen? Shamsadeen Baku? Why is Shamsadeen doing this to us? I haven't seen Shamsadeen since high school. That's been over ten years ago. I doubt if he would even recognize me if he saw me on the street."

"Look, dat's between y'all. We gittin paid for dis, and we gittin some pussy on top of it."

Vanessa could feel Memphis' fingers inserting Royal Crown hair grease into her vagina. She began to shake uncontrollably.

"Let me put some grease up your ass so we can slide in dar too. Bitch, you can shake all you want, all you doing is stirring it up for me. Big Daddy Memphis gonna make him a baby tonight. You said you already got two boys, you wanna girl dis time? You gonna name her Memphis after her daddy?"

"How you know it's gonna be yourn? Maybe it'll be mine. She could name it Jimmy, but have an i and an e on the end. Hey Memphis, maybe we be on Jerry Springer trying to find out which one of us is da faffer," joked Jimmy.

Vanessa felt him shove a swatch of grease up her rectum and then lie on top of her. He smelled of filth and alcohol. She could feel herself starting to vomit. She felt him searching for her opening. She felt his tongue licking her face.

Sleepy could not just stand there and watch this happen. And, he was certain that they were going to kill him and Vanessa. Why else had they so freely used their names? He had to do something. Jimmy turned his attention away from Sleepy to watch what was happening on the bed. He was dying for his turn with the light skin girl with soft pussy hairs. Sleepy lunged at him. They fell to the floor. Sleepy tried to wrestle the gun from Jimmy's hand. Memphis tried to get up, but his pants were too far down for him to get back on his feet. The gun went off. Vanessa screamed. Sleepy stood up. Blood was all over his left hand, he had the gun in his right hand. Jimmy stood up and then fell back down to the floor. Sleepy and Memphis' eyes met. They stared at each other, then they both raised their guns. There was a loud boom. Sleepy fell backwards and slid down the wall. Memphis collapsed on top of Vanessa. She felt drops of a thick warm fluid splatter of her face. She could not stop screaming. She kept her eyes closed. She was waiting for Sleepy to tell her it was alright, but she never heard his voice. Then, she heard a small voice.

"Lady, you all right? Lady, it's OK. Are you alright?"

Vanessa opened her eyes and saw a little girl standing beside her. She struggled to get Memphis' dead body off of her.

"Hey lady, you better put your dress on and get out of here before the cops come."

Vanessa looked around and saw Sleepy slouched against the wall. She started to cry. The little girl handed Vanessa a dress. Vanessa put it on.

"What's your name, sweetheart?"

"Cali."

"Thank you Cali. But I think you should leave right now. I'm sorry you had to see this. I have to stay. I loved that man over there and I can't leave him like that. Now you hurry up and get out of here." The little girl ran out as other people started to run into the apartment. Vanessa walked over to Sleepy and held him in her arms. She took off her weeding band and placed it on Sleepy's left little finger.

"I, Vanessa Jennings-Weintraub, do take you Ethan Smith, to be my only true love, until eternity do us part."

William and Lenora were the only ones at home when the phone rang. William picked up the receiver.

"Hello . . . Yes . . . I'm his son . . . Why? . . . What's wrong? . . . Has something happened? . . . Don't tell me to settle down . . . OK, I'm settled . . . Vanessa Weintraub is my sister . . . Is she alright? . . . Oh my god! . . . I'll be right there . . . Thank you." William hung up the phone and called for Lenora.

"Lenora! Lenora!"

"Tell who ever it is I'll have to call them back."

It's the hospital. They said Vanessa is down there. They need someone to come right away. They said she's OK. Let's go! Hurry up!"

Lenora stood still in shock. She couldn't move. She refused to believe that something had happened to Vanessa. She ran down the stairs and passed William. William followed after her. Neither of them spoke on their way to the hospital. Lenora had tears in her eyes. William had fear in his. William pulled into a parking space designated for visitors. They ran to the emergency ward. Vanessa was sitting in the corner with two uniformed police officers standing beside her. There was a man in a suit talking to her.

William walked up to them and excused himself.

"Excuse me, I'm her brother and she's her sister. Can we speak to her alone for a minute?"

The man in the suit identified himself. "Hello, I'm Detective LaPone. If I can talk to your sister for another minute, I'll be finished. It's real important that we complete our questioning of her while things are still fresh in her mind."

"It's alright. I'm fine," assured Vanessa.

"Ma'am, are you sure they said they were sent by a Shamsadeen?"

"That's the name they said. He said that Shamsadeen paid them to attack us."

Lenora and William turned and looked at each other. They could not believe what they just heard. Lenora began to cry. William felt rage racing through his body.

"Ma'am do you know a person named Shamsadeen?"

"No."

"Have you ever heard Mr. Smith mention his name?"

"No. In fact, Sleepy was couldn't figure out why this Shamsadeen person would want to harm him. It sounded as though they went to high school together, but that's it. Sleepy told them that he would be surprised if Shamsadeen would even recognize him."

"So, you have no idea why Shamsadeen would sic these low-lifes on you? Was Mr. Smith involved with drugs in any way?"

"No. Sleepy hated to take an aspirin. And I couldn't even imagine him selling drugs. No, I have no idea why this happened."

"Thanks for giving us the time. We have your number. If anything comes up or, if you remember anything that you forgot to tell me, here is my card. Call anytime. If anything develops, we'll contact you. Thanks again."

The Detective walked away. Vanessa looked helpless. William and Lenora walked over to her and held her. They all began to cry as they walked back to William's car.

"Where's mom and dad and the kids."

"They took the kids to Friendlys for dinner," answered Lenora.

"Please don't tell mom and dad about this? Please promise this will never go beyond the three of us? Not even my husband must know about this. Promise! I'll call Uncle Jesse. I know he's going to find out about it. I'll talk to him. Now Promise me."

Both William and Lenora raised their right hands and promised. William asked her to tell them what happened. Vanessa told them the whole story. Tears ran down their faces. Vanessa wanted to go home and take a shower. She felt filthy. She could still smell Memphis on her. She was thankful that he never got a chance to penetrate her with his penis, but she still felt violated. He had touched her and put his fingers inside of her. She still felt the slickness of the grease that he had inserted in her. She began to tremble and cry again.

"I can't believe that Sleepy is dead. They killed him for no reason at all. I don't know a Shamsadeen. Sleepy really didn't know him either. Who is this Shamsadeen person? I want to kill him myself."

He's William's new girlfriend's boyfriend, if that makes any sense," explained Lenora.

"What did you say?" asked Vanessa.

"Shamsadeen is Nafesa's boyfriend. Nafesa is the girl that William is changing his life for. I told him that she was nothing but trouble, but he wouldn't listen to me. I also told him that this Shamsadeen character wasn't going to let William just take his girl without doing something about it."

Vanessa turned and looked at William. He would not look at her. He could not face her at that moment. He had put his family in harms way over Nafesa. How could he be so stupid? He didn't know whether he should run or fight. He knew his uncle would get a hold of this. Lenora was right, he was ruining his life. And, he was ruining his family over a woman he barely knew. But his heart still pounded for Nafesa. He knew that she had nothing to do with this. He also knew that Shamsadeen would attack her to get at him. William wanted to protect everyone; his family; Nafesa; and himself. He had to think. He had to talk to Nafesa.

"I can't believe that Sleepy was killed and I was molested because of a pissing match between you and a goddamn drug dealer, over this damn Nafesa. William, what were you thinking about getting mixed up with a drug dealer's girlfriend? I guess the question is, what were you thinking with? How could you do this to us? Where do you draw the line?"

"It's about love. How do you draw a line when it involves love?" he asked.

"When I brought Sleepy home and told mom and dad I wanted to marry him, they drew a line and left it up to me to cross it. I decided that my family was more important to me than Sleepy. I was in love, but I made a choice. And I would make that same choice today. William, remember one thing about life, first there is God then there's your family. When love has walked out of the door on you, your family always has a door for you to walk through. Remember that if you don't remember anything else in life. Now promise me that you'll put an end to all of this?"

"Believe me Vanessa, I am going to put an end to all of this. This can't and won't happen to anyone else," he promised.

CHAPTER TWENTY-ONE

It was Wednesday night and Nafesa had not spoken to either William or Shamsadeen. She was tired and needed to get her head together. Jasmin's house was as good a place as any to do that. She was straining to stay awake for the eleven o'clock news, but she fell asleep by ten-thirty. She felt something shaking her. She opened her eyes and tried to adjust them to the darkness. It was Jasmin. She rolled over to see what was going on.

"Fe, wake up. Fe, it's Shamsadeen, wake up. I told him that you were sleeping, but he said it was very important."

"Oh shit, I don't feel like talking to him right now. I can't deal. What time is it anyway?"

"It's three-forty."

"Three forty in the morning?"

"Yeah, in the morning. Look Fe, I don't feel like being in the middle of this shit. You have to deal with this. It's not going away."

Nafesa knew that Jasmin was right. She had to deal with the situation. "OK, give me the phone," she said grudgingly. Jasmin handed her the phone and walked out of the room.

"Hello."

"What's up with you? How have you been? I've left a bunch of messages on your cell phone. How come you haven't called me back?"

"I've been tied up for a minute."

"Yeah, right. I guess you heard about what happened at the hotel. I've had to lay low for a minute until that whole thing blows over."

"Shamsadeen, you didn't call me three-forty in the morning to talk about that shit that happened at the hotel. So why did you call at this time in the morning? So, what's up?"

"No, you tell me what's up?"

"I don't know what you mean," she answered.

"Look Fe, stop the bullshit. What's up with you and white boy? I hear the two of you were hanging out in New York. I guess you took the car up there. Let me ask you this, what made you think that you could fuck around with him and I wouldn't find out about it? Are you out of your mind? Do you know who I am? Look out the fucking window right now."

"What are you talking about Shamsadeen?"

"Fe, stop playing with me. You know what the fuck I'm talking about. Now look out the window."

Nafesa walked over to the window and drew back the curtain and looked outside. The street light illuminated the sidewalk. Nafesa could make out a tall woman with what looked like platinum blonde hair, holding a cell phone. She was standing beside Nafesa's car. The woman picked up a can and appeared to be dousing the BMW with a liquid. Nafesa's mouth fell open with shock. The woman looked up at the window and waved at her. Then, she stood back, lit a cigarette and through the lighted match on he car. The car went up like a barn fire. Next, the woman casually walked over to a fire engine red Mustang 5.0, got in the passenger side of the car and rode away. Nafesa could not believe what she had just witnessed. She could hear people shouting and screaming. Jasmin was saying something, but Nafesa was too dazed to hear her. She walked back over to the bed and picked up the phone.

"Shamsadeen, why did you do that? You could have taken the car back. It's not that important. I feel like I'm in the South with the KKK. This was just an old fashioned cross burning to teach me fear. But it shouldn't be about fear, it should be about love. And, if you really loved me like you say you do, then you would have never done anything like that to me. This isn't love, this is like everything else about you, control and power. Well Shamsadeen, I'm tired of the power and the control. Stay with Lorraine, maybe she can tolerate this shit, but I can't. Right now, the only thing that's burning between us is that car. I'm leaving you and all of your bullshit!"

"Shut up Fe. You ain't going nowhere. You better not even think about leaving me. I'll tell you when we're through. Do you hear me? I said, do you hear me?" Nafesa refused to answer him.

"Look Nafesa, I'm gonna come by Jasmin's at three o'clock today to get you. I want you to have all of your stuff ready so that we can roll out. That car shit ain't my fault. That's your fault. You had no business fucking around on me like that. I was too good to you. But no, you had to embarrass me. Now you got an attitude. I'm the one who should have an attitude. Look, fuck all of this rap, have your gear ready when I come at three to get you. By the way, did you boyfriend get the message I sent him?"

"What message? What did you do Shamsadeen? Shamsadeen, what are you talking about?" The phone went silent. Nafesa immediately dialed William's cell phone. His voice box kicked in. Then, she remembered that his cell phone was in the glove compartment of her car. It was probably a mound of melted plastic by now. She tried to call his home number, but the answering machine came on after the first ring. She hung up the phone and crawled back into bed. She could hear the sirens pouring onto the street. She could also hear the commotion going on outside. Jasmin stood in the doorway looking at her.

"What's up girlfriend? You wanna talk?" Nafesa gave her a sighing "no".

"What about the car?"

"It's his car. If he wants it to burn, let it burn."

Nafesa looked at the clock on the dresser, it read six-thirty-three. She got out of bed and went to the window to survey the damage. The car was charred. She closed the curtain and sat on the side of the bed. She was tired. It took her over an hour to explain to the Fire Marshall and the police what had happened. It was time for her to leave Philadelphia and she knew that she had until three o'clock to put her plan into action. She took a shower and got dressed. She wanted to be at the bank when it opened at eight- thirty. Then, she would go to the car rental agency, the air line ticket agency, and lastly, to the airport. She was slightly amazed at herself. Normally, she would have been too distraught, but not this time. She felt a certain sense of control. What could Shamsadeen take from her? There was nothing left. She had to decide where she would go. California was her first instinct, but she wanted to rest on an island for a while. She had to tell Flavor about her plans. She couldn't leave without telling him and the band everything. She picked up the phone and dialed Flavor's number. Flavor picked up the phone on the fifth ring.

"Hello."

"Flavor, it's me."

"Hey Fe, where in the hell have you been? Ain't nobody heard from you since the meeting. Those people have been trying to get things rolling, but I've been putting them off until I heard from you. The band is starting to get nervous. We don't want this deal to get shaky. What's going on?"

"Flav, this whole thing with Shamsadeen and William is becoming a nightmare. Shamsadeen's turning into a madman. I'm scared."

"No baby, I've been telling you all along that he was a madman. You just didn't want to hear it. So what you gonna do now?"

"I've got to get away. He had my car torched last night. Then, he had the nerve to tell me that he was coming for me today at three o'clock. I have to get away from here."

"I told you before that I would step to him."

"Flav, be for real, Shamsadeen would just as soon kill you than look at you. That's not the answer."

"So, where are you going?"

"I'm not sure yet. You keep the plans moving. Just give me a couple of weeks to get straightened out. I'll come back and get with you and the guys. We can still make this happen. I'll call you from wherever I go. Cool?"

"Fe baby, it's about you. If you ain't right then the band ain't right. I think the record company wants you too badly to cancel out. I've hired an agent. Her name is Florrie Dupree. The sister is bad. She's already working with some real big names. I'll deal with her. I'm certain she can hold them off for a couple of weeks. I got to be honest with you Fe, if I don't hear from you in a couple of weeks, I have to start auditioning for a singer. Cool?"

"Cool. Look, I've got to go. Don't worry, I'll be alright. As soon as I get to wherever I'm going, I'll call you. Flavor?"

"Yeah baby?"

"I love you."

"Fe, you know I love you. You be careful. And although you don't think I'm built like that, if anything happens to you, I'll kill that mother fucker myself."

"Don't worry Flav, nothing is going to happen to me. You keep the band together and keep that pen working. I've gotta go."

"Peace my Nubian sister."

Nafesa smiled. "Peace my Nubian brother." She hung up the phone. Tears streamed down her face. Their conversation sounded too final for her comfort.

The clock on the wall read one-seventeen as she walked through Jasmin's front door. Jasmin and her mother had gone down to the police station to answer some questions about the car burning. There was a note from a Detective LaPone, asking Nafesa to come down to the station for some additional questioning. There was also a note from an insurance investigator. She ignored both of them. She took the phone off of the base and went into her room and dialed William's home number. She prayed that he would answer the phone. A female's voice answered.

"Hello."

"Hello. Is William available?"

"Who may I ask is calling?"

"Could you tell him it's Nafesa?" There was a long pause from the party on the other end. Nafesa thought that the person was going to get William. Then came a tirade.

"Why you little black, picky headed witch. How dare you call this house. You have no right to call here. First you send William on a downward spiral, then you have my sister raped and her friend murdered. Haven't you done enough harm to this family. You should stay with you own. You're nothing but a cheap, drug dealer's whore. You don't deserve my brother. He had a perfect life until you stepped in. Get out of his life before something terrible happens to him. That's what you want isn't it?"

"What are you talking about? I've never hurt William or anyone else in your family. I don't even know you. What are you talking about having your sister raped and somebody murdered?"

"Your drug dealing boyfriend sent some thugs to rape my sister and kill her boyfriend. They were probably going to kill her too. Whether you knew about it or not, you're still responsible for it."

"Oh Allah, I swear to you, I didn't know anything about this. I'm so sorry. Please believe me? Please let me speak to William?"

"He's not here. He's with his fiancée."

"Would you please give him a message for me? Please? This is real important. Tell him that I'm leaving for the Bahamas today. Tell him that I won't be coming back to Philly. If he wants to be with me, tell him to meet me at 3927 Powell Street, by two fifteen. Please give him the mess . . ." The phone went silent. Nafesa stood there with the receiver in her hand. She could not believe what was just told to her. How could Shamsadeen do something like that? Had she been that blind over the past few years that she could not see she was living with a monster?

"Oh Allah, please see me through all of this turmoil," she prayed.

William was lying in his bed when he heard the phone ring. He hoped it was Nafesa. He had not spoken to her since their return from New York. He left numerous messages on her cell phone. He had to talk to her about what had happened to Vanessa. He was both hurt and surprised that she had not called him or, returned his calls. He heard Lenora shouting at the caller. He put his head against the wall to make out what she was saying. From what he was able to make out, he knew that she was speaking to Nafesa. He jumped into his pajama bottoms and burst into Lenora's room. When she saw him thunder through her door, she disconnected the call. William snatched the phone out of her hands and placed the receiver to his ear.

"Hello, Nafesa." The phone was silent. He dropped the phone to the floor. It rang again. He grabbed it from the floor

"Nafesa?"

"No William, it's me," responded his Uncle Jesse.

"Oh."

"William, I'm calling you about this Nafesa person. Vanessa called me and told about your involvement with this Nafesa. It's real important that you and I sit down and talk about her. This is very, very, very serious. Do you get my drift? Things are really starting to escalate with Shamsadeen Baku. Bodies are turning up everywhere. And from what Vanessa told me, you may be smack dab in the middle of this whole mess. You have to leave this girl alone; at least until we can figure where she stands in this drug ring. And it's my guess that she's standing pretty tall in the saddle. We're looking for Shamsadeen as we speak. We know where the girl is. We're keeping an eye on her. Last night her car was fire bombed. She spoke to our people when it happened, but she hasn't come down to the station to give a written statement as of yet. So listen to me William, I asking you; no I'm telling you to stay away from her. She's too dangerous for you to be dealing with. What happened to Vanessa is just the tip of the iceberg. This Shamsadeen fellow will do anything to get his message across. Promise me that you will listen to me and leave this Nafesa person alone?"

"Unc, believe me, I already know what he'll do to get his message across. I promise you that I'll stay away from her until you guys get this whole thing under control."

"Good. I want you to stop in my office in the morning so that we can talk about this whole thing. Make it ten o'clock."

"I'll be there." William hung up the phone. He immediately thought about dialing star sixty-nine to reconnect with Nafesa. He tried, but his uncle's call interrupted the star sixty-nine sequence. He stared at Lenora. Although he knew Lenora had a right to do what she did, he was still angry with her. He walked out of her room and went back to his room. He was dying on the inside.

Lenora paced back and forth in her room. She hated Nafesa. Nafesa was what her parents had preached about; a home wrecking, evil black woman. William was too blind to see. He had Marla, but all of a sudden she was not good enough for him. He had to have this tar baby. Lenora almost wished that he would go away with Nafesa. That way, it would be over. They could run away and have little black babies running all over. Maybe they deserved each other. He didn't deserve his family. He had shunned his family for a Nafesa. Hell, she even had one of those ghetto names. And, what she caused to happen to Vanessa was horrible. Even if she didn't make Shamsadeen do it, she was still the cause of it. She looked at the clock on the wall. It was two-twenty-five. If she gave William the message, would he have sense enough to let her go, or would he run after her? He probably couldn't get there in time anyway. Besides, if they really wanted to be together, who was she to keep them apart? Let them ruin their lives together. He would be back with his tail between his legs. Maybe he had to learn the hard way. She walked out of her room and knocked on William's door. She didn't wait for an invitation to come in. She opened the door and stood there staring at William with tears in her eyes.

"What do you want?" he asked.

"Nafesa left a message that she's leaving for the Bahamas today. She's probably not coming back to Philly. She said if you wanted to go with her, you should meet her at 3927 Powell Street by two-fifteen. William, I'm begging you not to go there. You'll be ruining your life if you go with that girl. She's nothing but trouble. And her boyfriend is the devil incarnate."

William stood there looking at her. Then, he locked up at the clock. It was two-thirty. He knew that it was a half an hour ride to that address. He grabbed his pants and ran out of the door.

CHAPTER TWENTY-TWO

S hamsadeen looked up at the clock, it was two-forty. He took a couple of pain killers and headed for the door. This was his first time leaving the apartment since he had been shot. He and Lil' Larry had planned to lay low in New Orleans for a few weeks. Shamsadeen had a couple of friends down there that had set things up for him and Lil' Larry. Lorraine and her brother, LaShonda could keep things running until they got back. He was more than confident that they could handle things for him. Lil' Larry picked up their bags and headed for the front door. He rented a black Range Rover for them to drive to Louisiana in. Shamsadeen gave Lorraine a kiss and a slap on the ass.

"Let's roll Lil' Larry. You know where we have to go first."

"Man, I think you're making a big mistake going down there. You can deal with Nafesa when you get back. It's just too hot for us to roll into town like that."

"Look Lil' Larry, Nafesa is coming with me. Her and that white boy are done. I'm not leaving her here. This conversation is over."

Sergeant Shelmire was sitting at his desk when a call came through alleging to have information on the whereabouts of Shamsadeen Baku. The operator immediately put the call through to him. A soft spoken voice was on the other end. It was obvious that the person was trying to disguise their voice.

"If you want Shamsadeen and Lil' Larry, they're on their way to 3927 Powell Street. They're heavily armed."

The phone went silent. Sergeant Shelmire raced through the office getting his agents together. They all began to put on the bullet proof vests. Heavy artillery was issued to them.

The same person who called Sergeant Shelmire then dialed another number. LaShonda was in bed with his boyfriend when the phone rang.

"Hey LaShonda, it's me."

What's up sweetie?"

"It's almost over. If things go down right, you'll have Camden and I'll have Philly just like we planned."

"Alright sis, just keep me posted and let me know if I have to finish anything for you."

"Naw, I wanna take care of little Miss Black Beauty myself. When I'm done I'll call you. We'll get together tomorrow to work everything out. Talk to you later. Bye."

"Bye, sis."

Lorraine was proud of herself. Everything was going as planned. Raoul and Rockman had screwed up just like she knew that they would. And, Shamsadeen had fallen for that Mohammed bullshit, just like she knew he would. All she needed was for the police to do their job and she would be the Queen of Philly. LaShonda could run Camden. Together, the two of them were unstoppable. She loved Shamsadeen, but she was not going to work her ass off to help make him number one only to watch him drool over some twisted hair, black bitch. "If you fuck me, then you can be sure that I'm gonna fuck you back!" she said out loud to herself.

William arrived at Jasmin's house at five till three. He rang the door bell and waited with anticipation. Jasmin answered the door.

"You must be William. I'm sorry, but you missed her. Nafesa's gone. She left at two-fifteen. I guess you didn't get her message in time. Hold on for a second, she left something for you in case you got here late." Jasmin walked away from the door for a moment and returned with an envelope in her hand. "Here, this is for you."

William took the envelope. "Did she say where she was going?" he asked.

"Look, just read whatever's inside the envelope. That's all I can tell you. Take care." Jasmin shut the door and walked away. William stood there not knowing what to do next. He sat down on the top step of the porch and tore open the envelope. There was a letter and an airline ticket to the Bahamas. He unfolded the letter:

Dear William,

If you're reading this letter, things didn't go as I had hoped they would. I hope that you still have time to make the flight. If not, maybe you can catch the next one. However, I'll understand if you don't want to be with me. I've caused your family a lot of pain and suffering. Tell them I'm sorry. I do feel responsible for what happened to your sister and her friend. Please make her understand that I would have never allowed anything like that to happen to her. I guess your family must hate me. I just hope that you don't. Please do not come to the islands just to spend a little time with me. I am asking you to only come if you truly want to spend the rest of your life with me. I know this is a hard choice for you to make on the spur of the moment, but I'm asking you to make it. Well, I hope to see you soon. All the info on where I'm staying is inside the ticket jacket.

More than love,
Nafesa

William read the letter three times before he folded it and placed it back in the envelope. His mind was spinning. She was asking him to spend the rest of his life with her. What about his family? What about Marla? What about his career? What about Shamsadeen? His head was swirling. He looked at his watch, it was five after three. *"Good bye Philly,"* he said to himself. He started to walk back to his car when a black Range Rover pulled up. A well built guy with his left arm in a bandage got out of the truck and started to walk up the pathway. Their eyes met. They turned around and stared at each other as they passed one another.

"Shamsadeen?" asked William.

"Depends on who wants to know. Oh, you must be that wanna be white boy that's been sweating Nafesa. What's wrong, she kicked you to the curb?"

William's lips were trembling with rage. "No, she's gone. She left for the Bahamas. She left me a plane ticket to meet her there. So I guess she's kicking you to the curb. You know, I thought I would see something more when I met you. But, you look just like what you are, a low life drug dealer. It probably took you until you were twelve to learn how to spell your name. Seeing you makes me somewhat disappointed in Nafesa. She could have done better. I guess that's what I'm all about. I'm her step up, or should I say leap up from you."

"You white looking mutha fucka, I'll blow your brains out. How did your sister like the dick I sent her? I heard she even liked it up the ass. Next time I might personally give her some dick. But then, your family might not like me sitting at the dinner table. Who knows, maybe I'd end up fucking every bitch in your family. Your mother might even want to jump on some of this dick," laughed Shamsadeen.

"You can't keep the woman you have now. How are you going to get someone new? I heard that you sent those two bums to get my sister because you knew she would laugh at you if you tried to rape her yourself," retaliated William. The two of them began to move closer to each other. Lil' Larry was moving up behind William. Shamsadeen pulled his nine from under his shirt. Lil' Larry pulled out his forty-five.

"How typical, little Shamsadeen gets his feelings hurt, now he wants to shoot someone. Are you sure your parents weren't cave people?"

"Fuck you pussy. Ask them when you see them?" Shamsadeen had the gun pointed at William's chest. William could hear police sirens approaching them. His confidence level began to rise.

"Look Shamsadeen, the fucking cops are coming. We have to get out of here. Do what you have to do, but let's get out of here. I say leave this mother fucker for another time and place. He don't mean nothing," advised Lil' Larry.

"He means something to me," answered Shamsadeen. William could see the police cars speeding in. Officers were filing out of their cars with their guns drawn.

"Fuck! What are we going to do now Shamsadeen? How this many cops get here this fast? Look, the fucking D.E.A. is here. Somebody set us up."

Sergeant Shelmire slowly approached Shamsadeen, Lil' Larry and William.

"Look, if everybody put their guns down I'm quite sure we can work this out."

"Ain't shit to work out. I ain't going out like no slave. My people didn't go out like that and neither am I. So fuck y'all. If we gotta do this, then let's do it," hollered Shamsadeen.

Lil' Larry spun around towards Sergeant Shelmire with his forty-five in his hand. He tried to raise his hands in the air, but a bullet ripped through his chest and was followed by a hail of bullets. The bullets slammed Lil' Larry to the ground. Shamsadeen watched Lil' Larry fall. He began to scream. He turned and looked at William.

"See you on the other side my man," he laughed. Shamsadeen squeezed the trigger letting off three rapid shots. William felt solid punches to his chest. Then, he felt a burning sensation moving through his body. It was robbing him of his life. He thought he was still standing, but when he looked around, his face was plastered against the side walk. He didn't remember falling. Shamsadeen turned around and was met by a never ending volley of gun fire. He strained to stay on his feet. He refused to fall to the ground. He staggered over to the truck and collapsed along side of it. The gun fire stopped. Sergeant Shelmire ran over to William and checked for a pulse. What little pulse remained was fading fast. He shouted for someone to get an ambulance.

"Can you hear me? If you can hear me nod your head?"

William tried to nod his head, but his head felt unattached to the rest of his body. His mind was telling him to get up and walk away, but his body would not respond. Everything started to sound like one long word. Where just a moment ago he felt a burning heat racing through his body, he was now cold; an inner cold that moved through his body and left it numb. Everything started to fade into darkness. He knew he was dying. It felt as though he was dying in slow motion. The paramedic ran over to him and began to connect him to all kinds of portable machines. The paramedic looked at one of the machines for a reading. William was flat lining.

Lenora was home reading an article on a rock that some scientist claimed was a twenty-thousand year old work of art, when the phone rang. She lazily reached over and picked up the receiver.

"Hello . . . No, this is her daughter . . . No. she's not at home. Neither of my parents are at home. Can I help you? . . . William? . . . Oh my god! . . . No. No. No. No. No. No . . . Where is he? . . . God, please be wrong. I'll be right there." Lenora raced out of the house. She drove frantically to the University of Pennsylvania hospital. When she got there, the TV cameras, the reporters and the police were everywhere. She fought her way through the crowd.

"Where is my brother?" she screamed. She was approached by Sergeant Shelmire. She saw her uncle standing off to the side. She broke away from Sergeant Shelmire and ran over to her uncle. He looked at her with tears in his eyes. She stopped and looked in his face. She dropped to her knees and started to weep. Uncle Jesse walked over and picked her up from the ground. He held her in his arms, kissed the top of her head and chanted, "it just doesn't make any sense."

"Did he say anything?" she asked

"No, not that I know of. I'm still waiting for the report to come to figure exactly what happened out there."

"What about the girl Nafesa, was she killed?"

"No, there were only male bodies found." Uncle Jesse reached into his pocket and pulled out an envelope. "Here, he had this in his hand when they brought him here. I want you to go home. This is not where you should be. I'll handle everything down here. Someone has to let the family know. I think it should be you. Go home and take care of that. I'll be here for a little while." He pushed Lenora away and motioned for a uniformed police officer to come over. "Take her home," he ordered.

"I'll be alright to make it home. I can drive."

When Lenora walked through her door, the house seemed like a tomb. She could not believe what had happened to William. How could she tell her family? She couldn't. She went up to William's room. It was alive with him. She could smell him in the room. She sat on the side of his bed. The tears would not stop. She opened the envelope and read the letter. The tears flowed even faster. *"Maybe they really did love each other."* She picked up the phone and began to dial.

Nafesa landed at the Bahamian airport on schedule. She cried the entire flight. On her way to the airport she prayed that William would meet her there. He didn't. She still hoped that he would catch the next flight. A shuttle bus took her to the Marriot Inn. A polite man in a well tailored white suit and polished black shoes escorted her to the front desk. A young, deep black man with pearly white teeth and a lime green suit asked her for her reservation papers. She was fumbling through her hand bag when the phone rang. The young man excused himself and answered the phone.

"'Ello, Marriot Inn, Bahamas. "'Ow can I help you? . . . Let me check that for you. No, I'm sorry, I'm not showing a Nafesa Islam as being registered 'ere . . . Yes. I'm sure."

"Hey, that's me," shouted Nafesa. She was certain it was William.

"'Old on, there is someone at the front desk by that name," said the young man.

"Hello, this is Nafesa Islam. Nafesa recognized Lenora's voice. She felt disappointed and confused. Why would Lenora be calling her? Fear raced through her body. "This is William's sister right? What's up? . . . Oh Allah, please be wrong! . . . Stop it . . . Oh Allah, why have you forsaken me?" she shouted as she dropped the phone to the floor and fell to her knees.

CHAPTER TWENTY-THREE

I t had been over a year and a half since Nafesa had gotten the phone call in the Bahamas. She returned to the States and immediately moved to New York. She and the band cut their first CD and things were going well for them A tour was being planned for them at the beginning of next summer. They were playing in the top clubs in New York. She had limousine service to and from the clubs. However, for as much as she was a rising star, she still had not recuperated from losing William. He was all she ever wanted out of life. When Lenora called her and told her the news, her whole world fell apart. Shamsadeen deserved his fate; William did not. She didn't have the courage to return to Philly. She went straight from the Bahamas to New York. She had spoken to Jasmin a couple of times, but Jasmin was too close to the past she was trying to free herself from. She poured her heart and soul into her music. It was her refuge. They were currently playing at the Palace Chic'. It was the hottest jazz club in New York. Celebrities always frequented the place. Some of the top names in the business would stop in on any given night.

It was Wednesday, the band had arranged for their set to end with their hot new single. The club was packed. Nafesa was in a decent mood. She had given the people their money's worth. She sat down on her stool to begin her finale.

"This last song that we are going to do for you tonight is my favorite song. And, as some of you may know, it's a song about new love. When I first heard this song I fell in love with it. When I first sang this song I fell even more in love with it. The next time I sang this song I fell in love with someone. It was new love; it was good love. I want you to listen to the words and feel the rhythm. It's definitely a lover's rhythm." The keyboards began to creep into the atmosphere, followed by the guitar. Nafesa bounced her head for a couple of bars. She smiled and moved into the song. She filled the club with her rich voice. The crowd swayed as one to the melody. Everyone was feeling the song. It made lovers love and singles desirous for love. Flavor brought the melody down and Nafesa closed out the song with a long final note. The crowd roared. The applause seemed never ending. When the applause began to die down, there was a man off to the right of the stage who kept his applause going at full force. Nafesa thanked the crowd and turned around to see who her new fan was. The lights prevented her being able to get a clear view of him. He looked familiar. The rest of the club was now staring at him. The applause never ceased. Nafesa stood up. Her heart began to race. She moved closer to the front of the stage. Her heart was leaping. She raced off the stage and ran towards her fan. She saw that he was supporting himself with two metal crutches. Flavor began to clap. Not knowing why, the rest of the club joined in with Flavor. She saw his face; it was William. He tried to walk towards her, but each step was a struggle. Tears cascaded down her face as she ran over to him. He stretched out his arms as best he could for her. She fell into his arms sobbing with joy.

"I'm sorry I missed that flight," he joked.

"Oh William, I can't believe it's you. I can't believe this is actually happening. It's like it's happening all over again," she cried.

"What do you mean all over again? Nafesa, I never stopped loving you from the first time."

"Oh Allah, you are truly a wonderful God," she whispered in his ear."

THE END